DEATH AND THE IMMORTAL

Icy water filled Fitzcairn's lungs. His body was carried by the current beneath the ice, banging from rock to rock. Once, as he rolled, he could see up through a clear patch. The sky was white, too, he thought for a while.

It was his last thought for a while.

When he choked back to life, he found that he was no longer in motion. He'd become wedged between two rocks, face up, his head pointed downstream.

He drowned, again.

The next time he revived, it was dark. He sputtered, coughed, and began to feel the first faint stirrings of worry. What was the possibility that Duncan could find him? None.

His last thought as he drowned again was that if worse came to worst, the ice would thaw next spring . . .

ALSO IN THE HIGHLANDER SERIES

Available from
WARNER ASPECT

HIGHLANDER™
WHITE SILENCE

NOVEL
BY
GINJER
BUCHANAN

ASPECT®

WARNER BOOKS

A Time Warner Company

WARNER BOOKS EDITION

Copyright © 1999 by Warner Books, Inc.
All rights reserved.

"Highlander" is a protected trademark of Gaumont Television. © 1994 by Gaumont Television & © Davis Pauzer Productions, Inc. 1985.

Aspect is a registered trademark of Warner Books, Inc.

Warner Books, Inc.
1221 Avenue of the Americas
New York, NY 10020

Visit our Web site at
http//warnerbooks.com

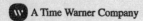 A Time Warner Company

Printed in the United States of America

First Printing: March, 1999

10 9 8 7 6 5 4 3 2 1

Dedicated to the memory of Laird Douglas
—*Father, we miss you still . . .*

ACKNOWLEDGMENTS

Thanks to:

Betsy Mitchell, my editor, for not laughing when I called and asked if I could pitch a Highlander novel.

John Douglas, my "other editor," for transcribing a large part of the beginning of this book, and for his patience as I nattered on (and on) about Immortals.

Donna Lettow and Gillian Horvath, for the obvious—inspiration, information, and support. And for the not-so-obvious—proving to me that you're never too old to make new friends.

Bill Panzer, for wanting to know what was going to happen next.

David Abramowitz and all of the writers who helped create the character of Hugh Fitzcairn.

And, of course, Roger Daltrey, for bringing Fitz gloriously to life. From him, I get the story. . . .

"This is the Law of the Yukon, that only the Strong
  shall thrive:
That surely the Weak shall perish, and only the Fit
  survive."

> —from *The Law of the Yukon*
> by Robert Service

Chapter 1

Amanda was wearing white. She fairly gleamed in the soft candlelight cast from the wall sconces on either side of the ornate vanity where she sat, obviously admiring herself in the oval mirror. A sight to give a man pause, even one who had known her for over two hundred fifty years. Duncan watched her for a minute, then gave voice to his question.

"White?"

Amanda met his eyes in the mirror as he walked across the room to stand behind her. She was not surprised to see him, of course. None of their kind could ever take another unaware. She smiled, a mere quirk of her lips.

"Hmm," she murmured. "Snow-white."

Duncan knew better, but could not resist.

"Like a virg—"

Before another syllable could leave his lips, Amanda swiveled on her seat, her skirts spread about her, her dark eyes narrowed. One slender finger stabbed out, poking him not-at-all gently just above the waist of his trousers.

"For your information, Mr. MacLeod, a merchant had a run of bad luck at the tables last week, and I now own a warehouse full of the finest silks that San Francisco has ever seen. Silks of colors that you are not capable of imagining. I intend to have at least one dress made from every single color. And, while we are discussing clothing, you"—she paused, sliding the finger higher—"could very much use a new waistcoat. There's one brocade I quite liked, dark brown and gold shot through with metallic thread, that would look splendid on your manly form. I could have my dressmaker take measurements. Or"—she smiled up at him through her lashes—"I could do it myself—later."

Duncan caught her hand and raised her fingertips to his lips. "As always, I bow to your fashion sense." He inclined his head and kissed the finger that had assaulted him.

Amanda laughed then and turned back to the mirror, to the rapt contemplation of her own image. It was Duncan's opinion, formed over a very long time, that Amanda's very favorite thing to look at was Amanda.

"Duncan dearest"—that was Amanda's helpless-little-me voice—"could you be a sweet and bring me my necklace? It's in the case on the bed."

Duncan crossed to the ornate mahogany bed. Until very recently, another of their kind had slept there. This hotel suite had been home to the Immortal named Kit O'Brady. He'd lived here, close by the drinking and gambling establishment that he owned. It had been called the Double Eagle. Then, like the silk merchant, Kit O'Brady had had a run of bad luck when gambling with Amanda. He'd lost everything to her. The Double Eagle became the Queen of Spades, by decree of the new owner. And Kit O'Brady had been forced to move to rather less expensive quarters. Amanda had taken over his rooms with great glee.

Kit kept coming around to the Queen of Spades, playing small-stakes poker, losing regularly. He was convinced that his run of bad luck wouldn't end until Amanda returned his lucky coin—the very one for which the saloon had been named. But he was not about to beg for it.

As Duncan found the flat gold velvet box, he smiled. The hotel room might have been Kit's, but Duncan doubted that the bed had been covered in peach-satin sheets with a matching quilted coverlet edged in white lace when he had spent his nights in it.

He returned to Amanda's throne of mirrors and placed the case on the vanity. Once more, then, he stood behind her, closer now, so that the rough material of his evening coat nearly touched the generous portion of her back that the dress revealed.

Amanda opened the jewel case and, almost reverently, took out the necklace within. She held it at her throat, signaling to Duncan that he should take the two ends and fasten the clasp. He did so, and they both stared for a moment at the glory that circled Amanda's lovely neck.

The necklace was an intricate riot of gold filigree set with an almost impossible number of diamonds. None was large, but there were a lot of them. Amanda smiled at her reflection and donned the matching earrings, delicate traceries of gold set with even more diamonds, that dangled to her shoulders. She finished and arranged her hair over them, just so.

He brushed the back of his hand over one of the earrings.

"Don't tell me. A diamond merchant had a run of bad luck at the tables."

"A gift," Amanda replied, sweetly, "from an admirer."

Possibly, Duncan thought. And possibly not. He had been spending the nights in his own bed, alone, the last little while.

Amanda might think that a rival—real or imagined—would renew his ardor.

She rose gracefully, arranged her skirts around her, extended her arms out to her sides, and turned slowly in front of him.

"Well?"

The dress was magnificent, and so was the woman wearing it.

"Aye!" He had to admit it. "There is indeed much about you to admire."

He offered her his arm. Time only for a light supper, then Amanda had to be at work, charming the wealthy patrons of her opulent saloon.

Duncan was caught now, by the glitter of gold, of diamonds, and of snow-white brocade. Tonight the odds were with Amanda. He thought he might well visit this room, and Kit O'Brady's ornate bed, once again.

Hours passed, pleasantly enough. Duncan was not much of a gambler, so although the Queen of Spades was busy as usual, he contented himself with drinking Amanda's fine brandy and smoking one or two of the very expensive cigars she kept for preferred customers. He paid, of course. They had had a huge row over that. Amanda had so wanted to be indulgent, but Duncan's "no" had been delivered with some force, and she had demurred. So now he ran a tab, and settled it scrupulously on a regular basis.

At the moment, he was standing directly outside the saloon, finishing one of those very cigars. The night was chill and damp, as it often was in this city by the Bay. Duncan stared intently into the darkness. You couldn't see the ocean, but Duncan knew it was there. And tonight he almost thought he could smell it, maybe even hear it. He was a Scotsman, a Highlander to the bone. He would never love the sea as did some he had met in his wanderings. But he knew that a swift ship with the right winds could take a man to places beyond the reach of horse or camel or donkey, or any beast that walked on land.

He sighed without realizing it, threw his cold cigar into the gutter, and returned to watch the mortals hover around the icy flame that was Amanda this evening. Duncan suspected that one particular gentleman, who sported a ruby stickpin that looked like glass but wasn't—judging from the attention he had been receiving from Amanda for the past two hours—was also about to have a run of bad luck.

As he settled at the bar, propping himself with one elbow, he idly wondered how often and how much Amanda cheated at cards. She swore, for instance, that the poker game with Kit had been straight. Duncan wasn't convinced. He was in the midst of a case-by-case consideration, when the feeling came over him.

He glanced first at Amanda. She paused for a second and laid her cards on the table. Her hand went reflexively to her throat as she sought Duncan with her eyes.

Another Immortal was near, perhaps even already in the room.

Kit? He'd not been around for a week or so. Or perhaps Alec Hill? Duncan had been trying for months to get his friend to leave his house, to leave off his futile efforts to conjure the spirit of his dead wife. Alec was unkempt, weak from lack of food, and near-incoherent from lack of sleep. Yet Duncan would not give up on him, had been to see him as recently as yesterday. Had he gotten through to Alec at last, and convinced him to live his life once more among the living?

But his moment of hope faded as a young man, a stranger, appeared in the arched entryway to the Queen of Spades. He had been, Duncan guessed, anywhere from twenty to twenty-five when he died the first death. Dark-haired, blue-eyed, a handsome open face, with a nose just a tad too big, too—what was the word?—aquiline, like the profiles on Roman coins. On the short side, but strongly built. He looked like he would handle his sword with some force. His straight hair was fashionably cut and his clothes were well-made, but seemed somehow ill fitting.

No, Duncan thought, as he looked more closely. It wasn't the cut of the clothes. However old the stranger was as an Immortal—and Duncan had long ago learned for himself the truth of what Connor had told him, that there was no way to tell—this young man was simply not used to large, brilliantly lit rooms, redolent with the various scents of expensive men and women.

Duncan nodded imperceptibly at Amanda and started toward the stranger. If he was here to give a Challenge—well, it would be a shame for the lady to have to soil her snow-white gown.

Danny O'Donal stopped just inside the entrance of the Queen of Spades. His teacher had said that they would meet here. A saloon he had said, called the Queen of Spades. And this must be that place, for wasn't that the name on the fancy sign outside? Danny had been in saloons before, of course. But here there were no spittoons, nor sawdust on the floor. Instead, there were white roses everywhere, in vases of the finest glass. And a bar of dark wood polished so that you could see yourself near as well in it as in the mirror behind. The walls were red, velvet he thought, and he'd never seen the like of the golden lamps hanging above, like upside-down trees they were, with candles blazing at the end of every branch. And who was the beautiful lady in the painting above the polished bar? Not naked, like some such paintings Danny had seen, but wearing a dress as dark as her hair and eyes, cut just low enough that the soft place between her pearly white breasts could be glimpsed. Danny was transfixed, assaulted by the sights and sounds and smells of this saloon, this Queen of Spades. Indeed, he near forgot to attend to that feeling his teacher had told him meant that another one of their kind was around. But the feeling was strong, and he reluctantly turned his gaze from the painting and connected it to a tall, handsome man who had just left the bar and was heading toward him. For a second, he felt a flutter of fear. But his teacher had said that the Immortals who would be at this saloon were friends, and could be trusted. So Danny stood his ground as the man approached.

The man stopped in front of him.

"Duncan MacLeod . . ." he said. His eyes were cold, cautious, ". . . of the Clan MacLeod."

Danny swallowed. "Daniel Patrick O'Donal of—uhh—the city of New York?"

The man was about to speak again when his eyes grew even colder. Danny felt it, too. Another Immortal. He thought—he hoped—he knew who.

He'd half turned as a clatter of footsteps sounded from the stairs to the foyer below. A familiar figure strode in, a full smile on his face, his mop of curly hair damp from the night mist.

Danny grinned hugely in relief, and from behind him, he heard Duncan MacLeod exclaim:

"Fitzcairn, ye worthless piece of British offal. What in blazes are ye doing here?"

"She was blond. Golden blond with the softest, downiest . . ." Hugh Fitzcairn noticed that Amanda had paused at the top of the staircase and was glaring back at him. She had been not at all pleased to have her plans for the night interrupted by their arrival, and had made that clear to him, if not to his young companion. Ah, it was a good thing that heads did not roll with a look, or the simple wishing of it! He chuckled. "Well, Danny, let's just say I was in a position to know how blond. 'Twas the wench we met in Versailles who had hair like autumn leaves, MacLeod."

The three men sat in a dim corner of the Queen of Spades, at a table littered with empty glasses, empty bottles of brandy and champagne, and a heavy brass ashtray holding the stubs of Duncan's cigars.

Filthy things, Fitz thought, as he drew on his pipe. It was one he'd had now for almost a hundred years, and he felt it was almost properly broken in.

A door slammed below. Duncan flinched slightly. Danny, who had spent several hours almost speechless in the actual presence of "the lady in the painting," raised his head at the sound. Fitz grinned.

"A thing of beauty. A joy forever."

"If you think so," Duncan said, draining his glass, "then why have you never turned your eyes her way?"

"Don't you recall, laddie, you asked me that once, long ago?" Fitz leaned back in his chair and blew out a stream of aromatic smoke. "We were drinking in a wayside inn that was hardly more than a sty. Somewhere near Heidelberg, it was, and though the ale was swill, we were much less discriminating then. It went down hard, but we managed to consume a vast quantity." He paused. "I don't quite remember how the subject of the fair Amanda came up—"

"Well, I don't remember any of it," Duncan interrupted. "It may be I'm getting forgetful in my old age. Tell me again. In the past three hundred fifty years, I've been witness to your wooing of all manner of women, from scullery maids to at least one princess I could name. So why not the fair Amanda?"

Fitz smiled, and leaned forward across the table. He nodded toward Danny. "Listen, my boy, and learn. A man must have standards in his life. Mortals have only so much time to find things out." He tapped a champagne bottle with the stem of his pipe, then a bottle of brandy. "Do I like wine, or spirits? Do I"—he tilted back and examined the crotch of his pants—"dress right or left? Do I prefer my women"—he leaned in again—"with some flesh on their bones, or as slender as lily stalks?

"However, those of us gifted with Immortality can, over the span of our years, refine our standards to the pure, clear essentials. I"—he pointed his pipe at Duncan, and used it to sketch lines in the air—"have three requirements in a woman. That she be beautiful"—a stroke of the pipe—"mortal"—a second—"and compliant." A third.

"Amanda is for certain beautiful, Hugh," Danny said, looking toward the painting above the bar.

"Ah, but one out of three just won't do," Fitzcairn replied.

MacLeod shook his head. "It's all coming back to me. The inn. The ale. The pain the next morning. Yes, I have heard this before. I remember it now. And"—he rose from his chair—"I also remember a time or two when you have compromised those refined standards."

"Sometimes, Highlander," Fitz responded with great assumed dignity, "I am presented with occasions to which I must arise."

Duncan laughed. "And someday, Englishman, some stubborn, plain Immortal lass will hold your heart at sword's point. I can but hope that I'll be there to see it."

"We're going to live forever, Duncan MacLeod, so you may well see that, and much else besides. But even if you live to be the One, you'll not see the day come when I risk heart or head with the lady in white." As he spoke, Fitz gestured toward the stairs.

MacLeod laughed again. Danny, after asking the whereabouts of the jakes, excused himself to make use of it. He paused on the way out to steal another long look at the portrait above the bar.

After he left, MacLeod poured more champagne for the two of them. Danny's glass sat, still half-full. Duncan hesitated.

"The lad's not much of a drinker, at least not these days," Fitz said.

"You've known him long, then?" MacLeod asked.

Well, Fitz thought, there was a long and a short answer to that question. And since the hour was late, he'd give out the short.

"We met in New Orleans about five years past. I was visiting a friend in an—establishment, in a part of the city where the gentry seldom go." He drank a swallow of the champagne. "I had a drop or two—though nothing as fine as this—and I got into a rather violent disagreement with another patron of the place. A much larger patron."

"One of us?"

"No, the brute carried no sword. But he did carry a nasty short club, studded with nails. And I was by way of getting the worst of it when Danny stepped in. He was working at the place as what a colorful fellow I met in Philadelphia called hired muscle." He paused, noting a fleeting look on MacLeod's face.

"Make no mistake, Highlander. The lad is on the small side, but he is strong and quick. He kept his head for quite a few years, pretty much on his own. Taught himself to use a sword, practiced by himself, faced a few Challenges. And I've taught him a thing or three since we met."

"Head-butting?" Duncan asked, innocently.

Fitz ignored him. "As I was saying, Danny put himself between the large fellow and me, at some risk to his own person."

"But he must have known what you are—that you weren't really in any grave danger."

"Of death, not. Of damage, oh my yes! So he stopped the fight, and got me back to my lodging. And lost his job over it, since the large gentleman was a regular customer, and I was not. And his bed, which was in the establishment." Fitz shrugged. "I owed him then, a meal at least. And a few lessons, to add some finesse to his swordwork. And a bit of advice about improving his position in the world."

"So you've been traveling together then—what—five years, you said?"

Fitz nodded. For tonight at least, he hoped that MacLeod would settle for the basics. For Fitz, man of words that he was, was not certain that he could find the exact words to tell his friend how he surprised himself when he had realized that he had—with no intention to do so—become Danny O'Donal's teacher.

Danny's return saved him the need to give the Highlander further details. Duncan then left himself, to attend to his own needs. The young Immortal did not immediately rejoin Fitzcairn. He roamed the room, running his fingers over polished wood, green felt, and brass railings. The place was spotless except for their table, cleaned after closing every night by instructions of the owner.

"When shall you ask him, Hugh?" the young man questioned. "Are you still thinking he'll agree? I'd wonder at that. To my mind, this seems a good place to be."

Fitz shifted in his chair; his pipe was out again. He found a match in his vest pocket, carefully played the flame over the bowl, and drew in deeply, as the tobacco glowed once more.

Of course Danny would think that the Queen of Spades was a good place to be. A lot of men, mortal or not, would find little to object to in living in a thriving city. Living well, judging by Duncan's clothes and the thickness of the stack of banknotes in his money clip, living with a woman as beautiful and successful and wealthy as Amanda.

But Duncan MacLeod was Hugh Fitzcairn's oldest friend, and Immortals measured friendships in centuries. Fitz knew that the Immortality that he savored for all the possibilities that it offered him—an attitude he was attempting to share with young Danny O'Donal—sometimes weighed on Duncan. The Highlander was prone to introspective musings, periods when his sense of honor and duty drained his life of joy.

Hugh Fitzcairn was an honorable man, as honorable as any Englishman ever born could be, Duncan would say. And if he took on a responsibility, he fulfilled it. But for him, Immortality was not about the Game, though he had fought and taken heads when he had to. Hugh did want to live forever—but he didn't actually expect to.

No, Fitzcairn thought, as fragrant smoke curled from his pipe, for him Immortality was an adventure. The extra time that he and his kind were given was to be used, was to be filled with new experiences, with exploring all the places on the earth that a simple English boy—called Hugh by the farmer's wife who found him in a rock-strewn field—would never have known existed, had he not died, struck down by a jealous husband, his body dumped into a storm-swollen river where he drowned, water filling his aching lungs, as darkness closed around him. Until, who knew how long after, far downstream, he sputtered back to life, and was pulled from the waters by a member of the King's Guard named Henry Fitzmartin. So he lived again, lived to become—to learn to become—the Immortal Hugh Fitzcairn.

Over the last few hours, Fitz had watched MacLeod closely, and listened to the words beneath the words. The Highlander was feeling restless. He was thinking too much. About his friend Alec Hill. About a woman named Sarah he'd known before he came to San Francisco. Something had happened between them that MacLeod wasn't easy with. He was thinking about his relationship with Amanda and his life here with her. It was as plain as could be. As his oldest friend, it was his obligation to save Duncan from himself. The man was in desperate need of a change, of a new experience, of—an adventure. *Hugh Fitzcairn, at your service!* he thought.

"Danny, boy, fetch a fresh lamp. The light is almost gone. And MacLeod"—he called to his friend, who had just reentered the saloon—"come here now. I've something to show you."

Danny brought the lamp, and Fitz cleared a space on the table, moving the brass ashtray and several glasses aside. The three men sat once more, as Fitz reached into the inside breast pocket of the jacket that hung on the chair behind him. He drew out a small leather pouch. Opening the drawstrings, he spilled the contents into the empty space before them.

Duncan whistled softly. "All that glitters . . ." he said.

"Actually, laddie, it *is* gold in this case." Fitz fleetingly thought of the two illiterate swordsmen they had been when they first met. Now they could quote one of Will Shakespeare's plays with ease.

The five nuggets, each about the size of the last joint in a man's thumb, did actually glitter in the light of the fresh lamp.

Fitz nudged one to the side with his pipe stem. "This is for our passage. We'd take ship from here to Seattle, and then another from there to Alaska."

A second.

"And this for lodging, and such, when we arrive. There are hotels there, I've heard, as fancy as any in this city. And places where a man can find entertainment, of all shapes and sizes."

A third and fourth.

"These for outfitting, gear. Food. A guide, I would think. There'll be those already there who will know what we need."

"And the last"—he picked up the nugget and held it between his thumb and forefinger—"for luck. One—what is it the kiddies say at birthdays?—one to grow on. There's many more like this there, just lying around, there for the taking, I've heard."

Duncan sat silent. Fitz watched him closely. Danny fidgeted, reached out to touch one of the nuggets, and drew back, as though it were somehow dangerous to handle.

Finally, the Highlander began fumbling at his watch pocket.

"MacLeod, ye thickheaded Scot," Fitz grumbled, "it's not the time to check the time." He tossed the fifth nugget back on the table.

"That would be two to grow on," Duncan stated as he withdrew a sixth nugget and tossed it on the table.

Danny gasped in surprise, as Fitzcairn, blue eyes sparkling, threw his head back and laughed aloud.

"A gift from the lady in white?" he guessed.

Duncan smiled. "After the *Excelsior* docked, this place was packed with men just come down from the north, with their suitcases full of gold. More than a few nuggets were gambled away that night. Amanda gave this one to me to work into a watch fob. But I guess it will be put to a different use now."

"So, you'll join us then, Highlander?"

"I'm thinking that I might regret this after a cup or two of coffee, but, yes, I'll join you."

Fitzcairn whooped with delight. He rose, grabbed a half-full bottle of champagne, long since gone flat, and a glass.

"Bring glasses, lads, and follow me."

Duncan and Danny trailed after the capering figure who, golden curls flying, danced across the Queen of Spades, down the stairs, and out the front door.

The sky was not yet light, but that gray that comes before the glow of the dawn. Fitz took a minute to get his bearings, then filled their glasses to overflowing, laughing as Duncan stepped back to save his boots from a splash of warm champagne.

Fitz positioned them and raised his glass for a toast in—he hoped—the right direction.

"North," he cried, "to Alaska."

Chapter 2

The next morning had brought a second thought or two. But Fitz went about booking their passage to Seattle while Duncan considered how best to broach the matter with Amanda.

The moment seemed right a few nights later, as they lay together in Amanda's bed, tangled in peach satin. But before he could turn the subject, a knock on the door summoned them to the disaster that ended Amanda's newfound pleasure in her identity as mistress of the Queen of Spades.

The saloon had burned down, reduced to blackened, smoldering ruins. Amanda wandered through the devastation, raging at fate—and at Kit, whom she somehow held responsible. Duncan had rarely seen her so distressed. His first instinct was to change plans and stay with her in San Francisco.

Then Fitz stepped in. He told Amanda what they were about, reminding her of the fortunes that had come off the *Excelsior*. At first she raged anew at Duncan for thinking of leaving her. But her rage turned quickly to cold calculation. Finally, she bade him go—with the promise that he would share any fortune he might find equally with her.

So here he stood, barely a week later, on the deck of a fine clipper ship, watching the waterfront of San Francisco fade in the distance.

Fitzcairn joined him at the rail, snug in a heavy pea jacket, a red knitted scarf wound 'round his neck.

"Oh, I say," he drawled, "look there. If you squint, you can see Amanda, still on the dock, gazing forlornly after you." He made a show of shading his eyes with one hand and peering toward shore.

Duncan snorted. "Well, she did take time to see us off, at least." He glanced around. "And where is young Danny? Still reeling from Amanda's farewell kiss?"

"Ah, the lad does have stars in his eyes, it's true. At the moment, however, what he's suffering from most is not *l'amour* but *mal de mer.* I left him, and a slop bucket, in the cabin."

They both laughed, laughter tinged with sympathy. Duncan could well remember his first time at sea. It was crossing the Channel to France. Fitz doubtless had his own similar tale to tell.

As the centuries rolled by, it was inevitable—even necessary—that older Immortals began to forget some details of place, time, and person. Some by choice but more by chance, simply by virtue of the fact that while the span of years given to them might be measureless, in most other ways they were like the mortals whose lives they shared. And what mortal husband had never forgotten his wife's birthday? Or what mortal woman did not sometimes have to stop to recall the color of her second lover's eyes?

So the memory lapses of the Immortals were to be understood. Indeed, Duncan had such himself. But he had never, in all his years, encountered one of his kind, friend or enemy, who did not remember—vividly—his or her first time at sea.

Belowdecks, young Danny was probably working on his own indelible experience.

"Should we tend to him? He'd be better on deck."

"Tried that," Fitz replied. "He just moaned and asked me to kill him."

The shoreline was no longer visible. All around, all that could be seen was the mighty ocean called the Pacific. For Danny's sake, Duncan hoped it lived up to its name.

"Come now, Highlander," Fitz said. "I've some rum in the cabin we can heat. There's maps to look over and plans to be made."

Together they descended the narrow wooden staircase that was almost a ladder and made their way down the corridor to the cabin that they were sharing.

It was on the small side, though well-appointed. If they had been willing to delay their departure, more spacious accommodations would have been available. But each man, for his own reasons, wanted to be on his way, so the three booked what was best available.

At the door, Duncan felt the presence of another Immortal. Fitz, too, hesitated a split second. Though they both knew it was Danny, Duncan opened the latch cautiously.

Oh, yes. It was definitely Danny. Inside, the odor of sickness was strong, and from the shadowy recesses of one of the lower bunks, a weak voice whispered hollowly.

"Hugh? Could you maybe be taking my head now? Please?"

Fitz moved past Duncan and went to attend to the young man. He emptied the slop bucket out of the porthole, and replaced it by Danny's head. Then he poured cold water from the pitcher on the table into a basin, soaked clean cloths in it, and laid them gently on his forehead.

Duncan busied himself by lighting the oil lamp, removing

the maps from the bag where they were stored, and spreading them on the table.

He marveled at Fitzcairn's solicitousness and wondered about Danny O'Donal. He'd talked to his friend a bit further about the young Immortal, gotten the basics of his background. Still, Fitz had played many roles in the years Duncan had known him—and teacher had never been among them. That he had taken on Danny O'Donal said much about the young man. So Duncan could not help but be curious about the details.

Well, there would be time for that discussion later. Now, by lamplight, Duncan trailed his fingertips over the thick paper that covered the table, tracing the outline of the landmass that made up the territory of Alaska. Over half a million square miles, the maps all said. Bought by Abraham Lincoln's secretary of state, William Seward, from the Tsar of all the Russias, for a pittance. Which, Duncan reflected, had seemed to be about what it was worth. Until just last year, when gold was discovered. Now, as had happened sixty years before in California, the rush was on.

Fitz left Danny, who had fallen into a fitful sleep, and joined Duncan at the table.

"Some rum, then?" Without waiting for a reply, he produced a bottle and two cups, and proceeded to pour them each a generous portion.

So they sat there, far into the night, drinking good dark rum, studying the maps, arguing about the days to come, these two Immortal men who had known one another for centuries. While nearby another of their kind, a child by their reckoning, moaned and tossed in his sleep.

So cold, it was. And wet. He'd woken up not knowing whether it was morning or night—they never did, down in the hold. He'd woken up in his mother's arms, and she'd been cold, colder even than he was. And he'd tried to snuggle closer between her breasts, had clung to her, waiting for her to hug him back. But she didn't. No matter how hard he'd squeezed, she didn't. She was still. And so cold. And he began crying them, soft sobs that grew louder and louder still, until one of the other women saw what had happened. She called her man, and they pulled him from Katie O'Donal's arms, as the great ship pitched beneath them. And Danny screamed, and closed his eyes, and pretended it was but a night terror, brought by a pookah. But it wasn't.

Danny O'Donal did not get his sea legs at all quickly. Fitzcairn continued to care for the young Immortal, cheerfully it seemed. He kept him clean. He fed him clear broth, when the lad could keep something on his stomach. And he woke him gently in the middle of the night, when Danny would cry out wordlessly in his sleep.

Finally, Danny felt strong enough to be up and about. And once he was no longer captive to the slop bucket, he was increasingly impatient to reach their destination. Though the days passed swiftly enough as the ship headed north following the coast of California, Danny spent much of his time pacing the deck. It was as if he were trying to make the winds blow stronger by sheer force of will. Duncan and Fitz, for their part, spent the time planning, then arguing about the plans.

They met a few of their fellow travelers, men from as far away as the coast of Maine, all struck by the disease the newspapers were calling Klondike fever. There were tables in the mess set aside for use of the passengers. Sometimes, at meals, the three Immortals were drawn into the endless conversations concerning the proper disposition of the wealth that they were all sure was waiting for them at journey's end. Some dreams were big, some small . . .

—"There's a sweet piece of farmland right next ta our'n. My pappy tried ta buy it once't . . ."

—"Horses, of course. Racehorses. Only the finest Kentucky blood. And a stable, and grooms, and trainers and—oh, all of that."

—"There's a gal back home . . ."

When the question came around to Danny, he answered, without hesitation. "A grand house, on a beautiful wide avenue. With a strong, dark, polished wooden door. And square in the middle of the door, a knocker of solid gold. There'd be more than one window made of bits of colored glass, so that when the light came through, it would be like having a rainbow of your own. And behind the house would be a stable, bigger and cleaner than the places most ordinary folks live."

"You know such a place?" Duncan asked.

"I did, when I was a lad. My—sister—was in service there. In New York City, it was."

Fitz spoke then, of buying fine things for fine ladies. And of not having to do an honest day's work, ever again. Duncan laughed along with the rest at that, but for the most part was silent.

Later, as they made ready for bed, Danny asked, "Are you not interested in the gold then, Mr. MacLeod? Is it that you don't need it?"

Duncan winced a little at the "Mister." "I've money enough right now, Danny. Though there have been times when that wasn't the case. Being rich—well, it is better than being poor, I'll not disagree. But it's not everything."

The young Immortal shook his head. "Poor. It's but a word, I guess. Like a lot of words, if you say it over and over, it doesn't seem to mean much. But if you *live* it over and over . . ." He turned away then, and said no more.

* * *

He'd gone to bed hungry again, an ache in his stomach, the taste of the thin stew that had been dinner sour on his tongue. In the other room, Big Tom and Mother Kelly were arguing again. About "the child." He was "the child." The extra mouth Big Tom did not want to feed. But I brought three coins home today, from the begging, I did, *he wanted to say.* Don't turn me out, I've seen those that live on the street, I've seen what becomes of them. *But he was too frightened to do a thing but softly cry himself to sleep.*

The crew was to be avoided. They didn't want the passengers underfoot while they were about their work. Besides which, there was no privacy to be had on deck. So Duncan had taken to doing his swordwork in the hold. It was cramped and dim, but without doubt, he had the space to himself.

Shirtless, he moved the *katana* gracefully through a ritual of cuts and slashes. His whole being, mind and body, was in focus. Forward. Back. Again. Then repeat. It was no task, but a joy to perform—until his concentration was abruptly broken. He turned, furious at the interruption.

"Fitzcairn, ye great annoyance, I told ye what I was a—" Then he saw that it was Danny O'Donal in the shadows.

"Hugh has told me often of your sword, Mr. MacLeod. And how skilled you are. I thought, if I might watch a bit?"

It would be rude to refuse, though he was not keen on an audience.

"All right, then," Duncan said. "But take care. There's not much space down here."

"I know," Danny replied, in an odd voice.

Duncan returned to his exercises, drawing his energy inward again and then releasing it in a glorious pattern of deadly motion.

When it was completed, he rested briefly before donning his shirt.

"I've not ever seen the likes of that, Mr. MacLeod," Danny said. "It's almost a dance, is it not? But a dangerous one." He hesitated. "Nor have I seen a weapon like yours. It came from across this very ocean, Hugh said. Could I see it closer?"

Duncan hesitated—any of their kind would—then handed the *katana* to the young Immortal.

Danny took it, running one hand gently, carefully, down the blade. He fingered the grip, the intricate carving. Even in the dimness of the hold, the beauty of the sword was apparent.

"I've been to a museum or two, with Hugh. And nothing there was the equal of this."

"It belonged to a very brave and noble man. A mortal," Duncan said. He extended his hand, and Danny returned the *katana*. "It was his dying gift to me."

Danny smiled, with a twist of his lips. "I carry a dead mortal's sword, too." He produced his blade. It was the first MacLeod had seen of it. A military saber, an officer's sword by the look of it, still bearing the gold-fringed tassel of rank.

"You were in the war, then?" Duncan asked.

"Aye," Danny replied. "But I did not kill for this, if that's what you are thinking. I died for it. In truth, when I got this sword, I'd died already four or five times."

He frowned. "I'd come to believe that I was an unnatural creature. A pookah, a thing that only the dead or dying can see. I thought that, when the war was over, if I went home, I would cease to exist. But there was none I could speak to about what had happened, so I kept on, marching and killing."

It was spring, 1864. The Union Army, under the command of General Grant, had moved south, taking the fight to the Rebs. For near a month, they fought clear down the state of Virginia, from a river in the north all the way to a city called Petersburg. History would say that those four weeks were the worst of the war. Danny O'Donal would not disagree. Men died by the thousands, Yank and Reb alike. Danny was wounded, more than a few times, and the others started to notice how quickly he healed. Even General Hays, who had led the men from Western Pennsylvania since the beginning, took note when Danny was one of but two of the thousands wounded to survive the fighting at Cold Harbor. Hays was killed the next day, though, so his noticing didn't matter. Then his troops were put under command of a general named Burnside.

By then the Union Army had Petersburg under siege. Burnside had the bright idea to tunnel under the city. He ordered a detachment of men from Western Pennsylvania, assuming they were all coal miners, to dig the tunnel and pack it with gunpowder. Danny was among them. And when the gunpowder was ignited and the explosion over, several Union divisions ended up trapped in the resultant chaos. Danny was among them, too, and he quickly fell to the Rebel fire from above. Wisely, the Union commander surrendered, and Danny, by then revived, was among those taken prisoner.

"It was there that I finally found out what I was. Not a pookah. An Immortal, though what that might be . . ." He smiled faintly, and continued. "I was chained to a wall in a stable they were using to hold the prisoners when I got the— feeling. I'd gotten it once or twice before, during the fighting, but I hadn't any notion what it was. Then a Reb officer, a captain he was, came into the stable. I could tell at once that the feeling was because of him. He ordered that I be unshackled and brought to his quarters.

"He sat me down, got me coffee, and a good meal. And he told me."

The officer's name was Lucas Desirée. He was a good man, fighting in a bad cause, and he wished he could do more for the frightened, inexperienced young man whom he had immediately recognized as another Immortal. But the damn war would not be over, and he had no time to take a student, certainly not a Yankee. He took the time, though, to tell the young Immortal what he needed to know—about the Game and the Rules. About how he could truly die. About how there were others like them who would hunt him, for his head, and his Quickening.

"And he gave me my sword"—Danny held it aloft—"a Union officer's saber. A brave man, Captain Desirée said, who'd died well. He told me to honor it." He touched the blade carefully. "The next day, the city fell, and I never saw him again. I hope that he is living still, that none of the worst of us ever found him."

"So do I, Danny," Duncan echoed.

"You knew him?"

"For a very short while. He was a true gentleman."

Danny regarded the sword. "I've tried to do what he asked of me, all the years since. Though sometimes, it's been terrible hard."

"It is for all of us. It's a part of who we are and what we do."

"And does it get easier in time, Mr. MacLeod?"

No, it does not, that was the truth of it. But it was not his place to say so. Answering such questions was part of what Fitz had taken on. So he simply shook his head, put on his shirt, and led the young Immortal back up to the sunlit deck.

They were nearing the port of Seattle. Crew and passengers alike were abuzz with excitement. But Danny, who had not slept well the previous night, was belowdecks, lying on his bunk, dozing.

It was snowing, big white flakes. They fell softly on the dark hair of the green-eyed girl child who lived in the fine house where Molly Kelly was in service. She nearly smiled at Danny as she swept by him. Then she stepped into her carriage, and a flutter of white linen fell toward the ground from the warmth of her white fur muff. Danny reached for it and it turned into the hem of the snow-white dress Amanda had been wearing that first night at the Queen of Spades. She smiled down at Danny, her dark eyes bright, and—

"Danny O'Donal" Fitzcairn shouted, bursting through the door. "Get yourself up, lad!" He pulled Danny from the bunk. "There's a sight you must see!"

He was nearly dragged from the cabin and up the narrow stairs. On deck, he saw that most of the passengers, Duncan MacLeod among them, were gathered on the left—port—side of the boat. Hugh pushed him forward with one hand and with the other pointed out to sea. "Look there, young Danny."

Danny looked. At first he was not certain what he was seeing. But then it became clear. Sea creatures. Huge gray beasts, swimming along beside the boat, rising and falling in the water.

Hugh seemed excited, near gleeful. Even Duncan MacLeod was smiling broadly.

Danny was remembering Father O'Malley, speaking from the altar of his wee dark church. The pews would be full, for many of the folk unfortunate enough to dwell in Five Points were good Irish Catholics, who had fled the famine—like Katie O'Donal, who had died on the boat, and Moira Kelly, who had taken him from her arms—and they heard Mass and took communion every Sunday. He was remembering, most particularly, the Bible story about the man named Jonah.

"Uhh, these beasts?" he began. "It's whales, they are? Are they—are we—should we be . . . ?"

No one was listening. A number of smaller gray creatures had been sighted.

"They're the babes, Danny," Hugh exclaimed. "See how the grown ones gather round them?"

"They're called calves, I think," MacLeod said.

"Calves? Are ye daft, Highlander? These are fish, not cattle!"

Danny edged closer to the rail. The whale fish looked fair big enough to swallow a man all right. But not a whole boat. He relaxed a little. They were a fine sight, indeed. Being here, seeing these beasts, being on the way to this place called Alaska—all this he supposed was part of the infinite possibilities that being an Immortal had given him. Hugh would say so. Right now, Danny would have to agree.

It was their last night at sea. And a fine clear night it was! After finishing their evening meal in the cabin, the three Immortals sat for a time on the deck, near the bow of the ship. Fitz had a small spyglass, and he and Duncan were pointing out the various constellations to Danny.

"Look, Hugh," The young Immortal pointed into the night sky at a fall of stars. " 'Tis a shower of gold! Will it land, do you think, where we can pick it up?"

Fitzcairn grinned and raised the spyglass to his right eye. "A pretty thought that, lad. All we'll be needing to find is a handful or three each and we can live like nobility for a century or so."

"And never do an honest day's work again, which would suit some of us, if I recall correctly," Duncan added.

Fitz swiped at him with the spyglass, and missed.

"Mr. Macleod . . ." Danny hesitated. "You never did say—why are you with us, then, if not for the gold?"

Duncan gazed into the distance, out over the midnight sea. "The man who lost that nugget of gold to Amanda—he didn't talk much of what he'd done to make his fortune. But he did speak often of what are called the Northern Lights." He gestured toward the sky. "Brilliant colors, sweeping across the stars. Sometimes in waves, like the tides. Only to be seen at the far edge of the world. It sounded like a sight that any man, Immortal or not, should see for himself."

"Like a rainbow of darkness, that's what it sounds to me," Danny said, eyes wide at the thought.

"Well, lad," Fitz said, as he handed Danny the spyglass, digging in his pockets for pipe and tobacco, "if luck is with us, there will be one of those pots of gold at the end of it. And admit it, MacLeod," he added, "if we were to make a strike, you'd find some use for the wealth. Unless you've filled that warehouse in Paris already?"

Duncan smiled. "There's space left. I've only had it for a hundred years or so, you know."

Fitz answered the young Immortal's unspoken question. "The Highlander collects, Danny. Odds and ends of things that catch his eye. A lot of it is plaid."

"I wouldn't expect you to see the value in anything that could not be eaten, drunk, or taken to bed, Fitzcairn," Duncan retorted. "But the day will come when some of those things will prove their worth."

"Do you have any fine glass?" Danny asked, obviously interested.

"Glass? Why, yes, I do in fact," Duncan replied, surprised. "Some crystal, Austrian-made. Amanda had one vase in the Queen of Spades—"

"Tell him about Temperanceville," Fitz said, as he made himself a comfortable seat on a nail keg.

Danny leaned back on the rail next to Duncan. "When I was sixteen or so, I moved there—to Temperanceville—with the woman who had raised me as her own. It's a town just by a city in the western part of the state of Pennsylvania. Pittsburgh, it's called. It was, they say, built first as a fort, at the fork of three rivers. Have you ever been there, Mr. MacLeod? The countryside is fair green, and hilly."

"No, but I know of it," Duncan replied. Pittsburgh had been fiercely abolitionist. Though he had had many contacts there around thirty years before, he had never actually seen the city.

In the dark a match flared, as Fitz attempted to relight his pipe. "One of the places where we fought the bloody French."

"We?" If it were possible, the single word was said with a distinct burr.

Fitz chuckled, as Danny continued. "There was work to be had in the area, in the mills and the mines and the factories. I found a place in one of the glass factories. The job was hot and hard, it was, but some of the things we made were lovely to see." He smiled in the darkness. "I often wondered what fine tables they might be setting."

"You were there before the war?" Duncan asked.

Danny sighed. "Aye. And after, too. Which was my undoing."

After his encounter with Lucas Desirée, Danny at least knew what he was. And the knowing helped. But when the war was over, he could think of nothing to do but return to Temperanceville.

When he got back, he found that he'd been reported killed, one place or another. Some that served with him who had been wounded were home, too, and he noted them giving him sideways glances. And Mother Kelly was in failing health.

He had been back a bit more than a year when the worst that could happen did. He was at the glass factory, working an extra shift one cold winter day, when a boiler blew. The explosion rocked the building. Hot shards of metal flew everywhere. Clouds of steam billowed. Danny, working closest to the blast, was lifted clear off his feet and thrown through the brick sidewall of the factory. He lay motionless in the rubble. The foreman knelt, felt for his pulse, and shook his head. *To come through four years of the war, and die like this,* he thought.

Then Danny moaned, opened his eyes, and sat up.

In a matter of hours, the story was all over Temperanceville. The old women made signs to ward off evil as he passed. Young wives pulled children from his path. He found his belongings on his landlady's porch, and she would not answer his knocks.

And standing by an open window of the Temperanceville Tavern, he heard John Kelly—brother to the long-dead Big Tom—talking to the men. About pookahs. And the evil fey. And cleansing by fire.

Though he thought he could not be killed by burning, Danny did not want to test the theory. His bags were packed—his landlady had seen to that. But there was one last thing he had to do.

"She told me then, Mother Kelly did, that I was not Katie O'Donal's son any more than I was hers. Katie had lost her husband and her wee infant to the famine, so when she found me in the very cradle where her babe had died, she asked no questions of God or man."

"We're all foundlings, Danny, you know?" Duncan said.

"Now I know. I didn't then. And Captain Desirée didn't tell me that part."

"Where we came from, lad, is not nearly as important as where we go," Fitz said. "Captain Desirée may have known that."

"She said that there were many who called me Katie's changeling child, left by the faery folk, an unnatural creature who would only bring ill to her. When she died on the ship on the way over, some who knew the story wanted to throw me overboard. But Mother Kelly would not let them do so, and fought with her husband, Big Tom, to save me." Danny paused. "Do you believe in the faery folk, Mr. MacLeod, that we might be of them? Hugh doesn't."

Who am I then? What am I? Duncan remembered the man he had been, begging an answer from the only father he had ever known. "That's one thing Fitzcairn and I do agree on," he answered, "though there are many who have thought that about us."

"Big Tom Kelly did, long before I—died. That was the reason of his not wanting me when I was a child. And John Kelly had heard the tale, too. After the accident at the factory, he was certain. But Mother Kelly said that it mattered not to her from where I had come—I was her son, as true as any she had borne.

"I cried a bit then—a man can do that, I think, and still be a man—kissed her cheek, and left."

There was a silence then, each of the three caught for a moment in his own thoughts.

"I've been called far worse than changeling, young Danny," Fitz said finally. "Far worse."

"With cause, no doubt," Duncan added.

Danny laughed, a bit awkwardly. He was, Duncan guessed, shy of having told so much, yet pleased to be able to talk to those who understood. He moved away from the rail, yawned widely, and stretched, one hand reaching toward the sky. "The stars are falling still, Hugh," he said. "Could I catch one to carry in my pocket for luck, do you think?"

"They say they're made of fire, lad," Fitzcairn replied, "so that wouldn't do. But"— he drew out the leather pouch and opened it—"you can take this." He handed Danny the smallest of the nuggets.

From his coat, Danny took a small snow-white linen handkerchief trimmed in cobweb lace. Carefully, he placed the nugget in the exact center, tied it up, and returned it to his pocket.

"A satisfying lump, it is indeed." He grinned. "Good night then, Hugh, Mr. MacLeod. I think I'll slip this beneath my pillow, and have fair golden dreams."

After Danny left, the two older Immortals were alone in the night. Fitzcairn sat on a nail keg, enjoying his pipe, watching his old friend watching the sea.

MacLeod, he knew, was considering Danny's story, considering how much alike they all were, all Immortals. Such deep silent thought was MacLeod's way. Hugh Fitzcairn's way was to give voice to thought.

"So, here we are, we three. MacLeod. Fitzcairn. O'Donal. And none of us true sons to any man."

"Aye. Nor bastard sons, either. Though that's been said of both of us, now and then."

"Many a time. And I've, a time or two, been accused of bringing a Fitzcairn marked with the bar sinister into the world." He shook his head ruefully. "And what does it say about a relationship when a woman will take your word as a gentleman that you will not tell her husband of her trysts, but won't believe you when you insist that the child she is carrying cannot be yours?" Affecting a bluff heartiness, he continued, "Well, my dear, I regret to tell you that you shall, in the fullness of time, be giving birth to a legitimate child. Buck up, now, woman. Some of England's finest men have been legitimate. Not many. But some."

Duncan laughed. *Good,* Fitzcairn thought. *He is much easier to talk to when he is not in one of his damn dark Scot's moods.* Fitzcairn wrapped his scarf tighter around his neck. The night was getting chill.

Duncan leaned on the rail and faced Fitz. "He's still very young, Hugh," he said quietly, "your Danny O'Donal. And so"—Duncan spread his hands—"he's had so little and wants so much. Is it good to *need* so, I wonder?"

"Highlander," Fitz said, rising, "when you were but a young lad, you were still roaming the forests and mountains of your misbegotten land. You couldn't read, you never bathed, and you wore a skirt."

"And you, you Brit twit—"

"I never wore a skirt. And I did bathe. On occasion. But my point, which I would have sooner made had you not resorted to name-calling, is that in time we became the fine specimens of Immortal manhood that we are today. Time, MacLeod, is the one single thing we all have a wealth of.

"We learned. Danny will, too. He's a good man, with a good heart. And if his golden dreams don't come true this time—well, if a Scot can learn to wear trousers, anything is possible for an Irishman."

MacLeod sputtered. Over the centuries Fitz had realized that Duncan hadn't the true gift for insult that he himself possessed. It kept a balance in their friendship.

"What's possible right now is that I might throw ye in this ocean, Hugh Fitzcairn. As I recall, ye can barely swim. It might be amusing to watch ye bob up and down a while."

Fitz laughed heartily and clapped his friend on the arm. "Look now, MacLeod." He pointed toward a faint star. "The North Star. We're headed straight there. And I'm"—he began moving away—"headed belowdecks. Whether we're changelings, pookahs, or the bastard sons of some distant god, we sleep as mortals do. And," he added softly, "perchance we all do dream."

Chapter 3

"MacLeod!" Fitzcairn shouted. "Behind you—jackass!"

For a split second Duncan thought that Fitz was referring to the North American Trading and Transportation Company booking agent. They had been arguing with him for over a week about their reservations aboard the steamship *Portland*. It was due to leave for Alaska in four days' time, bound for the port of St. Michael. There they were to take further passage on a boat that would travel down the Yukon River. Their final destination was the place the newspapers called "the Eldorado city of Dawson," just over the Canadian border in the Yukon Territory.

If they had any hope of making it to the gold fields before autumn, they had to reach St. Michael before this month was out. Duncan had closely questioned those who sold them their supplies. From what they had said, he'd gotten some sense of how short a time the river was passable.

So far, however, the fact that they had documents guaranteeing their passage had not impressed the man. Their names, he insisted, were not on the passenger list.

The sound of cursing, screaming, and thundering hooves increased. Duncan's instincts, honed by centuries of life-and-death confrontations, took over. He jumped to the right just as a thousand pounds of runaway mule swept by.

The beast was braying in terror, kicking out randomly as it ran. The wharf area was jammed with men and women. Some were bound for the gold fields. Some had come to see the adventurers off. And some were there to exploit them. Not everyone was as quick as Duncan. Bodies tumbled about in the mule's wake.

A few yards away, Fitzcairn planted himself firmly. He dodged as the mule swept past, and grabbed for the frayed rope dangling from its halter.

He caught it all right, but Duncan saw at once that one man's weight was not going to be equal to the task of halting the animal's panicked flight.

"Hang on," he hollered, sprinting toward man and beast. Fitzcairn was leaning backward, hauling with all his strength. The mule circled him, kicking furiously.

"Have I a choice, Highlander?" he said through clenched teeth as he tightened his hold on the rope.

A vicious kick narrowly missed Duncan as he ran to Fitz's side. He grabbed the rope above where Fitz held it, and joined his weight to his friend's.

A crowd was beginning to surround them. Duncan heard shouts of encouragement, and advice. One voice, rising above the rest, cursed the mule with an astonishing variety of obscenities. *No doubt the owner,* Duncan thought.

Men and mule struggled mightily. Duncan heartily wished Danny was there. A third man would make the difference. But the young Immortal was back in their hotel, guarding their possessions. Though the Rainier Grand Hotel was a first-class establishment—that reservation at least had been honored—they had been warned by the desk clerk himself not to leave valuables unprotected even in a locked room. So until they could arrange an account at a local bank, one of them had to be watchman.

Still, even without Danny, he and Fitzcairn were winning the battle. The mule was tiring, its frenzy decreasing. Duncan's arms ached. He would be glad to be done with this little adventure soon.

At that moment, the crowd around began to stir. Shouts rang out, and people milled about.

Another runaway? Duncan wondered.

The crowd parted to reveal a well-proportioned closed carriage drawn by a matched pair of sleek white horses. While they were not at a gallop, they were definitely being driven at a pace faster than conditions on the crowded dock warranted.

Duncan, Fitzcairn, and the mule were directly in their path.

"Bloody hell!" Fitz shouted. They had no choice but to drop the rope and leap aside.

The coachman, seeing them, pulled up sharply. The white horses reared. The mule, loose once again, spooked anew. Rather than running off, it continued to move in a circle, braying furiously, kicking continuously.

Like a wooden pull toy with a mad child at the string, Duncan thought, as he scrambled out of range of the flying heels.

Fitzcairn had fallen backwards after letting loose the rope. As he rose to his knees, the iron-shod hooves caught him squarely on the rump. He was sent sprawling, headfirst, into several stacked crates of chickens, part of some gold seeker's provisions.

Wood splintered. Chickens flapped free. One flew at the mule, sending it racing down the wharf, the owner in futile pursuit. The coachman had left his seat and stood at the side of his team, calming them with his voice and his hands.

After the chaos of the last few minutes, the wharf seemed almost silent. Duncan went to assess what damage had been done to Fitzcairn. As he helped his friend roll over and sit up, a chicken nestled gently on Fitzcairn's head. Duncan tried to shoo it away.

Laughter, bright shiny laughter, sounded in the air.

Both Immortals looked up. A woman, framed by the carriage window, looked out at them. She had dark golden hair and a delicate, almost elfin face.

"Are y'all all right?" she asked. There was a touch of the South in her voice.

Duncan stepped forward, leaving Fitzcairn among the chickens.

"No harm done. Except to my friend's dignity." He smiled warmly. "I'm Duncan MacLeod."

Fitzcairn scrambled to his feet. Picking feathers from his jacket, he jostled Duncan aside. "And I'm Hugh Fitzcairn. I do hope this little incident hasn't spoiled the day for a lady as lovely as yourself."

A feather wafted slowly past his nose as he spoke.

The woman stifled a giggle. She seemed about to respond when the coachman approached. He whispered something. She frowned, and nodded.

As he climbed up and took the reins in his hand, the woman gave a smile and a small wave to the two Immortals.

"Mr. MacLeod. Mr. Fitzcairn. 'Bye now. You two be careful, you hear?"

She sat back and the carriage pulled away.

Fitz sighed. Duncan turned, regarding him with a critical eye.

"You've more than just chicken feathers in your hair, I swear. I don't think we'll be impressing anyone at the Transportation Company this afternoon."

"Oh, and it's my fault the jackass got loose again, I suppose? Who let go of the rope first, Highlander?"

"And what was I to do? Stand there and have us be run down?"

"Well," Fitz replied, "that would have gotten the lady's attention." He cocked his head thoughtfully. "No doubt she would have wanted to nurse me back to health, tending to me personally, day and—"

Duncan pulled a feather from Fitzcairn's hair. A strand or two came with it.

"Ow," he protested. "Off with you now, Highlander."

"Off with ye, ye endless lecher. Back to the hotel with us both."

Fitz nodded. "We can clean up." He brushed at his sleeve. "And give young Danny a chance to wander about if he wants."

They began walking toward the steep streets that led away from the water.

"Should we have supper in the room tonight, do you think?" Duncan asked. "If Danny goes out, it might be best to eat in."

"The room. The restaurant. It matters not to me." Fitz grimaced as he ran a hand through his curls, combing out more feathers and bits of unidentifiable debris. "As long as supper does not involve, in any way, shape, or form, chicken."

They were all alike then, Danny thought. All the places where the ships came and went. He remembered walking the levee at midnight, the Mississippi sparkling under a golden full moon. The air was so still and thick that you could near reach out and grab it. Yet the men were there, working. Black, white, and all the colors in between that New Orleans folk had a string of names for. They were loading and unloading the ships that came downriver from the North and upriver from the Gulf.

He stood at the end of Schwabacher's Dock staring up at the huge bulk of the *Portland.* Though it was late in the day, the sun was only now setting. He could see the ship clearly. Supplies were already piled on deck, and the crew were making her ready to set forth.

At supper, Hugh and Mr. MacLeod had concluded that since all else had failed, they must needs try bribing the booking agent.

And if bribery did not work? Danny did not want to ask. He did not want to have it said that their adventure might end here. It was a fair city, surrounded by mountains on three sides and the ocean on the fourth. Earlier in the week, he had found the area where the fine big houses were, all built to face the sea. He wandered the streets for hours, looking through windows, drinking in details.

A fair city indeed. But not one that held the promise of riches.

Danny sighed and walked on. The docks were crowded still. He heard a splash, and thought of summer evenings, decades past. The Kellys had moved uptown by then. The area, far better than Five Points, was still bad enough to be known as Hell's Kitchen. The boys of the street would swim the Hudson River, careful of the wakes of the big ships.

And the ships would pass by to dock at wharves like these. To be unloaded by the pas and uncles and brothers of the swimmers.

Big Tom had such a job. And one day when a half ton bale of cotton fell, it killed him.

Danny stopped for a minute and felt in his pocket for the scrap of white lace and linen that was always there. Once, there had been a gold coin wrapped in it, a coin given to him casually by the green-eyed girl, who'd mistook him for a beggar boy.

But, when Big Tom lay dead, Mother Kelly had no money to bury him. And it fell to Danny, her changeling child, to see to it that he had a proper wake. Money he'd put by from his job at the livery stable saw to that. The gold coin had gone then, to Father OMalley, to buy Big Tom a plot on holy ground.

When it was done, there was little left. Mother Kelly took in washing. Danny worked, and then worked more, sometimes eighteen hours a day. And, a time or two, stole from the produce wagons to put food on the table.

So no wonder Mother Kelly wept with joy when John Kelly offered her a place with him. She would come, she replied, and of course her Danny would come with.

The memory was a bitter taste on Danny's tongue. A short distance away, he knew, were places where the men who worked these wharves could stop and have a pint or two when their workday was done. Not fancy establishments like the Queen of Spades. These were raw, rough saloons, more akin to John Kelly's tavern.

He crossed the street, careful of the traffic. The sounds of cursing and tinny pianos beckoned him.

The door of the Golden Nugget swung open just as he reached the rough sidewalk. Was that not a sign, then? He started in—

But—he'd told Hugh that he'd not be long, that he'd just needed a breath of air. He and Mr. MacLeod would be wanting an early start, to be about their bribing. And he'd need to be in the room awake, to stand guard.

Danny shook his head. He'd go back to the room—and a grand room it was—and have a wee drop with Hugh, if he still felt the need. He'd walk, though. The night was clear and pleasant and he could, in truth, use the exercise.

The hills were steep, and he'd gone scarce three blocks when a sound in a narrow passage ahead stopped him short. He'd spent time enough in just such dark alleys to be immediately on guard. The danger was not from an Immortal. But it was real.

A scrape on the sidewalk behind—Danny threw himself forward. He felt a blow on his shoulder and his arm went numb. He hit the ground, and rolled over, kicking out and up. His bootheel struck bone. His assailant went down with an oath, clutching his knee.

Danny rolled again, trying to rise. But another man emerged from the alley. He swung a heavy cudgel in a vicious downward arc.

Training and experience took over. If the man held a sword, aimed at your head, you'd block with your own blade. Danny couldn't get to his sword. So he raised his already numb arm and took the force of the blow. Ignoring the pain, he drove his other fist into the man's groin with all his strength.

A third man appeared. Danny groaned. These odds were less and less to his liking.

But the newcomer was picking up the first assailant and booting him down the hill. The man from the alley had collapsed against the side of the building, clutching his privates, whimpering.

The newcomer helped Danny to his feet.

"Can you run, mate?" he asked. "These two might have friends about. Best to make ourselves scarce."

Danny nodded. His arm ached, but the pain would soon pass. He'd had more than enough experience at street fights to know that.

They headed back down toward the waterfront, toward the sounds of cursing and tinny pianos.

They stopped in front of the Golden Nugget.

"That was some close call, mate," the newcomer said. "Fighting always gives me a thirst. Join me?"

Well, Danny thought, *it would be rude to say no. Hugh would agree, I'm fair certain.*

They entered the Golden Nugget, shoving their way to the bar. Danny ordered whiskey with a beer chaser. His rescuer had whiskey straight.

They found a corner of the bar and huddled there.

"Jim Foster's the name, mate," the man said, extending his hand. "Most folks call me Slim Jim."

And it's no wonder why, Danny thought. The man was some six feet tall, but rail-thin. He had brown, curly hair and a pleasant, open face. He reminded Danny of a scarecrow or two he'd seen while marching through Pennsylvania.

"Daniel Patrick O'Donal. I'll be thanking you for your help, sir."

Slim Jim sipped his whiskey. "Just luck I was there, mate. You need to be careful these days, you know? Careful where you walk and such. There's thugs aplenty after a man's stake."

"Well, I'd not be carrying it on me now, would I?" Danny laughed.

"Some might." Slim Jim replied. "I guess you're all booked and loaded, then?"

Danny drank down the beer. "We thought we were."

Slim Jim raised an eyebrow. Danny chose to ignore it.

"Are you bound for the gold fields, too, then, Mr. Foster? The *Portland* sets out soon, I hear." Maybe he could find out something that would be useful to Hugh and MacLeod.

"The *Portland*? The Water Route? Not on your life. By the time those argonauts get to Dawson City, all the gold in the Klondike will be in other people's pockets."

Danny frowned, and downed his whiskey. He'd left the deciding of the route to the two older Immortals. They'd settled on the voyage up the Pacific Coast and then down the Yukon River.

But several drinks later his rescuer had convinced him: a short water trip to the Alaskan town called Skagway, followed by a forty-five-mile overland trek across the Canadian border to the Yukon River below Dawson City was the quickest and easiest of routes.

After all, Slim Jim said, whoever gets there first, gets the gold.

"It's Goo-no, laddie," Fitz said, as he passed a glass to Danny, "not Gow-nod. The Frenchies have a thing about d's and t's and such." He handed a second glass to MacLeod, who'd just returned from the gents.

It had taken all of Fitz's powers of persuasion to get the two other Immortals to come with him this evening. He had had a box at the Seattle Opera reserved for weeks, even before he and Danny had arrived in San Francisco. His passion for opera, nurtured at first by a buxom brunette soprano, had not diminished over time. He'd wanted to see this opera, a new one for him. *Though the story goes way back,* he thought.

MacLeod sipped his drink. "Well, this Gounod is better than some I've heard. That Austrian abomination you dragged me to the night Robert and Gina met—what was his name?"

"Lost and forgotten, thankfully." Fitz laughed. "This music sits well, I think. The actor singing Mephistopheles is beyond his range, though. But the Marguerite—as Monsieur Gounod would say, '*magnifique.*'" He kissed his fingertips and clutched his heart.

"Hugh was telling me that this man Faust is one of our kind, Mr. MacLeod," Danny said. "He promised me the truth of the story later."

"Hold him to that promise, Danny. It's quite a tale. Even without the music." Duncan swirled the liquid in his glass.

"Do you think that Johan has seen this particular version, Fitz?"

"It's 'Jack' now." Fitz corrected.

"Jack?" Duncan raised an eyebrow.

"He's living in Oxford, running a bookstore. 'JACK FAUST—FINE BOOKS AT FINE PRICES."

Duncan shook his head. "And the student body no doubt is taking endless delight in teasing him about his name."

"You know Johan, Highlander," Fitz replied. "He's more stubborn than that mule we encountered yesterday. And still determined to be the most guilt-ridden Immortal alive. He keeps the name to ensure that he'll be teased—it's part of his never-ending punishment."

The interval bell rang, and Fitz added, "Actually, he's one of the few of us who make you seem lighthearted." Duncan glowered, as Fitz took his glass and placed it on the bar. He urged his two friends back toward their box. They joined the crowd. Fitz excused himself, to answer a call of nature, he said.

In a moment, the lobby fell silent. The heavy interior doors closed. Fitz moved quietly across the thick carpet. He could faintly hear orchestra sounds. He glanced briefly to the right. MacLeod and Danny should be settled in their seats by now.

Fitz turned left.

All through the first act, he had done all he could to direct MacLeod's attention toward the stage or the orchestra or the floor below. Anywhere but the box directly across from theirs.

For there, half-hidden in the shadows, an elusive vision in what looked like rose-petal satin, sat the woman whose coach had nearly run them down on the dock.

Fitz first knew she was there when he heard her silvery laugh. Casually, he glanced at MacLeod. The Highlander was watching the stage intently. Casually, he raised his opera glasses. Casually, he trained them on the box opposite.

It was she. And she was alone.

Now, the act done, the interval over, MacLeod and Danny out of the way, Fitz was about to alter that situation. It was, to his mind, an affront to nature that a woman so lovely be alone. Once more, Hugh Fitzcairn to the rescue!

He paused just behind the heavy curtain that marked the entrance to her box. He adjusted his scarf, ran his fingers through his hair, and stepped forward.

Indeed it *was* her. And the dress *was* rose-petal satin. She smiled up at him and held out her hand. He took it and bowed.

"Why, Hugh Fitzcairn. Whatever took you so long?" she said with a light drawl.

Startled, he raised his head. "You remember me then, my dear?" Her eyes were, he noted, as blue as his own. "But how did you know I was coming to you?"

Then he felt it—the unmistakable presence of another Immortal. He turned, as the curtain was once more swept aside, and a familiar voice answered his question.

"She knew because I told her to expect you, ye great oaf," Duncan MacLeod said.

Duncan found Claire Benét fascinating. She was beautiful—fine-boned and petite, with honey-gold hair and sky-blue eyes. She looked fragile. But after only a short time spent with her, Duncan suspected that she was anything but.

She lived in a huge suite of rooms, on a higher floor of the same hotel where the three Immortals were staying. She invited them all to join her there after the opera, for a late supper. Danny had declined. He'd made plans to meet the man who'd helped him to fight off a pack of would-be thieves the night before.

Fitzcairn bade him take care, and went with Duncan and Claire. Their banking business had been done that day, so they were no longer prisoners of their own quarters. A thief might carry away some clothing and other odds and ends of gentle-manly attire. But their money and anything else of worth was now safe behind steel doors.

The three sat now, still in their evening clothes, in an enormous formal dining room. Claire's rose-petal gown matched the delicate tint of her lips and cheeks.

She rang a small silver bell, and a servant appeared.

"We'll be havin' our coffee in the sittin' room, Anna. And brandy for the gentlemen?"

"The lady's presence may be intoxicating enough," Fitzcairn said.

Duncan smiled. "Sometimes he speaks the truth. But if the lady would join us, brandy would be welcome."

She grinned. Not a sedate polite smile, but a full-out grin.

"The lady would love to join you. Three glasses, Anna. And the cut-glass decanter on the second shelf."

They adjourned to the sitting room. Though it was no larger than the one in their suite, Duncan noted that it was much more richly appointed. Some of the furnishings were actual antiques. He had, for instance, sat on a chair much like the one Fitzcairn now occupied a hundred years before. When it was new. Other pieces *were* new, but imported from the Continent.

The brandy glasses were the thinnest of crystal—Duncan had a fleeting thought of Danny—and the brandy was beyond superb.

Whoever Claire Benét was, she was very, very wealthy.

"So," she said, making a wry face, "we've been talkin' on all evening about the opera, and the city and the weather. I think that you've been very kind to me—you've not so much as mentioned the word gold. But now, before I just lose my heart completely to you both, I have to know—when does your ship leave?"

Duncan laughed. "Our ship is the *Portland.* It's scheduled

to depart in three days' time. But it seems less and less likely that we'll be on it."

He told her then, with regular interruptions from Fitzcairn, of their plight.

"Today, we even stooped to bribery," Duncan admitted.

"Yes," Fitz added, "only to find that we were dealing with the sole honest employee of the North American Trading and Transportation Company."

Duncan winced at the memory. "He threw us out of his office. Said that if we didn't go immediately, he'd summon the police."

Claire laughed her silvery laugh. "An honest booking agent! What next on Schwabacher's Dock? A unicorn? I will have to tell Uncle Witherspoon of this!"

Fitz looked up sharply. "Would that be Silas Witherspoon?"

"Why, yes. Don't you tell me, Hugh Fitzcairn, that you know Uncle Witherspoon?"

"No, my dear Miz Benét, I do not. But since we have been in this fair city, I have often seen his name in the local newspapers. The *Times,* the *Post-Intelligencer*—"

"Uncle Witherspoon," Claire said, "is a rather prominent man in Seattle, it is true. In fact, he owns one of those papers. You might have met him tonight. Unfortunately, he had a more pressin' engagement. Involvin' Mrs. Witherspoon." She grinned, and poured another brandy.

"On the other hand, had he been there, it might have been awkward. Three can be company, under certain circumstances. But four would most surely be a crowd."

Duncan raised his glass. "Uncle" Witherspoon, indeed! He wondered if Mrs. Witherspoon knew about Claire.

Their eyes met as they drank.

As it turned out three was company only during the day. At the end of the evening, Claire Benét did not care for crowds.

It was Duncan who began spending nights as well as days with the lady. While her "Uncle" did have first call on her time, she made it obvious that she was her own woman. Though it had been a long while since anyone had struck her fancy, she was free to pursue that fancy wherever it might lead.

Fitz shrugged and made the acquaintance of the diva who had sung Marguerite.

The *Portland* did indeed leave without them. The supplies they had bought lay waiting in a warehouse by the dock.

And the days passed.

"Tell me, Hugh. What was the fault with the boat you looked at this morning?" Danny demanded, angrily. As time went on, he'd gone from morose to frantic.

His teacher sighed. "The *Eliza Anderson* hasn't been to sea in years, Danny. She was used as a gambling hall. I'm no sea dog, it's true. But even I could tell the bloody scow wasn't fit."

"If it's not been one thing, it's been another," the young Immortal said. "It's MacLeod himself that insisted we had to be on our way before the month ended. And where is he? Not down on the docks, that I can see."

"He's been following a lead or two on his own, Danny. Claire Benét is well connected—"

Danny interrupted him with a rude noise and an even ruder comment. He'd not taken the Highlander for a man who lived off rich women. But since he'd started bedding the blond lady with the fine carriage and the grand suite of rooms, he seemed to have lost all interest in their quest.

"Mind your tongue, lad," Hugh said, sharply.

Danny scowled. *Hold your temper, boy-o,* he thought. *MacLeod is Hugh's oldest friend. It's not in his heart to criticize the man.*

"What are these leads, then?" he asked. "If there's some plan being made, sure and I don't know of it."

"We do need to talk, the three of us," his teacher responded. "MacLeod was supposed to see some politician today. We both should know what came of it. And I have an idea about trying our luck in Tacoma."

"I've one better," Danny said. "There are men with tickets in their pockets to be found wandering the waterfront after dark. They'd be easy prey for the likes of us."

"Thievery?" Hugh was taken aback. "I would hope that it wouldn't come to that. And MacLeod would have none of it, you know."

"He had a part to bribery, did he not?" Danny retorted. "It would be that much worse?"

But Hugh was adamant—taking advantage of mortals was out of the question. Danny lost his temper then, and the quarrel that followed was a bitter one, by far the worst exchange that the two had ever had.

It ended only when Danny tore from the fine room, his throat thick with despair, his eyes blurred with tears of frustration. He headed for the Golden Nugget. There at least, he could drink and dream, and keep the vision of the grand house with the colored-glass windows alive for a few hours more.

Danny was gone the whole rest of the day. Alone in the suite that night—Duncan was four floors above—Fitz fretted to himself. He knew where the young Immortal was—in some dockside bar. He could find him, fetch him back. But—he remembered his own wild days. Danny's passion was for fortune; Fitz's was for romance. In pursuit of that passion, he had done some things he'd always kept to himself. Though, on long nights alone, he would sit in the dark and remember. Those splendid foolish years spent serving the cause of that tragic woman who sought to be queen of both his land and the

Highlander's! He had done some night deeds then he was not proud of now.

Ah, but she had been bonny!

Best let the lad make his own mistakes, Fitz decided, *earn his own midnight memories. He's in no danger. He'll return.*

Which he did, the next morning, disheveled and sick from drink. Fitz cared for him, as he had on the boat, and left him to sleep.

He was settling down with his pipe and a cup of tea when Duncan came in.

"Top o' the morning to you, as young Danny might say," Fitz greeted him.

"Is he back?" Duncan asked. "I know you've been worried. We could go down to the waterfront—"

Fitz pointed with his pipe. "In there. Sleeping the night off. He'll be none the worse later on. Although"—he laughed—"he got himself a tattoo along the way. An extremely colorful rainbow with an overflowing pot of gold at the end. That will be a surprise when he wakes, I'll wager."

He smoked silently as Duncan poured coffee and sat down opposite him.

"The lad was a bit overwrought yesterday," Fitz said. "But he did pose a valid question. What do we do next?" He watched MacLeod closely. Despite his defense of his friend, he had begun to wonder himself how much of the man's passion for this adventure had been burned off in Claire Benét's arms.

Duncan sighed. "This is the second time this morning I've had this conversation. I told Claire that the congressman she'd sent me to wasn't able to help us."

"And did the beautiful Miz Benét have any further suggestions?"

"The beautiful Miz Benét thinks that gold fever is a disease worse than the pox. She listened. She was not overwhelmed with sympathy."

Fitz shrugged. "She's not yet grown weary of your manly charms. Give it a day or two."

Duncan leaned back and closed his eyes. "I think I've just been insulted. But I'm too tired to take offense."

"We must do something about that, laddie," Fitz replied. He rose and solemnly poured the contents of the cream pitcher on Duncan's crotch.

Later in the day, Duncan found a pale rose envelope on the floor of the suite. Obviously, it had been pushed under the door. Inside, handwritten in a flowing script, was a dinner invitation for that evening. It was from Claire Benét, addressed to all three of them.

At eight o'clock sharp, they presented themselves, dressed for dinner, in the formal dining room.

Claire was wearing fuchsia velvet, garnets at her throat and ears, as she presided over what was arguably the best dinner Duncan had ever had.

The conversation was pleasant, superficial. Fitzcairn kept up most of it. Danny was withdrawn, sober but brooding.

Duncan felt oddly ill at ease. He tried to catch Claire's eyes, but she avoided his gaze. He knew that somehow, something that had barely begun was about to end.

Finally, Claire rang the tiny bell and ordered coffee for the sitting room. There was no suggestion of brandy.

After they had settled, she began to speak. There was a note of amusement in her voice.

"First off, I have to say that I know what it is to be poor. I was born poor. And I did what I had to do to change that." She paused, looking them over one by one, with her penetrating blue eyes dancing with intelligence. Her gaze lingered longest on Danny.

"I don't believe in luck, or the easy way. And I do believe that those who are lookin' for the easy way are fools."

She shook her head, made a small *tsk* sound. She stared directly at Duncan. "Y'all aren't fools. But it seems you are helpless victims of these foolish times." She sighed.

"I guess not a soul is immune. Why, even Uncle Witherspoon, though he has no earthly need for more wealth, has been feelin' a touch of the gold fever. Of course, considerin' his age, he can't go prospectin' himself."

She paused, rang the little bell, and whispered something in Anna's ear. "So, I convinced him today that the next best thing to bein' there would be to stake some deservin' group of argonauts."

The three Immortals were silent, their coffee untouched.

"Uncle Witherspoon has a good-sized yacht. Named the *Belle Claire.*" She grinned then. Duncan caught his breath. "He'll lend it to you, with a full crew."

"Were it up to me, my dear Miz Benét, I would do whatever you might command, simply for the pleasure of seeing you smile," Fitzcairn said, with a bow of his head. "But from what I've heard, Silas Witherspoon is quite a shrewd businessman."

Claire rewarded him with a smile.

"A businessman who owns a newspaper, Mr. Fitzcairn. 'Member? Folks are just wild to read about this gold-rush business. Uncle has been tryin' to get one of his regular reporters to go north to cover it, just like the papers back East have done."

She paused as Anna returned, with a bottle of vintage champagne and four chilled glasses.

"Problem is, those that want to go prospectin' don't want to be bothered with writin' about it." She poured the sparkling liquid carefully, filling each glass to the brim.

"So I just told him what a very experienced journalist Mr.

MacLeod was. How he'd even run a newspaper himself a few years back in Davidsonville." She handed the glasses around. Duncan brushed her fingers lightly as he took his.

"Uncle Witherspoon was most suitably impressed. Why, any reluctance he'd had to allow y'all the use of the *Belle Claire* just dissolved away when he found out that Mr. MacLeod would be sendin' back regular dispatches!"

She raised her glass.

"A toast then, to success. I do most sincerely hope that y'all find what you're lookin' for." Her voice was light, but there was a shadow in her eyes.

Fitzcairn and Danny raised their glasses. Fitz looked bemused, Danny stunned. Duncan hesitated.

Claire grinned widely at him.

"It will take a day or two to get the boat ready, of course," she said.

He clicked glasses with her and returned the smile.

This part of the country held so many memories for him already, good and bad. Claire Benét, her golden hair, silver laugh, and elfin grin, would soon be yet another.

In a day or two. Meanwhile, there was still tonight.

Chapter 4

A sword cutting the darkness. Danny knew what he had to do. Lucas Desirée had told him. He raised his blade to meet the Challenge—and Jim Foster was there calling his name, breaking his concentration. He shouted at Foster that he must stand clear. But it was too late. The sword bit deep into his heart. As he died, he saw the face in the darkness. It was the face of the stranger, the first Immortal he had fought to the death. His vision blurred and the face was Lucas Desirée's, Duncan MacLeod's, Amanda's, Hugh Fitzcairn's. Then, a burst of light brought him awake. But before he opened his eyes, he saw. It was his own face . . .

The *Belle Claire* had real windows, like the proper floating hotel suite it was. Jim Foster had pulled back the drapes. He was urging Danny awake. He stumbled from his bed to the window. For a heartbeat he stopped, chilled by the ghostly sight of his face in the glass. But he saw the town beyond, glowing golden in the rising sun. He caught his breath. The dream was forgotten.

"If Seattle was an anthill," Duncan said, "this place is a nest of ants stirred up with a stick."

The three Immortals followed Jim Foster, picking their way carefully down the rutted, muddy main street of Skagway.

"The ants are a quarrelsome lot, laddie," Fitz added, as two shots and one scream rang out close by.

Duncan winced. In the scant few hours since the *Belle Claire* had docked it had become obvious that shots, screams, curses, crashes, and other noises best not investigated were the commonplace sounds of daily life in Skagway.

"Can't be too careful, mates. That's true," Foster said. "There's a lot here just waiting for newcomers off the boats. Cheechakos they call 'em. They'll take 'em for all they're worth." He deftly jumped a puddle. "With cards. Or with guns." He stopped. "Hold up. The office is right across Broadway." He pointed at a storefront. Lettering painted on a large glass window proclaimed it to be Reliable Packers.

As they waited until a cart drawn by a moose passed by, Duncan reflected on Slim Jim Foster. It certainly *seemed* a bit of luck that Danny had met the man. He knew his way around Skagway, all right. He'd helped them get rooms at the Golden North Hotel. And he was now taking them to what he assured them was one of the few honest equippers in town.

So far, Foster hadn't asked for anything in return. Free passage on the *Belle Claire* had been more than enough, he'd said. He'd gone to Seattle to collect some money owed him. That he'd not had to spend any of it on his return trip was like a gift.

There was sense to that. Still, Duncan was uneasy about the man. He was *so* accommodating, *so* helpful—

The street cleared, and the three Immortals followed Foster

into Reliable Packers. The place was full. Men leaned on walls and filled the wooden benches. Duncan frowned. Some of the crowd looked less than savory.

Slim Jim took them directly to the counter. "Claremont," he said, "these are my friends. O'Donal, MacLeod and Fitzcairn. Three argonauts just off a private yacht up from Seattle. Bound for Dawson. You do right by them, mate."

He left then, promising to see them later.

Claremont produced a clipboard. He began questioning them about the size of their outfit, filling in a form as they answered. Duncan explained that their supplies were still on the *Belle Claire,* back at Juneau Wharf, under the watchful eyes of Silas Witherspoon's crew.

"And we're not sure what more we'll be needing to cross the White Pass," he added. "We'd planned the Water Route. But Mr. Foster convinced us to go this way."

"Right as rain, he was." Claremont nodded. "The race is to the swift, you know." He made a note on the form. "You'll be needing horses, of course, and packs. And a guide. Not that the Pass isn't well marked and all. A guide just makes it safer." He frowned, crossed something out, then made a final notation. He extended the clipboard to Duncan. "That's a fair total, I think. You'll not do better."

Duncan motioned for Danny and Fitz to come closer. The three Immortals looked over the form. After a brief discussion, Duncan returned it to Claremont.

"All right. We have a deal. How long will it take to get all this together?" He smiled at Danny. "We're anxious to be on our way."

"Oh, maybe two days," Claremont answered. "You're at the Golden North? We'll be in touch." He produced a pen. "Sign here at the bottom, then. And you understand, we have to ask for a deposit? Just to guarantee that your business isn't given elsewhere."

"That's reasonable," Duncan said. Claremont named a figure. Duncan turned to Fitz, who was carrying their money. The gold nuggets had been exchanged for currency in Seattle. Fitz's leather billcase was bulging.

Before Duncan could caution him, Fitz drew it out. In an instant, a burly figure darted forward and grabbed it from his hand.

An uproar ensued. Claremont produced a wooden truncheon. He slammed it on the counter.

"Stop, thief," he shouted.

Men rose from the benches and left the walls. They began darting around the room. As Danny made a grab for the thief he was knocked from his feet by someone rushing to his aid. Fitz, too stunned to react at first, turned in time to see the man racing out the door. Duncan struggled to follow him, pushing through the crowd that seemed suddenly to fill Reliable Packers.

Clearing the door, he saw the man already across Broadway. He gave chase, heedless of the human and animal traffic bearing down on him.

The thief disappeared between two buildings. Duncan ran after. His quarry, he guessed, knew the town well. He could easily slip through some back door, and be gone forever. With all their money.

Duncan rounded a corner and saw a flash of movement. He sprinted forward, guided now by the string of expletives that rent the air.

Behind the building, two men lay in the mud in a tangle of arms and legs. One was the thief. They were struggling to rise. Their efforts only succeeded in churning up even more mud. They kept losing their footing, falling back in the muck. It would have been funny were it not for the violence of the thief's anger.

"Goddamn injun. *Get off me!* I'll kill you. I will."

Duncan grabbed the man by the back of his collar and hauled him to his feet.

"You'll not be killing anyone, you scum."

The burly man took a swing at Duncan. It was all the excuse he needed. One quick fist to the gut, another to the jaw. The thief fell back, spread-eagled in the muck.

Duncan offered his hand to the Indian. The man took it, and scrambled to his feet. He backed up two steps, then turned and ran. His hat—a broad-brimmed red felt trimmed with an eagle feather—lay in the mud. Duncan picked it up and called after him. But the Indian was gone.

"I can't believe that there's no jail in this town." A gunshot sounded from outside. "If ever a place needed one . . ."

The three Immortals were finishing their dinner—a surprisingly good one—at the Pack Train Restaurant. Duncan viciously stabbed a last piece of baked salmon belly with his fork. He frowned even as he chewed.

"Jim said that there was no law at all here for a long while," Danny offered. "Those that decide such things couldn't settle on whether the place was in Alaska or Canada."

"And the winner is"—Fitz pushed his plate back and slapped his hand on the table—"Alaska!"

Duncan scowled. "So the blackguard who nearly wiped us out sits, all cozy and comfortable, in a spare room at the back of the town hall. Until a judge happens to come by."

"We'll be long gone by then, Mr. MacLeod," Danny said.

"I know that," Duncan replied, with an edge in his voice. "Long gone and far away."

"Well, at least we got our money back, laddie," Fitz said, patting his vest pocket. "I'll pop by Reliable Packers in the morning and finish our business. And I can assure you that I'll look twice before I take out even a coin." He produced his pipe and tobacco.

"Aren't we supposed to be meeting Foster at some saloon?" Duncan asked. "I could use a drink."

Fitz shrugged. He slipped the pipe back into his pocket and called for the check. Duncan rose and went outside.

"Hugh . . ." Danny began.

Fitz shook his head. "The Highlander likes to *see* justice done, Danny my boy. When you've known him as long as I have, you'll understand."

They found Duncan leaning, arms folded, against the front of the building. The night was cold, but clear. The town was ablaze with light, pouring out of the string of bars and dance halls that lined the street.

"Mr. MacLeod," Danny said, his breath visible in the air, "Jim Foster knows near everyone here, it seems. He might know of the Indian who owns that red hat."

Duncan nodded. "That he might, Danny." He pushed off from the wall. "Let's go ask him."

Fitz gave the young Immortal a quick pat on his shoulder as they followed MacLeod into the noise-filled Skagway night.

Danny saw the girl straightaway. She came through the door to the right of the dark wood bar. She was still for a minute. She seemed to be looking about at the crowd packed into Jeff Smith's Parlour. Then she went over to the upright piano that stood facing the back wall. It wasn't far from the door that led to the room where Slim Jim said the gambling went on.

The girl sat down next to the Negro who'd been playing jagtime tunes for the whole of the time the three Immortals had been in the place.

Danny lowered his glass. It was his third drink from the bottle Slim Jim had bought. For them to celebrate their luck in actually catching a crook in Skagway, he said. Danny had planned on it being his last, anyway. The memory of his night out in Seattle, like the tattoo on his forearm, still had bright colors and clear edges. Unlike the tattoo, it would shortly fade away. In the time 'til then, he'd vowed to hold himself to just a drop or two.

The girl had a cloud of long dark hair, down to her waist it was. Held back from the pale blur of her face by a simple ribbon. Her dress was white, all ruffled. She didn't look like any of those that he'd seen slip through the small door to the room beyond.

In his time Danny had known many a girl who worked the saloons. Some were sweet. Some sour. Sure, he'd spent more than a night or two with some of the sweeter ones. He held nothing against them. To survive, he'd had to kill—his own kind most often. Killing was a grave sin, Father O'Malley had preached. To survive, some girls committed another on the list of the priest's terrible sins. Well, if they were damned, then so was he. He'd not cast stones. Mother Kelly had taught him *that*.

This girl—she was different though. Any man with but half an eye could see.

She slid over on the bench. The Negro got up and left. Then she began to play. At first, so soft that Danny couldn't hear. But in a bit, the sound grew, rising above the noise of the crowd.

She didn't play rinky-tink, but sweet, slow melodies. Some Danny knew from the war. "Sweet Lorena" and "Tenting Tonight." One he'd heard from boyhood, a song from Londonderry, in the Old Country.

He found he was holding his breath. The piano could be clearly heard now. *Why, the room's gone quiet,* Danny thought. He glanced around the table. Hugh, MacLeod, even Jim, who must have heard her before, were watching in silence.

As the last notes of the song called "Aura Lee" echoed, the girl lifted her hands from the keyboard. She lowered her head. A well-dressed dark-haired man stepped to the side of the piano.

"Gents—and ladies—Minnie Dale." He extended his hand. The girl rose, turned, and bowed. The room fairly shook with the clapping and whistling.

She'll be coming out among the tables now, Danny thought. *Jim will know her. He can call her over here.* But the girl withdrew through the door next to the bar. Danny waited, absently pouring himself another drink. After a time, he sighed aloud. He knew she would not be back.

Aura Lee, Aura Lee. The price of loving a mortal. Duncan thought of Alec Hill, sobbing over the broken body of his beautiful young wife. Young Danny's face was far too easy to read. He caught Fitz's eye. His friend looked amused and indulgent as the young Immortal left the table. Foster had told them Minnie Dale would play again later. Danny wanted to be much closer to the piano.

But Foster was still with them. So Duncan knew that a conversation with Fitzcairn—however futile it might be—on the subject of Danny's love life would have to wait. He poured another drink.

"Gentlemen?"

He looked up. The man who'd introduced Minnie Dale had approached their table.

"I'm Jefferson Randolph Smith," he said. His voice was low and pleasant. "Might I join you?"

"It's your Parlour, isn't it?" Fitzcairn said, gesturing toward Danny's empty chair.

Smith laughed and sat down.

"Duncan MacLeod." He extended his hand. Smith's hand

was small and well cared for. "The pipe-smoker is Hugh Fitz-cairn. And this is Jim Foster."

"I know Foster," Smith replied. "His brother is the bartender here." He picked up the whiskey and examined the label. "That's how you came by a bottle of my private stock. Right, Jim?"

"I told these argonauts yours was the best place in town, Mr. Smith. Tom was just helping me prove it."

Smith had an easy laugh. All in all, he seemed a gentleman. Good manners. Good clothes, including a heavy gold watch fob prominent against his silk vest. His dark hair and beard were neatly trimmed, and his clear gray eyes were intelligent.

A gentleman, Duncan thought. *Or a very effective imitation of one.*

"You're the men who were accosted this afternoon at Reliables, are you not? I just wanted to say that the good citizens of Skagway—and there are some of us—are pleased that at least one of the villains was caught."

"There was just one," Duncan said, "and for all the good it did, he was indeed caught." He swallowed his whiskey straight back.

Smith looked puzzled. "I'd heard there was an Indian involved."

"Yes." Duncan nodded. "But he helped bring the thief down. I want to thank him. And I've not been able to find him."

"Foster here knows everybody," Smith said.

"So I've heard," Duncan replied. He reached for the bottle. He wondered if he might get an opportunity to speak with Smith alone. The man treated Foster with a certain disdain. Duncan suspected that he would be a good source of information about Slim Jim.

"This fellow must be new around here, Mr. Smith," Foster said. "I can't place him."

"Try me," Smith said. "Up here, Indians and white mix pretty well. Your man might have been in my Parlour."

Duncan described the Indian as best he could, aware that his fleeting contact hadn't given him a clear impression.

Smith looked thoughtful. "Sounds like any one of a half dozen tribes. Athabascan. Skookum. Siwash. Chilkoot. They're all pretty much the same. The hat, though. That's something more specific."

He rose from the table. "I'll ask around. I admire a man who pays his debts, Mr. MacLeod. Even a debt of gratitude."

"I'd appreciate it, Mr. Smith," Duncan replied. He extended his hand again.

"Soapy," Smith said. "That's what some call me. Everyone up here has a nickname. Like Slim Jim." He nodded at Foster. "Holler, 'Hey, Kid' right now, and twoscore fellows would answer. Including my piano player. He's the Chocolate Kid. So, I'm Soapy." He shook Duncan's hand.

"Foster, tell your brother the bottle's on me. If you haven't already." He winked and walked back into the crowd.

Close up, Danny had seen that Minnie Dale's eyes were blue, a dark blue that was near black. She closed them sometimes as she played, and her black lashes fanned on her pale cheeks. Her face was a child's face, round and soft, with a small bow of a mouth. The dark cloud of her hair made her seem even paler.

Danny reached up and ran his fingers through that hair. He pulled Minnie down beside him. She lay on her side, pressing her naked breasts to his chest.

They lay together on the double bed that was all of the furniture other than a tiny table and two chairs in her house. The house was one in a row, all joined, all alike, behind the main buildings of the town.

The whores lived there, she'd explained to Danny when

he'd approached her in the Parlour. He could walk her home as he'd asked. But he should know what home was.

Danny touched her eyebrows with his fingers

"You don't make love like a whore," he whispered.

Minnie sighed. "You've had so much experience, then? You can't be much older than me, Danny O'Donal."

Danny smiled in the darkness. Hugh had taught him one of the first rules of seduction—never ask a woman, mortal or otherwise, her age. But he wanted to know.

"And that would be?"

"Twenty-two this month past." Her long fingers stroked down Danny's arm. She sat up, letting the lamplight fall on him.

"And where did you come by this?" She traced the tattoo.

Danny felt heat rise in his cheeks. "In the port of Seattle. I was being foolish that night."

Minnie kissed his forearm, then lightly touched the puckered scar beneath his shoulder blade. "And this?"

"A Reb bullet, the first of the fighting at Antietam. It's lucky I was. That day, at least."

She frowned. "Antietam? But—" Then she laughed softly. "Ah, well, Danny O'Donal. Have your secrets then. It may be that someday you'll tell me the truth of it."

Danny rolled her over on her back. He raised himself above her.

"Someday, Minnie Dale, I promise I'll tell you a secret that will take your breath away. This minute, I've other things on my mind."

Fitz speared another two griddle cakes with his fork. Placing them on his plate, he proceeded to generously ladle syrup over, under, and between them. He was humming under his breath, one of the tunes Minnie Dale had played.

Across the table, Duncan sipped his coffee.

"You're in a fine mood this morning," he said.

"And why not?" Fitz replied. "We've got our money back. We'll be on our way by week's end toward fortune, if not fame. And the food in this restaurant at the end of nowhere is much better than it has any right to be." He filled his mouth with griddle cake. "Did you know," he said, syrup dripping down his chin, "that they're actually serving oysters poached in champagne this morning? It's nearly enough to make me want to learn to cook."

"And how much skill does it take to burn beef and boil potatoes, my fine English friend?" Duncan asked.

Fitz wiped his chin. "Ah, MacLeod. Do you really want me to mention haggis while we're eating?"

Duncan poured more coffee. "You lost no sleep last night worrying over Danny, then?"

"Tilda, my dear," Fitz called to the waitress, "more of these splendid hotcakes, if I may?"

Tilda, a tall plump blond, giggled and hurried to fetch the food.

Fitz turned to Duncan. He spoke softly. "It's true, the lad's not got hundreds of years of experience in matters of the heart, as I have. But he's hardly a virgin. You do recall that I told you he was working in a brothel when we met?"

"I've seen that look on other men's faces, Fitzcairn. This girl isn't one he'll want for just a night."

"You've seen that look in the mirror now and then, I'll wager," Fitz said, shrewdly. He knew of a number of Duncan's past loves. But he suspected that there was at least one, no doubt long dead, whose memory his friend kept locked in his heart.

Tilda brought a platter heaped with cakes, steaming from the griddle. As Fitz kissed her hand, sending her into a fresh torrent of giggles, he had to admit to himself that the Highlander was right. In the time they had been together, he had taught Danny much about taking love lightly. It might now be the time for a word of caution about love taken seriously—particularly when one of their kind lost his heart to a mortal.

He sighed as Danny appeared in the doorway. There would be no putting it off.

The young Immortal joined them at the table. He looked tired. But the hint of a smile pulled at the corner of his lips.

Fitz knew what *that* look meant, too.

"Have some coffee, lad. And tell us about the girl, if you want. Is she as lovely as her playing?"

"Aye, that she is, Hugh." Danny took the coffee gratefully, spooning in sugar. He blew on the coffee, then gulped a mouthful. "She's a Canadian. She and her man came up here from a place called Vancouver."

"It's a city not far north from Seattle," Duncan said. "They would have come up the Inland Passage, like we did."

Danny nodded. "Months back, though. They'd be in Dawson counting their gold by now. But they were hit by bandits going over the White Pass." His voice grew somber. "Everything they had, all their gear and their stake, was taken. And her husband was killed."

"So, she's a widow stranded here in Skagway," Fitz said. "The poor lass."

Danny stirred his coffee. "This Jefferson Smith, the man who owns the Parlour, he's got a fund set up for those like Minnie. She draws some money from that. And he pays her to play the piano. All she wants is to save enough for passage home."

He hesitated. "She takes a man back to her place, sometimes, for the money. She told me that right off. But she wouldn't take anything from me." He looked at Duncan, then at Fitz. His blue eyes were steady. "I've known more than a few women, Hugh. I've told you of some of them. Minnie is different, though."

"And I've known many more than a few in my time, Danny—Don't say it Highlander." Fitz replied. "To find one that makes your blood *and* your heart sing is—well it's a thing as wonderful and as fortunate as finding the gold waiting for us across the mountains."

"Rare and precious," Duncan agreed, softly. Fitz wondered briefly of whom he was thinking.

"Minnie Dale might be such a one for you lad. But for two things. There is the gold. And there's the fact that she's mortal."

"We *can* love mortal women, Hugh. We all have."

"And we can watch them turn away when they find out what we are," Fitz said. Across the table, Duncan looked up in surprise. *So, Highlander,* Fitz thought, *you're not the only one with secrets of the heart.*

"If they don't turn away, we can watch them age and die," Duncan added. "While we live on. Alone."

"Ah, Danny, you've only just met her." Fitz clapped the young Immortal on the back. "Give more thought to what you want here."

"I want the gold across the mountain," Danny said, "and I want Minnie Dale."

Chapter 5

Duncan left the two Immortals, old and young, still sitting at the table, deep in discussion. He stood silent for a while outside the Pack Train, lost in the memory of an autumn night in the Highlands. He'd been with Connor, his kinsman and teacher, only a short time. They'd stopped earlier that evening at a tavern. The wench who'd served them had russet hair, falling in curls over her shoulders. And great green eyes that favored him as she went about her work. His heart had nigh stopped at the sight of her.

He'd fallen into a dark mood then, and it had taken some urging from Connor before he had finally spoken of Debra. Bonny Debra, who he had loved with all his heart. Dear Debra, who had died of her love for him. Dead Debra, whose ghost he would now have to live with for all of his endless life.

Connor had listened, and said little. But the next morning, he told Duncan to ready himself for a journey. They traveled many days, until they came to a ruined keep, on a hill over-looking a loch. In the shadow of the broken walls, Connor knelt beside a grave marked with the broadsword of the MacLeods.

They die, he said. Quickly, like your Debra. Or slowly, like my Heather. But they die, and we live on—

Alone. Duncan shivered. Although it was only August, a cold wind was blowing off the cloud-wreathed peaks that cupped the town. He pulled his coat collar higher. Skagway was almost peaceful at this hour, covered in a light blanket of snow that had fallen overnight. But on the Juneau Wharf, men were astir. Duncan thought to try again to find the Indian who'd helped him. He had the red felt hat stuffed in his jacket pocket. Perhaps someone on the wharf would recognize it.

He'd give it an hour, and if he had no luck, go back to work on the first of his dispatches. Though Witherspoon, when he met him to make the final arrangements for securing the *Belle Claire,* had been puzzled by the decision, he'd refused to have his name on the column. The reports would be run simply as "An Argonaut's Journal."

He set out, snow crunching beneath his boots. As he approached one of the few side streets in the town, a flash of movement and color caught his attention. To the right, just off Broadway, stood Jeff Smith's Parlour. And peering into the glass top of the shuttered door was the burly thief.

Duncan stopped short. The man, after rattling the latch, slipped into the narrow passage between the Parlour and the building adjacent.

Duncan's first impulse was to raise a hue and cry. But the man's actions had piqued his ever-present curiosity. So instead he followed, squeezing silently through the opening.

At the end of the passage, behind the building, was a small open area, bounded by a white wooden fence. The fence was around six feet high. Duncan approached cautiously, bent low, then slowly raised his head.

The courtyard was empty, save for the recent snow. But fresh footprints led from a gate to the back door of the Parlour.

Suddenly, the door burst open. A figure flew out, and fell facedown. The burly thief followed. He cursed and kicked the fallen man in the side.

"Hold up there, Zimmer." Another man appeared in the doorway. Duncan recognized him, too. Foster had pointed him out the night before. Burns was his name. Big Ed Burns. The bouncer at the Parlour.

"Mr. Smith don't want no trouble here," Burns continued. "Leave the injun be now. We'll take him up the mountain a way, and deal with him there."

Ignoring Burns, Zimmer lashed out again. The fallen man rolled, seeking to avoid the blow.

He was, Duncan saw, the Indian from the alley. His face was covered with blood, the snow stained where he had first lain.

Duncan stood. He backed up a few paces, then launched himself, vaulting the fence easily. He faced Zimmer, startled in mid-kick.

"So you're a bully as well as a thief?" he said. "Well, let's see how you handle yourself against a man who can fight back."

With an oath, Zimmer rushed Duncan. His weight carried them both back against the fence. This close, Duncan could see every detail of Zimmer's battered face, from the scarred eyelid to the crooked nose to the wart half-hidden by the scraggly beard. The man's teeth, bared in a snarl, were black with decay. His breath was hot and putrid.

Duncan's back flared with pain from the impact. The two men hammered at each other, trading body blows. Then Duncan freed his arms. He raised them and clenched his hands together. Then, with all his strength, he struck Zimmer on the back of the neck.

The man released Duncan, shaking his head. Duncan pressed his advantage, lashing out with his right foot.

But Zimmer was quicker and tougher than he'd thought. The burly thief dodged the kick, and rushed Duncan again. Clearly he was used to overwhelming his opponents with his bulk.

Two quick kidney punches left Duncan doubled over gasping. Zimmer struck him on the back with one powerful fist. Before he could deliver the next blow, however, Duncan butted him in the stomach with his head.

Zimmer staggered back, tripping over the still prone Indian. His head hit the frozen ground with a sharp crack. He lay still.

"Hold it." The command was followed by the unmistakable sound of a gun being cocked.

Through the haze of his anger, Duncan saw Big Ed Burns still standing in the doorway, gun drawn and ready.

"That was kinda interestin', seeing someone beat on Zimmer for a change. He's gonna be powerful angry when he comes to, though."

Duncan narrowed his eyes. "Maybe I'll not be here then."

Burns shrugged. "No never mind to me. You can go. But the injun stays."

"The Indian goes."

"You cheechakos." Burns shook his head. "You just don't know the rules up here." He leveled the gun. "Which is, there ain't no rules."

"Shoot me here, and there'll be trouble," Duncan replied. "Mr. Smith won't like that now, will he?"

Burns's eyes flickered. He hesitated. Duncan tensed.

Then something whizzed past him, striking Burns square

on the forehead. The man crumpled to his knees, and pitched forward. The gun fell from his hand. Duncan picked it up and turned.

The gate burst open. A fourth man—an Indian—entered the courtyard. Quickly he went to the side of his fallen comrade. Murmuring in a language that Duncan almost understood, he helped the blood-spattered man to his feet. Then he spoke.

"We go now."

Duncan was holding the gun on Zimmer, who had begun to stir. "Wait. Don't just leave. Fetch the town constable. Or you take the gun, and I'll get him."

The Indian shook his head. "No good. These Soapy's men. No law for them."

"This man robbed me and my friends." Duncan gestured at Zimmer. "And he beat your friend senseless."

"Brother," the Indian said. "I must take him away from here or he die."

The injured man groaned. His knees buckled. Tucking the gun in the waistband of his trousers, Duncan helped support him.

The Indian regarded him. His black eyes were calm, his voice level. "I am called Sam. Siwash Sam. You come with me. Maybe then we all live."

Duncan blew out his breath in exasperation. It fogged the air.

"All right then. One thing, though. Can you hold your brother alone for a minute?"

The Indian nodded.

Duncan crouched down.

"Zimmer?"

"The hell with you." The man groaned.

"Zimmer, you'd best hope we don't meet a third time. Your face is ugly and your breath is worse. I don't want to see—or smell—you ever again."

He rose and joined the Indian. They half dragged his brother through the broken gate, along the back alleys of the town, away from Jeff Smith's Parlour.

Duncan sat cross-legged before a fire burning brightly in front of a large hide tent. He could see the whole of the town below. A good place to camp, he thought. A smart place.

In the tent, the Indian who called himself Siwash Sam was ministering to his brother. Duncan had offered to help, but Sam had shook his head. Instead, he had nodded toward the fire and disappeared inside.

Siwash. What had that blackguard Smith said? The Siwash were one of many tribes who lived up here. These Northland Indians were not familiar to Duncan. But as he looked around the camp, he could make some judgments.

They were hunters, no doubt. The hides of the tent, the fur robes scattered around, the weapons he had seen when he'd helped lay the injured man down—all of that indicated men who knew how to live off the land.

But these two also knew more than a little of civilization. Some of their clothes—the bright red felt hat for instance— came from white men's stores. He'd taken note of the fact that their weapons included at least one very new-looking rifle. And though the two sleds that lay at the edge of the camp were fashioned by hand, the tools piled neatly around them were equal in workmanship to the very expensive gear he and Fitz had bought in Seattle.

Suddenly, Duncan felt hot breath on his neck. He turned his head slowly. A big black-and-gray dog stood inches away, eyeing him warily.

If the beast wasn't tied up like the rest, he had to have a special status, Duncan thought. He sat motionless and let the animal smell him thoroughly. Finally, the dog gave a satisfied sniff and lay down a few feet away.

"Dog approve." Siwash Sam said. He stood just in front of the tent. "Good."

"And if the dog didn't approve?" Duncan asked. He began to rise, but the Indian waved him down.

"Very bad." He shook his head. "Much blood. I have enough of that for this day." He sat down across from Duncan.

"Your brother?" Duncan asked.

"He be fine. Only nose broken. Not first time."

"I am Duncan MacLeod," he said. "My friends and I—our money was stolen. Your brother stopped the thief."

The Indian nodded wordlessly.

"Is he awake? I would like to thank him. I've been looking for him."

"We know you looking," Siwash Sam said. "My brother go to find you this morning. I tell him not to. I tell him Soapy's men find him first."

Duncan winced. "I—I am sorry that I caused pain to the brother of Siwash Sam. But Smith—I thought he was a respectable businessman."

Sam shrugged. "You are cheechako. That what you supposed to think." He spit to one side. "You want to know what Soapy is? I tell you."

So he did. And when he was done, anger swept through Duncan. It had been a long, long while since he had felt like taking his sword to a mortal. But this Jefferson Randolph Smith who preyed on the men—and women—who poured into Skagway, men and women made foolish by their fever for gold, made his warrior blood run hot.

Siwash Sam sat staring at him, his black eyes level.

"Scotsman, do not take on Soapy. This his place. You will lose."

Duncan frowned. "I should go on then? Forget what was

done to your brother? To all of the others that you've told me of?"

"He is *my* brother," the Indian said gently. "And we will go on. Before this day is done. We not wait to find men to guide across White Pass. It not safe here for us."

"The Pass," Duncan said, as he scrambled to his feet. "Fitz was going back to Reliable Packers this morning!"

"Then you must return to the town. I will tell my brother of your thanks when he wakens."

Duncan turned, hesitated and turned back. Siwash Sam sat watching him intently.

Squatting down, he spoke hurriedly.

"If my friends and I are to take our leave quickly from this unsafe place, we will need guides we can trust, who do not come from the ranks of those who work for Soapy Smith."

The Indian gave a slight nod.

"Siwash Sam and his brother are guides. We would hire them to lead us away from here. If they could stay a day or two more, until we have our gear together."

Duncan waited a breathless moment. Then the Indian nodded once again, more emphatically.

"You come back. We talk more of this. We will be here." He took Duncan's extended hand and shook it firmly.

"But now you must hurry. Or you will have no money to pay Siwash Sam and his brother."

Duncan smiled briefly in response, and set off down the hill. He knew the Indian was right—there was nothing to be gained by taking the battle to Soapy Smith in the town that he owned. Still, if he were to run across the man anytime soon—

The look on Duncan's face was one that had been the last sight of countless men over the centuries. As he sought Fitzcairn through the streets of Skagway, even the hard-bitten thugs on the prowl cleared out of his way.

But Jefferson Randolph Smith did not cross his path that

morning, and Duncan was not certain if he was sorry or relieved.

"What a lovely thing this is, Danny O'Donal," Minnie said, holding the delicate square of white linen and lace. "Now don't tell me it belongs to some special girl waiting for you back home?" she asked, half-teasing.

Danny took the handkerchief and put it in his pocket, smiling. "A special girl, aye, Minnie. But one I knew when I was only a boy."

They'd eaten a light lunch at the table in her small house, then spent the afternoon in the soft comfort of the bed—and each other.

Minnie sat brushing her great mass of dark hair, while Danny lit a lamp. "Night comes early up here," she said softly. "Oh, how I dread the winter!"

Danny sat beside her. He held her close. "I've a plan, Minnie. I can't tell you yet. But I give you my word—you'll not spend many more a night here."

"Oh, Danny—my Eamon had plans, too—"

"Hush," he said, as he kissed her. "Now, you finish with your dressing, and we'll walk a bit before supper."

She pulled away and sat still, looking down at her lap.

"I'll not be able to eat with you this night, Danny. I've an engagement."

He shifted beside her.

"It's one I made before you even came to town," she hastened to add. "Someone from home—he was in our party. He went on with another group, after . . . the bandits. Now he's back from Dawson City. I promised him I'd hear his tales. And I've letters for him to take to my mum."

"All right, then, my love," Danny said. "But look for me later. I'll be waiting by the piano."

She smiled then, and drew him close to her once again.

* * *

Fitzcairn looked down the length of Juneau Wharf. It was dark on the deck of the *Belle Claire*. The one lantern he had with him barely penetrated the early-evening gloom. He picked it up and moved closer to the rail, wincing at the weight. His arm still hurt from the force of MacLeod's grip. The Highlander had burst into Reliable Packers like a man gone daft, dragging Fitz away before he could give Claremont any of their money. Fitz had fairly sputtered with anger, but MacLeod had refused to explain until they were aboard the *Belle Claire*. It was, he'd declared, safe to talk there, far from the eyes and ears of the town of Skagway.

Which was, as Fitz soon learned, to all intents and purposes owned by the genial gentleman host of Jeff Smith's Parlour. Reliable Packers did little except act as a stage on which thefts were routinely carried out. The *Skagway News*, which spoke so glowingly of Smith's good deeds, was run by one of his flunkies. The town constable was another.

The big toe on Fitz's left foot throbbed—from kicking a barrel which happened to be full of picks and shovels. He had named the barrel for another of Smith's gang—Mister Slim Jim Foster. The attack hadn't lessened his anger. However, it had actually raised a brief laugh from MacLeod, his first since they'd come to this bloody town.

There were still a number of men and women out, even in the lowering dark. Still, Fitz easily recognized the figure headed down the wharf. It was Danny. He'd gotten the message they'd left at the hotel, then. Fitz took the lantern, wound his scarf tightly around his neck, and went to meet him.

The young Immortal's lips were white with anger, his dark blue eyes fierce. Fitz had never seen him so furious.

"Foster's coming to my aid in Seattle—are you thinking that too was a part of the scheme?" Danny asked.

"Possibly," MacLeod replied. They were in the lounge of the *Belle Claire*. Silas Witherspoon's fine store of liquor was being put to use this night. "Probably."

"We'll never know for certain, Danny," Fitz said. "Smith and his gang are, it seems, such a nefarious group of scoundrels that nothing is beyond them." He paused.

"For an instance, Minnie Dale"—Danny's lip thinned—"she's most likely even more a victim than us. The Indian told MacLeod that the guide who led her party was one of Smith's men. And he led them straight to the bandits."

"Who were also in the pay of Mr. Smith," Danny finished. "But if these things are known to be true, why then isn't he stopped?"

"Because half the town thinks he's a fine, upstanding businessman," Duncan said bitterly, "and the other half is on his payroll." He stood abruptly and began pacing the cabin. Fitz suspected that he was once more berating himself for his previous night's conversation with Smith.

"And I," Duncan continued, confirming Fitz's suspicion, "I did everything but hand Sam's brother over to him."

"That's past and done, laddie," Fitz said. If Duncan were not distracted, he could spend hours, days, even weeks, brooding. "If your Indian friend has the truth of it, there's naught we can do about Mr. Call-me-Soapy Smith. But what we can do is—oh, what that's Latin saying? I got it from a gorgeous young thing, Sister Immaculata her name was, the youngest daughter of the duke of Napoli. Sent to a convent for no other reason than that she'd taken a liking to me!—"

"Fitzcairn." Duncan said. He folded his arms, his face set.

"Ah, yes." Fitz said. "*Carpe diem.* I think that's it. It means seize the day. Or in this case, the night. *Carpe noctem?*"

Duncan and Danny both stared at him.

"What I mean is—what do we do now?"

Duncan frowned.

"Well, perhaps it's not quite the right turn of phrase for the situation. But you get my drift?"

"I must go and talk to Minnie." Danny said. "I'd—this is not the best time for it, now, but—I'd been intending to ask you, Mr. MacLeod, if she might not travel back to Seattle on this boat. I was hoping that you would be willing to write Miz Benét and ask her to look after Minnie?"

Fitz and Duncan exchanged a glance. That was a far more sensible plan than any they had thought Danny would propose concerning Minnie Dale. It seemed the lad could let his head guide his heart.

"I can't think of any reason why not," Duncan said. "She can give Claire my first report for her—uncle."

"With a few facts in it about Jeff Smith," Fitz added. "We can't do him harm here, but we can tip others to the truth."

Danny brightened. "I'll tell her straightaway, then. I don't want her to spend another night beholden to that bastard." He rose.

"Danny. A moment. Fitzcairn's right. We do need to make plans."

The young Immortal smiled and shrugged. "We cross that mountain out there. We've come too far to do otherwise."

Sure and I'm fortunate, he thought. He'd not wanted to raise the town looking for Minnie and the gent she was supping with. So he tried her tiny house the first thing, and found her there. She was in her undergarments, the flouncy white dress she wore for her piano playing spread out on the bed.

As quick and simple as he could, he told her then of what they'd found out about Smith. She paled and grew faint when it came to her that the man who she'd been working for was behind her husband's death. But before she could take on, he gave her the good part of his news—that he'd found her a way home. In but a day or two, when he and his friends went on, she could board the *Belle Claire* and be gone from this vile place. Long before the winter set in. Just as he had promised.

"You could stay on in Seattle a bit, if you want. Or go on from there back to Vancouver." He smiled tenderly. "As long as I know where to find you. And when we're rich, we can live wherever it pleases you most."

They had been sitting at the small table, chairs drawn close together. Minnie rose and fetched her wrapper from the foot of the bed. She drew it on slowly, her back to Danny. She turned, pulling the belt tight, and sat down again. She took his two hands in hers. Danny felt a flutter in his belly. Something was amiss.

"Danny," she spoke softly, but did not raise her eyes to his, "the man I met with tonight? His name is Fergus, Fergus Cooley. He's someone I've known a good while. He worked with Eamon. Danny—" She squeezed his hands and looked him full in the face. Her eyes were bright, near feverish. "He did it! He found the gold! A rich claim, one of the biggest since the first lot, they say!"

"That's a happy thing for a man that's just setting out to hear, Minnie," he said, carefully. Why was she flushed so? And why was she telling him this?

Abruptly, she pushed back her chair and crossed to the corner of the room where her heavy coat hung on a peg. She reached into a pocket, and took something out. She turned but stayed in the corner.

"He took me to the Pack Train for dinner. And a grand dinner it was! We had the finest of food. And champagne so light it fizzed on my tongue. And sweet chocolate afterward. I've not had chocolate since even before I came up here."

She walked to the table, carefully unwrapping the scrap of red silk she held in her hand. "After the plates were cleared, he told me to close my eyes. And when I opened them this was in front of me."

She showed him then. It was a ring, gold with one big diamond. Danny knew nothing about diamonds, if they were to be judged by size for instance. But he could see that the ring looked like a gift from someone who had money.

"He's asked me to marry him, Danny. He came back to Skagway just to ask."

For an eyeblink, Danny was back once more in Temperanceville. It was the evening of the explosion at the glass works. He'd found all his belongings sitting on the porch of the boardinghouse, packed up by the widow who ran the place. Though they had been sharing a bed for more than a year, she'd not answered when he knocked and called out her name. He had not loved her. But he had thought that she might love him.

Love. "Do you love him then, Minnie?" he asked, with a dreadful calm.

She hesitated. "He's a good man, Danny. He was a good friend to Eamon. I think that Eamon would want this for me." She sighed and sat by him once more. "We came up here, the two of us, so that he wouldn't have to work behind a counter doing another man's bidding. And I wouldn't have to spend my days teaching piano to little girls who dressed far better than me.

"Fergus Cooley is rich, Danny! He can give me everything that Eamon and I dreamed about!"

Danny grabbed her hand and held it fast. The ring lay between them. "I'll be rich, too, Minnie. If you can wait but a while longer, we'll be able to live those dreams together!"

"No." She shook her head. The dark cloud of her hair fell over her shoulders. "I've lived too long the months I've been here. There's a hundred times a hundred men I've seen pass through. And a hundred times a hundred stories I've heard of the few that made it and the many that didn't. I know now what fools Eamon and I were to have ever left home. And bless you, Danny O'Donal, you and your friends are no different."

She was weeping now, silent tears staining her pale cheeks. "It makes no sense, coming so quick as it did. Still, it's true. I do love you, Danny. But I'll not wait in Seattle in hopes that you'll come back to me with a pocketful of gold."

Danny stood. His voice was harsh. "I'll not be begging you, Minnie Dale. But I will return, with bags full of gold. Whether there's any one waiting for me or no." He swept the ring from the table with the back of his hand. Then he picked up the chair and threw it against the wall. It struck the small mirror above the washbasin, shattering it. "And when I do, it may be that I'll come looking for you and your new man."

Minnie cringed. He was frightening her, he could tell. He had seen that look on a woman's face a time or two before. But this woman had herself been an argonaut. She had no lack of courage. She stood, facing him down. Sobbing the while, she asked him to leave. With a muttered oath, he did so.

The night was crisp and chill. Fergus Cooley. It was a name that a barkeep would likely remember. Danny set out for Broadway.

"Mr. MacLeod."

Duncan stopped and turned. Coming toward him along the snow-dusted street was none other than Soapy Smith.

"You're an early riser, MacLeod," Smith said. "I asked after you at the hotel, but they said you'd been up and about for quite some time."

"What is it you want, Smith?" Duncan asked.

"To do you a favor." He smiled. It did not reach his eyes. "I like to help people out. I'm sure you've heard that said about me."

"I've heard quite a bit about you the last little while," Duncan answered. "I'm not sure if my friends and I need any more of your help. Now if you'll excuse me, I've business elsewhere."

"Well, I thought you might be concerned about young Mr. O'Donal." Smith shrugged. "If not . . ."

Duncan hesitated. Fitz was at the moment gone to Minnie Dale's to fetch Danny. They'd assumed he'd spent the night there.

"What about Danny?" he asked, an edge in his voice. This was not a game he cared to play.

"He went a bit wild last night, I'm afraid. You know Mrs. Dale? The woman who plays piano in my establishment? She'd accepted the proposal of an old friend earlier in the evening. O'Donal spent hours drinking and looking for her intended." He shook his head in mock dismay.

"Never found the man. But he did run across Jim Foster. They got into a fierce row. Some of Foster's friends came to his defense and, well, not to put too fine a point on it, your young friend got the crap beat out of him." Smith held Duncan with his clear gray eyes, gauging his reaction.

"And where might he be now?" Duncan asked, levelly.

Smith gestured across the street. "The boys locked him in the back room of Clancy's."

Duncan started towards the bar, Smith following behind. "Of course, if I'd known about this earlier, I'd have made sure he got medical attention. But no one told me 'til this morning."

The bar was closed. Smith produced a huge ring of keys from inside his coat. After three attempts, he found the correct one. The two men entered, passed through the deserted room, and stopped in front of a small door to the left of the make-shift stage where the dancing girls performed. Smith sorted through the keys again. He turned the lock and pushed the door open.

The room reeked of whiskey. Inside, Danny lay curled up

in a dark corner, snoring loudly. Duncan shook him awake. He got to his feet, with some assistance, and shuffled into the light.

There was a good deal of blood spattered on his coat front, and dried blood around his nose and in his hair. He was clearly hungover. But other than that, he was fine. The damage done to him had healed during the night. And judging by the look of surprise that Smith could not hide, that damage must have been major.

"Go outside, Danny," Duncan said. "I'll be along in a minute."

The young Immortal left, and Duncan faced Soapy Smith. "Hear me well, Mr. Smith. I know what you are. I know your game."

"Yes?" Smith said coolly. "That would be?"

"At the least, you're a cheap crook and a lowlife grifter. At the worst, you're some sort of human vulture, feeding on the hopes and dreams of decent people. You've had a piece of luck here in this town up to now. But that will change. You'll go down. I've seen it happen more often than you would believe."

Duncan moved closer to the man. Only a few inches separated them. "I almost wish I could be here when the good people of this town—and I do believe there really are some—come for you. However, my friends and I are leaving Skagway. By noon tomorrow, we'll be gone." He reached out and fingered the fur collar on Smith's coat.

"Between now and then, it would be in everybody's best interests if none of the boys cross paths with us. Or with Siwash Sam and his brother."

Smith moved back a step. He took out his gold watch and made a show of consulting it. "Noon tomorrow you say? I hope, Mr. MacLeod, that I can count on that." He clicked the watch shut and inclined his head. "Good day, Mr. MacLeod. And Godspeed."

Siwash Sam was native to the land. He was not old by the standards of his people. But compared to the cheechakos, he was as ancient as any of the elders.

He and his brother had been working with the white men for many years. The Canucks, the squaw men who lived among the Indians, the red-coated Mounties who tried to bring a law based on books to the land. And for the past two seasons, they had made much money by guiding the men (and some women, too) who had poured in from the south and the east. They came like the vast herds of elk, driven by a hunger not for food but for the gold that hid in the rocks and streams.

The wealth the white men coveted had been buried for time beyond time. The land did not give it up easily. Sam had seen more, many more, fail than succeed. But he and his brother were paid, whatever the outcome of the quest. It was their life.

Siwash Sam had known from early on what manner of white man Jefferson Randolph Smith was. Accordingly, he and his brother had avoided Skagway, hiring out instead to haul gear from Dyea, north of Skagway, over the fearsome Chilkoot Pass. But an avalanche at Chilkoot had recently closed the pass (and killed scores of luckless cheechakos). So they had come to Soapy Smith's town, where his brother had nearly lost his life by being in the wrong place at the right time.

That he was alive was due to the Scotsman—and Sam's true aim with a snow-covered rock. Now the Scotsman and his two friends—the wiry little Englishman and the young Irishman—were to be Sam's responsibility. He had made an agreement, settled by a handshake, to guide them over the White Pass, and on to Dawson. Where they would no doubt be lost to the gold fever.

They were cheechakos, these three, like all the rest. Yet Siwash Sam knew, in the way that he knew where best to look for the winter hare when all the land was white, that they were somehow different.

But for now, he kept those thoughts to himself.

Chapter 6

From AN ARGONAUT'S JOURNAL

My party left Skagway on a Thursday morning near the end of August. We numbered five—my two companions, our two guides, and myself. We had with us roughly two tons of supplies. Most are lashed on two flat-bottomed sleds drawn by two teams of seven dogs apiece. But each of us also has to carry a huge pack, carefully balanced on our backs.

To the gear that we had purchased in Seattle—the tents, blankets, cooking utensils, tools, ropes, saws, lanterns, coal oil, soap, candles, matches, baking powder, lard, and salt—we added more foodstuffs. Tea and coffee, chocolate (an excellent source of energy), dried potatoes, mincemeat, cornmeal, bacon and beans, dried fish for the dogs, various kinds of dried fruit, sugar, and condensed milk.

We left behind all but one good suit apiece. It is said that some of the hotels in Dawson City rival those of Seattle, so we felt that we should be prepared in case the tales are true. We wear the uniform of the gold seeker now—mackinaw trousers, a flannel shirt, a heavy coat, and rubber boots. We have each purchased a broad-brimmed hat, designed to protect the head and neck from damp and drips.

The going is slow. The White Pass, though well marked, is narrow. And so many have come here to seek their fortune that at times, we must walk single file, like schoolboys on an outing . . .

"Fitzcairn," Duncan called, "take care."

Up ahead, Fitz half turned. To his right, the narrow trail dropped away five hundred feet to the rocky ground below. The bottom was littered with carcasses, animals that had fallen to their deaths. Horses mostly, lying sprawled and broken. Carrion birds covered the freshest, intent upon feeding before the corpses froze. It was a pitiful sight, Duncan thought. He'd seen the like in battle, where arrow or shot and shell had struck down horse as well as rider. But never so many, in heaps along the way.

"Why should I worry, MacLeod?" Fitzcairn said. "Don't you remember? This is the easy way across the mountains!" He threw his arms wide, nearly losing his balance. Only the steadying hand of Sam's brother kept him upright.

Duncan did not bother to reply. The White Pass, forty-five miles of switchbacked trail that sometimes would lead them across the same river twice, *was* the easy way. Even at its highest—the aptly named Summit Hill—travelers still had only a thousand-foot climb, over ground that was difficult, to be sure, but not impossible. The Chilkoot was more direct, but it was thirty-five hundred feet up from the town of Dyea. And the top of the always snow-covered mountain could only be reached by climbing a single trail, so narrow and steep that men and beasts had always to go single file.

He'd been in mountains like this before. Fitz's complaints notwithstanding, the terrain was no more rugged than some he'd encountered in the Northwest Territories.

No, the true challenges of the White Pass were twofold. Dealing with the hundreds of others on the trail. And coping with the difficulties of moving five men, fourteen dogs, and two flat-bottomed sleds loaded with close to two tons of supplies.

Could such a task ever be said to be easy? Until he'd met Darius on that snowy battlefield, he'd always been a warrior. And as a warrior, he'd never given a thought to those in charge of the wagons with the food and the blankets and all of the equipment that kept the army alive—until the army could die for the cause, whatever it might be. He was beginning to consider that fighting and dying were perhaps the simpler jobs.

He stepped carefully around a fall of loose rock. Sam, who was in the lead, had stopped again, pulling his dogs to a halt with a grunted command. It was the third time in the past two hours. Once more, they waited while the group ahead—a half dozen men who had all been neighbors back in Boston—struggled to negotiate a particularly difficult section of the trail. Their overburdened pack animals were weary and skittish. It was obvious to Duncan that their experience with horses had probably been confined to riding in streetcars. Yet the way was too narrow for him, or any of their party, to be of assistance.

So they waited, Duncan and the Indians, with various degrees of patience, Danny as sullen as he had been in the two weeks since they had left Skagway, and Fitz with many a loud complaint. Duncan passed the time remembering with some fondness the moment, centuries before, when he had run Fitz through.

Finally, Sam whistled the dogs to their feet. And the long journey continued.

The easy way, Fitz muttered under his breath. Over a month of up one bloody steep hill and down one bloody soggy valley after another. The White Pass Trail. Porcupine Hill. The horror of Dead Horse Gulch.

They'd nearly lost a sled in a mudhole just after they crossed the border into Canada, right at Summit Hill. Fortunately, one of the Royal Canadian Mounted Policemen on duty there had come to their aid. He'd gotten himself quite mucked up doing it, too, Fitz remembered.

The Mounties, with their colorful uniforms and rigorous sense of duty, fascinated Fitz. He'd shared a smoke and some conversation one night with a party camped nearby at Summit Lake. From them, he'd learned that the Mounties were *the* law in the Yukon Territory. The old-timer prospectors—the ones called sourdoughs—and most of the Indians were in awe of them. But the thousands of newcomers pouring into the country were straining their resources—and their patience.

After Skagway, it pleased Fitz to know that there *was* law in the Yukon. Although, of course, that was Alaska and this was Canada.

Well, it looked just the same to him. More rocky hills, more endless bogs. More piles of supplies, left behind by those who had given up. They'd seen dozens of them, weary, defeated men headed back to Skagway, their dreams abandoned with their gear.

And, he would swear on his sword, they had seen one of the horses that belonged to the fools from Boston commit suicide. The poor creature, whipped past the point of exhaustion, had simply walked off the side of the trail, falling to the rocks below.

But they had kept on, through the icy rain, the wet flurries of snow, and the gray gloom that only lifted at the very top of the mountains. They were now, according to their map and Si-wash Sam, in the Tutshi Valley, a day away from journey's end. They'd camped for the night at the base of a wooded hill beside a small lake, on a spot of land that was almost dry. Campfires dotted the valley, though none were nearby.

Fitz was glad of that. He was gregarious by nature, but for the past several months he had scarcely had a moment of solitude. The journey so far had been from one crowded place to another. Even this supposedly vast wilderness was teeming with gold seekers. They were loud. They were raucous. They were competition.

And, worst of all from his point of view, there was not an available woman to be found among them.

Fitz stood outside the large tent in the misty gloom of early dusk. The night was silent, the camp quiet. Vixen, the light brown–and–white bitch that was the swing dog for Siwash Sam's team, whined softly and pawed at his foot. She was a handsome beast, Fitz thought. Most of the dogs were mixed breeds, a bit of this, a bit of that—even a bit of wolf here and there. But she was a husky, purebred from her mix-matched gold-and-blue eyes to the tip of her plumed tail. Her bark was a high-pitched yip, her small size belied by her prodigious strength.

She'd taken a fancy to him from the first. And he, never one to disappoint a lady, had reciprocated. She sat, ears pricked, tongue lolling out. He smiled and tossed her the bit of salted fish she'd smelled in his pocket.

Rip, Sam's lead dog, came over, wagging his tail. Though the black-and-gray was the dominant male of the pack, even he deferred to Vixen. She snarled. He stopped, then turned away, wandering over to where the rest of the dogs were staked out. Some had already curled up, asleep after their day's labors.

Sleep. He'd be for that soon himself. There was hardly a stir from inside the tent. MacLeod, Danny, even the two Indians, all had turned in soon after their meal. Early to bed, early to rise would bring them all the more quickly across the one last bloody mountain to their destination. He'd wanted a moment or two with his thoughts and his pipe before joining them.

Vixen growled, a low rumble in her throat.

"Now, my pretty," Fitz said, reaching down to ruffle the fur on her neck. "Don't be so demanding. I've nothing left that you can eat." He stopped. The dog's ruff was up, her ears back. He raised his head, peering into the foggy darkness.

A shot rang out. Fitz felt a hot pain in his side. As he fell face forward into the embers of the campfire, he heard first Vixen, then Rip, then all of the dogs fill the night with barking.

In that darkness, in that time before he breathed again, Fitz remembered the first time he'd been shot. He had died many a time before then, by the blade for the most part. And once, when he'd jumped out of a window just as someone's husband came in through a door. But he'd not died from the gun until one summer's dawn. There had been a duel, fought over the honor of a lady, of course. And he had lost.

The ball had taken him in the chest. The pain was like some hideous flower blooming, spreading through his lungs. A sword, a dagger—those were bright, swift pains. Over and done, until the light returned. This gunshot—quite something else again.

Afterward, he'd made it a point to learn to shoot straight. But since then, he'd tried to avoid pistol duels.

And, he thought as he gasped back to life, *I'd also prefer to avoid being set upon in the dark by armed brigands, thank-you-very-much.* He rolled over, his face covered with ashes, and struggled to his knees. Now the night was filled with sound. The dogs were still barking. Gunshots could be heard and seen, as rifle muzzles flared.

"Hugh!" Danny was by his side. "You're back, then."

Fitz nodded.

"Here," the young Immortal said, thrusting a rifle into his hands. "We've got them pinned down."

He disappeared into the night. Fitz followed, cautiously. Though a pale moon had risen, it would be hard to tell friend from foe in the darkness. He had no desire to be shot again, by either.

He found the two Immortals huddled together in the shelter of a boulder. As he approached, MacLeod stood and fired up the hill toward a stand of trees. An answering shot followed, barely missing Fitz's head.

"Why don't ye just stand atop this rock and be done with it, ye great idiot?" MacLeod muttered. "Haven't you had enough of dying tonight?"

Fitz crouched beside them.

"According to Danny, you have our assailants pinned down." He ducked his head as a bullet struck the boulder. Small chips of rock flew through the air. Danny jerked back, a thin rivulet of blood running down his cheek. "If they're pinned down, then why are we the ones kneeling in the mud, being shot at? Is there some great strategy here that I'm missing?"

"Sam and his brother have gone up the hill." Duncan replied. "They should be in position soon. We'll have them then on two sides."

"It's a good thing that the dogs made such a fuss when you were shot, Hugh," Danny said. "It was a warning to us."

"Hugh Fitzcairn at your service," Fitz said, through gritted teeth. "Always glad to die in a good cause."

Danny lowered his gun. "I didn't mean—"

"Quiet." MacLeod said. Farther up the hill, a light appeared briefly.

"Sam and his brother, I presume." In the dim moonglow, he could just see MacLeod's nod.

"Now!" MacLeod shouted. He rose and began a volley of shots. Danny joined him. Fitz, keeping his head carefully down, fired also, aiming toward the flashes of muzzle fire that flared in the trees.

Though the three Immortals could not see the Indians, the results of their attack were quickly evident. Cries of pain echoed down the hill. A body fell from a tree, rolling like a rag doll down the slope. To Fitz, the exchange of gunfire seemed an endless series of explosions in the night. The smell of sulfur hung in the air.

In truth, it was over in a moment. Two men appeared out of the trees, holding their hands above their heads. They called out their surrender, fairly running down the hill in their desire to give up.

A short time later, they were securely tied up, sitting back to back at the entrance to the tent. Vixen, her head on her paws, lay not far away, watching them intently. Rip circled them several times, then lifted his leg. A stream of urine soaked the men. They cursed the dog. Rip walked away, and settled down close by.

MacLeod smiled. It was not, Fitz decided, a smile that anyone with any sense would care to see, even in the light of day.

"They not go anywhere," Siwash Sam said. "You all come with me."

He led them back into the night, and up the hill. Three more bodies lay under the trees. The Indian's brother bent down and rolled one of them over. Sam shone the lantern in the dead face. The man was as ugly a specimen as Fitz had ever seen. Broken nose, scarred eyebrows, and a wart on his chin that his scraggly beard could not quite hide.

Fitz thought he had seen the face before. But where?

MacLeod rarely swore. So Fitz was startled when he did so now. He followed the oath with a name.

"Zimmer?" Fitz repeated. "Zimmer! The heinous thief who stole our money!" Now he recalled the brief glimpse he had gotten as the man snatched the wallet from his hand.

"Did you not tell us, Mr. MacLeod, that he was one of Smith's men?" Danny asked quietly.

Duncan confirmed the fact. Fitz was astounded. "You're saying that Soapy Smith sent his men after us? That we've been followed for all these weeks, clear across that trail of infamy?"

"These all Soapy's men," Siwash Sam said. "I know them to see."

When they questioned the two prisoners, they found that the Indian was right. The six were indeed all in the employ of Soapy Smith. Zimmer had volunteered to lead the group, anxious for the chance to settle his score with MacLeod. But the plan had been Smith's. He'd wanted them all dead, argonauts and Indians alike. "For the principle of the thing," he'd said.

"We've been a mile or less behind ya clear 'cross the Pass," the more talkative of the two said. "If it'd been up ta me, we would have laid inta ya long ago." He nodded his head toward the dark hillside. "Zimmer said no, said that Mr. Smith didn't want his business done in the open. Said we had to wait 'til we could do the job and get clear away. All that damn way, all those damn dead horses," he said bitterly, "then Zimmer tips ya by shooting too soon."

"Soapy not be happy with you." Sam said.

The man winced.

No one, bound or free, slept well that night.

The next morning, though MacLeod raged quietly about it, they decided that there was nothing for them to do but to let the two go free. There were most probably Mounties ahead at Lake Bennett. But that was still a day's journey away. Adding two bound men to their party would not only slow them down, it would be dangerous.

Better to let them return to Skagway, to face the wrath of Jefferson Randolph Smith.

They collected all of the guns. What they didn't keep, they threw far out into the lake. Then they waited until the two men had vanished over the hill, back toward the border. The bodies they left where they lay.

As they broke camp, the carrion birds were already circling.

Dear Claire,

We're camped now by the headwaters of the Yukon River, on the shores of Lake Bennett. Although "camp" doesn't really do justice to the situation. For it is here that the travelers who have climbed the Chilkoot and those who, like us, have crossed the White Pass converge. So great is the number that what might in time become a small town has sprung up. It was thus that Skagway came to be, I've been told.

There'll be no Soapy Smiths here, though. The Mounties are present, as they were at the border. They keep order, supervise the boat building that is the occupation of the citizens of this "town," and generally see to the common good. They are a marvel! How I wish they had been nearby when we were attacked in the Tutshi Valley.

I'm sending this letter, and my dispatches of the last month on to you by the hand of an American named

Peter Moore. He and his friends are leaving this morning to return to Skagway. It seems that they had thought that the Klondike was just the other side of the mountains. When they reached here, and realized that a water journey of five hundred miles still lay between them and Dawson City, they lost all heart.

Moore intends to travel home by way of Seattle and has promised, for a price of course, to see that this gets to the Rainier Grand. I'm not sure what part, if any, you will want to share with Witherspoon. You would know, far better than I, whether or not it would be best for him to keep his illusions about this expedition.

For myself, Claire, the trail of dead horses has blasted any illusions that I might have had left after Skagway. Yet there is something that compels me to continue. And I have more confidence that this peculiar adventure may come to a positive conclusion since the Indian who calls himself Siwash Sam has joined with us.

He has proved his worth time and again. Most recently, it was only because of him that we were numbered among those given permission by the Mountie commander to continue our journey. This late in September, heading for the Yukon is a risky business. Only the soundest of crafts and the soundest of argonauts are being let by. The rest will winter here—except for those, like Peter Moore, who will turn back.

But our boats were solidly built, to Sam's specifications. And the commander was impressed with his knowledge of what lay ahead.

And so we will go on, bound for—what??

The Irishman has done this work before, Sam thought, as he watched the young man load gear onto the second of the rafts. *The Englishman—well, he is strong enough and willing enough.*

As for the Scotsman—Sam still doubted his claim that he had lived for a time with a tribe of the Southland. White men were known to be liars. But the Scotsman had, sometime in his life, lived off the land. Sam had watched as he'd felled the slender spruce that ringed the lake, and shaped them into planks in the whipsaw pit. He'd watched as the man lent his hands to the building of the two raftlike boats that would carry them down the river. And he'd watched as he caught a string of trout, then cleaned the catch with no questions or hesitation.

Now he watched as the Scotsman stood on the first of the rafts, lashing down the sled and the supplies. When he had finished that, Sam would have him secure the extra rope to the deck. Later, Sam would look at what he had done. He knew that the work would be good.

Danny sat alone in the dark, leaning against a sled. After the wet snow and chill rain of the mountains, it was almost pleasant in the camp by the lake. Pleasant, but still damp. There was a fine mist in the air. He pulled his hat brim down to shield his face and stared across the water. The rafts were ready, anchored in place. They would leave before dawn. Tonight, at the insistence of Siwash Sam, the five of them would keep watch in turn. The first shift had fallen to him.

He'd taken the small square of white from his pocket. Long, long ago it had held the scent of the green-eyed girl-child. Through the years, Danny would hold it in his hand and think of her.

Now, the pale linen reminded him of Minnie Dale's face. He wondered what she was doing and where. Were she and Fergus Cooley back in Vancouver yet? Had they married in Skagway beforehand? Or was Cooley planning a Church wedding?—a High Mass with a full choir singing the Gloria, the priest in heavy white vestments, lilies on the altar, and Minnie a vision in white satin and lace.

He wondered if he would really have killed Cooley. He'd killed a mortal once before, by plan. It was not a thing he spoke of. Even Hugh did not know of it.

The man—Michael Sheehan, his name was—had needed killing. He and Danny had both worked for the great political machine called Tammany Hall. Tammany ran the city of New York after the War. Not all of the job was on the up and up. But the Organization was there, if a man had to step over the boundaries, now and then.

Sheehan had had some education at the Church schools. And he affected manners that he'd learned when he was in service. So he thought he was better than the likes of Danny. He tormented him without end, in ways both large and little. They'd come to blows a few times. Though Danny was by far the smaller of the two, he had no trouble holding his own. The practice work he did with his sword had given him skills that were of use in many a fight. And the fact that he could not trounce Danny seemed to make Sheehan hate him all the more.

Still, for the most part, Danny held his temper. He'd learned a lesson in Temperanceville—it was best not to call attention to himself. Too many bruises that healed in a day's time would raise questions.

Then one night, Sheehan told Danny that one of their regular contacts, a crooked copper named Russell Grady, wanted to meet with them on a certain street corner at a certain time. Danny arrived—and found himself in the cross fire of a gang fight. As he died in the gutter, coughing up bright blood from a torn lung, he realized that Sheehan must have known that the two gangs had plans for that evening. With his last breath, Danny swore revenge.

A week later, he'd followed Sheehan—who'd been mightily surprised to see him alive the morning after the shooting—as the man made his way home along the gaslit paths of Central Park. In the shadows of an underpass, he ran up behind. As Sheehan turned, Danny shot him once, square through the forehead. Then he took his billcase and the flashy ring from his finger. He'd thrown both into the lake.

That night, he'd drunk himself to sleep. His dreams had been troubled. He knew that what he'd done was wrong. But he had done it anyway.

And I could have done it again, wrong or not, he thought. *Fergus Cooley, you are a lucky man indeed. If I had found you that night—*

"Blast!" Hugh's voice startled him. He looked up. His teacher stood on the shore, slapping at his cheek.

"Is it time for you to take my place already?" Danny asked.

"No," Fitzcairn answered. "But MacLeod and the Indian are busy jabbering at one another in two different heathen languages. There wasn't a lot I could add to the conversation."

"Come out on the raft, then. But I should warn you—the bugs are just as bad here."

"Mosquitoes!" Fitzcairn muttered, as he joined Danny, stepping carefully over some coils of rope lying on the deck. The dog called Vixen followed him, settling at his feet. "Is this not the Frozen North? Why then, I ask, haven't these intolerable pests been reduced to mere bits of insectoid ice?" He swore again, swatting at his sleeve.

They sat for a while in silence. Danny continued to stare out at the lake. Fitz took out his pipe. As he went about the business of filling it, he hummed softly. The tune was one that Minnie had played. Danny drew his breath in sharply.

"She was a lovely girl," Fitz said. "You'll carry her memory with you for a long time, I've no doubt."

"And as I am an Immortal," Danny said, bitterly, "the time could be measured in centuries." He turned on Fitzcairn, fiercely.

"We've talked of this before, Hugh. But I must ask it again—what is it for, this living forever? What good is it to be able to rise when you are done to the death, if your rising brings you nothing more than just another day?"

"Consider the alternative, lad." Fitzcairn said. "Consider those four left rotting back on the trail."

"That's no answer, Hugh," Danny said. "Sure and I know that any mortal would say he wanted to be like us."

He heard Hugh sigh. "Well, yes, most would. Until they heard the part about the swords." He drew up his knees and rested his arms on them.

"Some would say that we are what we do. That we live for the Game, for the chance to be the One. For them, that's reason enough." He drew on his pipe and blew out a plume of smoke.

"It's not for you, I know. Nor has it ever been for me." He turned and leaned forward. Danny could read the concern on his face.

"I asked the same question of Henry Fitz six hundred years ago. He could give me no answer. But, after he was gone, I came to realize that he had lived all his long life to prove, over and over, to mortals that were long dead that he was worthy of their family. That was his answer, the one he had came to for himself." He paused.

"My friend Darius—you'll meet him someday when we go to Paris—he's one of the oldest of our kind. In his lifetime, he found two answers. And very different they were. For centuries, he lived for conquest. Now he's a man of peace. The Highlander—"

"He lives for justice," Danny broke in. "You told me so in Skagway. And I saw that it was true when we had to let those two thugs go. It pained him."

"It's his way," Fitz said. "It always has been, I think. Though he used to be more inclined to seek that justice at sword's point." The dog stirred. Fitz reached down and scratched behind her ears.

"Ah, Danny, here's all the wisdom I'm capable of. Your Immortality—it's a treasure given to you. The great luxury of time to find your own answers. Whatever span of years the search consumes, you'll live on to pursue it. And all those men camped here . . ." He gestured toward the shore. "They'll be gone, dying with their own unanswered questions. And no time left to ask them."

Danny stood abruptly. The dog pricked up her ears, growling softly in her throat. He turned his face away, and spoke with great intensity. "I hear the truth of what you are saying Hugh. I know there are times when you must doubt that I've a brain in my head. But I do. And that part of me understands." His shoulders slumped.

"But there's a part still that can't fathom the notion that you and Mr. MacLeod were alive before white men ever saw this land. That I will be alive when the grandchildren of the men who stood beside me at Gettysburg are dust in the wind. That part feels—well, it's dark and bleak, it is." His voice broke.

"Do we get less like mortals as the time passes, Hugh? It might be a thing to be wished for, not to be human . . ."

Fitzcairn rose to his feet. "I should hope not, lad. If we were not human, why then we couldn't love." He put one hand on Danny's shoulder.

"But we can love, lad. We can lose our hearts, and have them badly handled. Yet as long as we don't lose our heads, we can go on living and learning." He drew the young Immortal into a brief hug.

"Ah, Danny. Think what a blow it would be to the women of the world if Hugh Fitzcairn could not love! Imagine the lamentations!"

Danny laughed, shakily. Impulsively, he returned the embrace. His teacher's words had comforted him. Though a black core of his anger remained, he felt a new hope, a new resolve.

If Fergus Cooley, a mere mortal, could find his fortune in the Klondike in a matter of months, then the odds of striking it rich were even more in favor of men with all of time on their side!

"Look there," Fitzcairn said. The two rafts had just rounded a bend in the river. He stood and pointed. On the shore, tied to a tree, was a piece of red cloth. Directly beneath it, a hand-lettered sign bore the single word "CANNON."

"Are we to be under fire now?" he shouted.

As the dull roar ahead became more pronounced, Siwash Sam spoke to him tersely. "Englishman—sit down. Hold on to sled. Not gun. Big water."

Fitzcairn sat, crouching in the midst of the dogs, who were tethered tightly to the deck. At the back of the raft, Danny knelt at the sweep, the long heavy oar that served as a rudder. He steered at the Indian's direction.

The second raft, with Sam's brother at the front and MacLeod handling the sweep, was directly behind.

And spread out behind them, over the fifty or so miles back to the shores of Lake Bennett, was an assortment of boats that looked as though they had been whittled by the hand of a small demented boy. Rafts of all sizes, boats with sails of all description, even a craft that looked like a side-wheeler in miniature. It was hard to comprehend that this strange flotilla was the cull, the best of the hundreds and hundreds of floating conveyances that had been brought piecemeal or whole and entire over the mountains, or built painstakingly by the side of Lake Bennett.

But it was. And now they were all, each and every odd craft, headed inexorably toward the "cannon" that lay just ahead.

Not a gun, oh no. A canyon, filled with big water, rushing water.

The sound grew ever louder. It was not music to Fitz's ears. The rafts picked up speed. The cliff walls seemed to press in, as the river narrowed.

It's like being poured through a funnel, Fitz thought. *Or down a drain.*

The two Indians wielded their oars and shouted instructions to Danny and MacLeod. Sam's brother had enough English for that, thank the saints. Thus they steered past the whirlpool in the center of the river, coming so close to the black-basalt cliffs that Fitz saw places where travelers had dared to leave their marks, names scrawled hastily as boats bobbed on the current. As they skimmed along, he was able to make out a few of them: there, in a looping script, the initials J.L. Above it, at a height that indicated some fool had stood to make his mark, a lopsided heart. Farther along, in block print, the name BUCK and a half-completed date.

A small canoe carrying three men had been caught in the whirlpool. It turned in dizzying circles, the men crying for help. MacLeod called to them, but there was nothing that could be done. The rush of the river would not be denied.

They were past the whirlpool now, but not past danger. Siwash Sam ordered them all to get down low, and lash themselves to the raft. The coils of rope that had been a bother underfoot now were to be put to their intended use. For the river narrowed even more, until it was scarcely thirty feet across. And at the other end of the canyon, it spat the rafts out onto the jagged rocks of the rapids beyond.

As they rode over the boulders, foam rising above them like sea waves in a gale, Fitz could see, here and there, the shattered remains of craft that had attempted the journey before the Mounties had come to impose order. It was not a comforting sight.

He had his right arm locked around one of the ropes that secured the sled and his left around Vixen. The dog lay half in his lap, a look of pure canine delight on her face.

"Well, I'm pleased that you're enjoying this," he muttered into her ear. Then he looked back. MacLeod was sprawled at the front of the raft. His face was alight with excitement. The raft dipped, and a spray of water cascaded over him. Even above the din of the river, Fitz could hear his laughter.

"Mad dogs and Highlanders," he said to Vixen, who yipped in response.

In the next instant, the raft tipped forward, sliding down the face of a huge boulder.

"Whooooaaa!" Fitz exclaimed. He kept his grip on the dog, as the deck became nearly vertical. Danny slid downward, too, headfirst, scrabbling for a handhold. *He must have left too much slack in his rope,* Fitz thought. All he could do was extend his leg to try to stop the young Immortal's fall. Drowning was not a death he would wish even on the worst of their kind.

But as the raft continued to tip, Fitz realized that it wasn't just Danny who was in danger of going for an unwanted swim. For a heartbeat, they teetered on the brink of overturning. Then the Indian reached for Danny, pulling him back. The balance tipped again, and the raft skimmed off the bottom of the boulder. The crash of spray when it hit the river soaked them all.

MacLeod's raft was ahead of them now. Fitz wiped the river from his eyes, and watched it career along. The Indians used the oars to push away from the larger rocks, when they could, but the way was still a foam-filled chaos.

Vixen whined, and he realized that he was holding her so tightly that she could barely move. He loosened his grip, and she got to her feet. A second later, he was drenched anew, as she shook herself thoroughly. Then the raft hit another boulder. Fitz grabbed the dog and once more held on for dear life.

A breathless few minutes later they were through the rapids, skimming along on the current. The river flowed into another lake, blue-green and peaceful under the cloudless sky. Mountains rose all around. Fitz looked up to see their peaks sparkling white. Then he looked out over the lake. The still, clear water mirrored the mountains and the sky to perfection. Certain now that he would not drown this day, he allowed himself to be transfixed by the beauty of it all.

Siwash Sam was on his feet, oar in hand, moving the raft smoothly across the calm surface.

"Water holds the sky," he said. "Sky holds the water. They all the same." Fitz was taken by surprise. Usually, the Indian spoke freely only to MacLeod or to his brother, in their own language. He searched for a response.

But Sam had already turned away. He grunted a command to Danny, and they headed toward the shore.

A handful of days later, Duncan sat crossed-legged on the raft, anchored by the lakeside for the evening. The night was still, save for the sound of Danny moaning in his sleep. In a while, if his distress continued, Fitzcairn would wake him.

During the day, the young Immortal seemed to have put Skagway behind him. At night—well, dreams were not where logic ruled. And no matter how good a job Fitzcairn was doing in his role as teacher, he could not go wherever it was that Danny went when he was asleep.

Duncan had a fleeting memory of Connor shaking him

awake once. He'd been dreaming of what? His first death? The old hermit in the cave? Debra, falling? He couldn't remember. But he had woke up screaming in the night.

He put the thought aside and returned to the map that he was examining by lanternlight, tracing with one finger the route they had traveled. The latest of his Argonaut reports lay next to him, half-completed.

"Lake Bennett to Marsh Lake." he murmured to himself. "Through Miles Canyon and the Squaw and White Horse Rapids. Down the River Lewes to Lake Labarge. From there, to the river called Thirty-Mile." He made a note on the map. Thirty-Mile had been difficult. Hidden rocks and sand bars had made the going treacherous.

"Then through one last set of rapids. Called the Five Fingers." He made another note. There was a trick to getting through, a trick that Sam knew. One of the five channels held a whirlpool. It looked dangerous, but in fact it turned the boats right, and set them safe.

"We're on the Yukon now, just about here." An X marked the spot. "And tomorrow, we reach Dawson City."

"This morning, we pass the cabin of Carmack. He the sourdough who made the first strike. I point it out to the Irishman."

Duncan looked up, though he did not turn around. He hadn't heard Sam approach. It had been a long time since he'd been taken unaware.

"I'll write that down. My friend in Seattle would find it of interest."

Sam sat next to him. He took the map and the pen. "Here," he said, making another X. "This where it is."

"George Carmack, wasn't that his name?" Duncan asked. "And wasn't one of his partners an Indian?"

Sam nodded. "Both were. They rich now, too. They not Indian anymore." He made a sound that Duncan recognized as a laugh.

Duncan responded in Siwash. He hoped he was saying something on the order of "lucky bastards." He'd been listening to Sam and his brother talk, and comparing what he heard to the Lakota that he knew.

Sam laughed again. "Pretty good, for a cheechako. I think maybe story you tell about living with Indians is true."

"I had a—wife," Duncan said. "And a son. They are dead now. I wouldn't lie about that."

This was not strictly true. Little Deer had not lived long enough to become his wife. Her son had not been his child. But these were things he could not tell Sam, things he had trouble speaking of, even after so many years.

Sam shrugged. "Most squaw men do not belong in the lands where they were born. They can live in the wild. In city places their hearts dry up." He faced Duncan, his black eyes level.

"You not like that. You different from other men. But not in way squaw men are different."

Duncan was uneasy. What had Sam noticed?

"If I were that different," he replied, as casually as he could, "I wouldn't be here, would I?" He folded the map. "My friend in Seattle thought that all argonauts were fools off on a fool's journey. She would laugh to see us now. We've not bathed in weeks, our clothes are filthy, and we smell of wet fur."

"But you go on," Sam said. It was not a question.

"Yes." Duncan agreed. "When we stood on the top of Summit Mountain, above the clouds—that was a sight meant for the eyes of eagles. I want to see more." He smiled. "I want to see the lights in the northern sky that I have heard so much about."

"Scotsman," Sam said, "there is more. I could show you." He was silent. Duncan waited.

"Tomorrow, many come to Dawson. Some stop there. Some not. They go along the Klondike. They strike the land with their axes. They sift the waters with their pans." He snorted.

"They are the fools. The land does not give up the gold to the soft men. It waits. For one like you."

"If they are fools, then what would a wise man do?" Duncan asked, carefully.

"Ten mile beyond Dawson there is a village. It not Siwash. But the tribe does trade with Siwash. A wise man would go there, to buy more dogs and another sled."

"And then?"

"A wise man would hire Siwash Sam and his brother. They would take the man and his friends to a place in the mountains. A place where land and water have not been touched."

"Why would Siwash Sam do this?" Duncan asked.

The silence stretched between them. Finally, Sam answered. "Maybe Sam a fool. Maybe he want to be rich Indian." He looked at Duncan from the corner of his eyes.

"Maybe he curious . . ."

Dawson City. Duncan would never forget the first sight of the town that had grown, in barely a year's time, from a few scattered tents pitched on muddy riverbanks to a thriving metropolis. The rafts rounded one last bend. Beyond the turn, the river widened. Already, even in early October, ice chunks could be seen floating along with the current. Here the mighty Klondike rushed into the Yukon. On the right, a snowcapped mountain rose, dominating the horizon. And in the triangle of land formed by the junction of the two rivers, back to the foothills of that mountain, what looked to be a thousand or more buildings were clustered. Ranging from individual canvas tents to a four-story hotel, they were built haphazardly wherever there was space. No city planner had been at work here, Duncan thought. The morning sunlight, shining through the mist that rose from the mudflats, made it seem indeed like an Eldorado. Though they went on, bound for the Indian village, he stood looking back at the odd flotilla that had shared their journey. As the boats came close to shore, men leaped out, wading the last distance, eager to pass through this final gate to the fabled wealth of the Klondike. How many, Duncan wondered, would find what they had sought for so long? And would he and his friends be among them?

Dawson City. Fitzcairn swore he could hear the sounds from the dance halls, the whoops of appreciation as the ladies raised their petticoats and shook their shapely legs to the music of the upright pianos.

Oh, for the sight of a beardless face—and the touch of a soft hand! And a hot bath!

Even better, the touch of a soft hand *in* a hot bath.

If he had known—if he had even suspected—how long this journey would be, how long he would be without the sweet solace of the fairer sex . . .

But their course was set—so as they floated by, he lost himself in the memory of a certain senorita, and a deep pool of water, heated from the earth. The place had stunk of sulfur, but he'd been too occupied to really notice.

Dawson City. Danny felt a hollowness in his belly that was like a hunger. The gold was *there*. He knew it. He heard the stories. Gold dust and gold nuggets were the currency of the place. Why, a man could find his fortune just by sifting the sweepings from the saloon floors!

Hugh had said to trust MacLeod. The Highlander had lived among the heathens—he knew their ways and their wisdom.

If he would follow the Indian called Sam, then they should likewise follow him.

Yet as Dawson came into view, he gazed toward it with longing. A rainbow seemed to shimmer above the town.

The sun on the damp morning air or his imagination? Danny didn't know. Yet long after Dawson has disappeared behind them he sat looking downstream.

He was there still when Fitzcairn called out the first sight of the Indian village, a rough circle of tents and sheds, scattered on the shore to the right.

Chapter 7

From AN ARGONAUT'S JOURNAL

We left the Indian village in early October with
three new sleds and three new dogs. The sleds were a
kind with runners. The snows had already begun,
and they were, our guide said, better suited to the terrain that lay ahead. The dogs—two bitches and an ill-
tempered, burly male—were the only animals he
could find that he judged worth adding to their fourteen. So two of the sleds were pulled by teams of five.

At the village, we replenished our supplies, adding
to the store of beans and bacon that are the staples of
a prospector's diet. And we laid in fifty more pounds
of dried salmon. The dogs thrive on it—even a small
amount is a solid source of nourishment and energy.

At the suggestion of our guide we traded some of
what he called our Southland clothing for items made

by the Indians. Wool greatcoats have given way to sealskin parkas, leather boots to high-topped fur-and-hide moccasins.

Claire Benét had wanted them to take a camera along, to supplement his Argonaut reports with photographs. Photography was all the rage these days. Duncan had demurred, claiming that the contraption would be more a bother than it was worth. In actuality, this invention called the camera concerned him. It was not in the best interests of men and women whose lives spanned centuries for there to be proof of it. Before he'd reasoned that through, he'd allowed a lover to have his portrait painted. A decision he'd lived—barely—to regret.

That had been some two hundred years past. Since then he'd made certain that no image of Duncan MacLeod in the eighteenth century would appear to confound those mortals who knew him now.

But photography had been steadily growing in popularity, and the day was coming when anyone, rich or poor, would be able to freeze a moment in time, capture it forever. An old woman could look upon herself in the bloom of her beauty. A father could see his grown son once again as an infant.

Already, pictures were being taken as a matter of course of classes as they graduated, couples on their wedding days, and men marching off to be killed. The battlefield photos of Mathew Brady were famous the world over. It was likely, Duncan suspected, that Danny appeared in some of those from Gettysburg.

He and Fitzcairn had discussed his concerns back in Seattle. Fitz was sure that photography was a passing fashion, like painting in miniature. No one he knew ever really liked how they looked in sepia tones, after all. Woman particularly were never happy with the results. Perhaps the device might find continued use by newspaper reporters and the like. But in the main, he was certain, people would prefer the art of brush and paint, which could alter life in pleasant ways.

But Duncan was just as certain that the camera would cause great grief to his kind in years to come. So he had declined Claire's offer. It would not do for someone he might come to know a hundred years hence to find the face of Duncan MacLeod among images from the Klondike gold rush.

At this moment, however, he almost regretted his decision. Though the flat black-and-white of the photograph wouldn't truly be sufficient, still it would be good to have a record more permanent than memory of this valley that Sam had led them to.

After they'd left the village, they'd mushed along the north side of the Klondike until the river ran out. The dogs were fresh, the path was clear. The going had been easy. Then they followed a trail into the mountains that wasn't there unless you knew where to look.

That trail had led them to this glorious place. In his homeland, it would be called a dale—a long, narrow valley, running arrow-straight in the midst of the Mackenzie Mountains. There was a small lake at the bottom, fed by the frigid runoff from the snow-covered slopes. The water seemed to be both sapphire blue and crystal-clear at the same time.

Stands of dark green spruce trees covered the lower hills along the sides of the lake, sweeping up from the shore. At the head and foot, the trees grew more sparsely. The rocky ground sloped gradually, and then soared upward thousands of feet, topped by white peaks that jutted into the misty blue sky. At night, which came ever earlier as winter approached, that sky was filled with a multitude of stars. They were stars strange to Duncan.

He stood now by the water, a short distance from the camp they had set up at the far end of the lake. In his mind, he worked on his next dispatch. The poets among his kind could perhaps have done justice to this land, he thought. But he was a warrior. He felt the lack of wit to conjure a picture in words. Still, he would do his best. And wish again, fleetingly, that he could send along a photograph to speak for him.

The Indian had said to look not where the stream was now but where other streams had been. The notion made no sense to Fitzcairn. But MacLeod went along with it, though it made more work. So Fitz shrugged, collected the prospector's tools that they had carried with them for thousands of miles, and set to the task at hand.

Already today, he had spent several hours on his knees, digging beneath the hard topsoil to the earth below. Then he would fill a pan with the dirt, pour water into it, and swirl the contents. The gold, if it were there, would settle on the bottom.

He moved a few feet to a new spot of ground. He dug, filled, poured, and shook. Grit. Mud. Foul water. He rose and tossed the contents of the pan to the side, raising a shout from MacLeod, who was unfortunate enough to be in the way. He looked down at the camp, snug against the hillside below. A mug of tea might be just the thing. And perhaps a bite of sourdough bread, spread with some of the sweet preserves the Indian had with him.

But it was nearly time for them all to take a break. Something was cooking. Fitz could see the fire and smell the delicious odor rising on the smoke. The valley was filled with small game, birds and beasts that hadn't yet vanished for the winter. And the lake teemed with fish. They had been eating well this last while.

Fitz felt renewed at the thought of food. One or two more pans, then, and he would be more than ready for a meal. He knelt down. Vixen, who had been dozing a few yards away, rose to her feet. She bumped against him, wagging her tail.

Fitz shooed her away. There now, a pan of dirt. Add a dipper or two of water—Vixen was drinking from the bucket. He laughed, ruffled her ears, and began shaking the pan gently.

In a second, he knew. Specks of light settled out, shining in the grit. And not one or two here and there—the bottom of the pan was covered with them. He sat back on his heels, and opened his mouth to call MacLeod. At first, no sound came out. Then he started to laugh. His laughter grew, until he was fairly gasping for breath. Vixen caught his mood. She ran in circles, barking loudly. When MacLeod and Danny came to him to see what was the matter, he showed them the pan. And they knew, too.

That night, he broke out a bottle of expensive brandy that he had bought in Seattle. He had carried it with him, keeping it safe. In case there was need of it, in case there was something to celebrate. He opened it slowly, savoring the aroma. They had no fine crystal glasses to hand, but it didn't matter. The brandy was heady liquid fire, drunk from battered tin cups. One round of toasts followed the other, until all of them, the Indians included, were drunk. From the brandy. And from a renewed attack of the disease called Klondike fever.

It had been that easy, then, to find the gold. The months of the journey north, the weeks on the trail through the mountains, the days spent setting up the camp—then Hugh cried out, and it was done.

Since then, they'd worked hard during the short hours of the daylight, all of them. Even the two heathens took up picks and shovels. The strike was a rich one, it was plain to see. Why, Danny himself had panned out nuggets as big as a man's thumbnail! It didn't seem but a moment until they had two leather pouches, made from the hides of moose, filled with gold. And more being found every minute.

At night, exhausted yet still somehow filled with energy,

Danny slept hard. And he dreamed. But these dreams, unlike the nightmares that had tortured him all of his life, he would remember with the rising of the pale, distant sun.

It seemed in the dreams that a door that he had long thought closed to him was beginning to open. It was much like the heavy dark wooden door on the grand Fifth Avenue house—the door with the golden knocker through which he had watched the green-eyed girl vanish from his sight. He'd never so much as caught a glimpse of what was behind that door.

Now, though, he could see the entrance hall. The walls were covered in gold wallpaper with a pattern in it. Flocked, it was called. He remembered that from the whorehouse in New Orleans. A great crystal-and-gold chandelier hung from the ceiling. It looked much like the one in the Queen of Spades. A staircase of gold-and-green marble, with a solid gold banister, led to the second floor of the house. Had he not seen one such through a window of a fine home in Pittsburgh?

Just where the stairs curved up, there was a window made of bits of colored glass, like those in the churches that were important enough to be called cathedrals. The window had three panels. The two on the side were of angels, dark-haired women wearing snow-white dresses. Sometimes he could see their faces clearly—Amanda, Minnie, the green-eyed girl all grown up. And sometimes they were only pale ovals. In the center was another angel, a man this one was, holding a flaming sword. He was smiting the wicked who cowered at his feet. The faces of the wicked often changed. But the angel always had Danny's face.

As the days went on, and more pouches were filled, Danny began to venture into other rooms in the house. In his sleep—and sometimes with his eyes wide-open.

* * *

"There's easier ways for a man to make his fortune," Fitz-cairn complained. "I haven't ached this much since Henry Fitz taught me the proper way to sit a horse."

"Do tell us, then, about these easier ways." Duncan stopped and turned. "From your vast experience."

Fitz mumbled a reply.

"What?" Duncan asked, cupping his hand behind his ear. "What was that you said? Could you speak up a bit?"

Fitzcairn spoke loudly, "I said 'no.'"

"No—what?" Duncan was relentless.

"No," he shouted, "I can't speak on the subject from experience!" A grackle, startled by the noise, flew from the bushy cover. Vixen, who had followed along with them, bounded off after it.

"No experience?" Duncan shook his head. "But what about that trading ship you had a stake in? All the wealth of the Indies, bound for the New World?" He frowned. "Oh, I'd forgotten. It sank."

Fitz tried to push past, but the trees were thick around, and Duncan was not about to move.

"And didn't you once have a da Vinci sculpture to sell?" he continued. "A lovely female nude, done in bronze? Except that . . ." he paused. "Oh yes, now I remember—it turned out to be a forgery."

Danny, who had been lagging behind, caught up to them. "What ship was that, Hugh? You'd never mentioned—"

Fitzcairn stood between the two Immortals. He turned first to Duncan. "She was a tight ship with a good cargo, Highlander. It was just bad luck that the weather went against her. And the statue was an excellent fake. As you well know! You had the opportunity to examine it closely after the fair Amanda got her thieving hands on it." He faced Danny and continued.

"The point I was endeavoring to make before I was rudely

attacked by this Scot's git"—Duncan snorted loudly enough to disturb another bird—"was that even my Immortal bones are feeling the strain of our efforts. It's hard on the back, bending to dig up gold! I'm not certain that I'm in condition for any swordplay."

"You've been saying that since we left camp. And I say that's all the more reason you should do it," Duncan insisted. "If you're worried, ye needn't be—I promise I'll not run you through this day."

"I've learned a thing or two since Verona, laddie." Fitzcairn replied. "If you're determined that we're going to do this, then we'll just see who gets the best of whom." He strode off into the woods. Danny went to follow, but Duncan held him back. In a minute, they heard Fitz calling, followed by the barking of a dog.

"Where the bloody hell are you, MacLeod? Where the bloody hell am I?"

After finding Fitzcairn, they continued to pick their way through the forest. As they went along, Duncan carefully marked the trail, cutting wedge-shaped blazes in the trees. Finally, they came to a clearing large enough for their needs.

Duncan unsheathed the *katana*. It felt good to have it in his hand again. He'd been able to do his exercises a few times during the journey. But this was the first time since one evening on the shore of Lake Bennett that he had found an opportunity to practice with his sword.

The valley was sheltered, the mountains blocking the worst of the chill winds. And it was warmer still here among the trees. The three Immortals were able to shed a layer or two of clothing. That allowed them to move about more freely as they played at the Game that was the center of their lives.

Danny sat at the edge of the clearing on a felled tree. He held Vixen by a piece of rope tied around her neck, as Duncan took on Fitzcairn.

They'd not really crossed swords since they'd first met, though they had fought side by side more than a few times. Fitz had gotten better since Verona. He still carried the cavalier's blade that he'd been given by his teacher, and he used it, as always, with style. But over the centuries he had added more power and control.

As they fought back and forth, Fitz kept up a steady stream of insults. Duncan gritted his teeth and ignored him. He was far more practiced and experienced, so bit by bit he was wearing Fitz down.

Suddenly, Fitzcairn feinted a downward slash to the right. Duncan moved to block it. With a swift motion, Fitz transferred the blade to his left hand, and thrust forward. Duncan was only able to avoid the blow by falling backward. He rolled quickly back to his feet, and raised the *katana* defensively.

"One of the things you've learned?" Duncan asked, as they circled one another.

"In Spain," Fitz replied, grinning, "from a swordsman named Montoya. He had a sister—"

"Don't they always?" Duncan said, as he closed in. A flurry of movement, and the cavalier's sword went flying.

Fitz laughed and offered his hand to Duncan. "Ah, I should know by now not to think of women when I've a sword in my hand. Such sweet distraction!"

"Aye, it's true. There's just no room in your tiny English mind for more than one thing at a time," Duncan said. They shook hands. Danny tied the dog to a tree and retrieved his teacher's blade.

"We'd best let the Highlander rest, Danny," Fitz said. "And pick pine needles off his britches."

Duncan stood to the side then and watched Fitzcairn and his student. Rather than insults, Fitz kept a running commentary—advising Danny, correcting him, complimenting him on a particularly good pass.

The young Immortal had no style—he hadn't really had enough time to develop one. Still, Duncan could see how he had survived. He fought with his sword as he no doubt fought with his fists. He was quick, strong, and brutal. Even an ill-aimed blow, if delivered with enough force, can make a nasty wound. A wounded opponent was a weakened opponent. A weakened opponent was an easier kill. And there was no rule that said that a kill had to be clean.

Duncan did recognize one or two moves that obviously came from Fitz—a certain way of parrying a two-handed thrust and a swift stabbing motion with the blade held sideways. But the student was no match for the teacher, overall. He wondered though—in a real fight, how brutal could Danny be?

He was vaguely aware that Vixen had been whining steadily. Suddenly she broke into furious barking, throwing herself forward, straining to break free.

Distracted, Danny slipped and fell, muttering under his breath. Fitz turned toward the animal.

"Hush, beastie. It's only a kind of game we're at." As he turned back to help Danny to his feet, the sound of a great disturbance came from the trees to the right.

The three Immortals stood frozen.

"Something wicked this way comes," Fitz muttered.

"Something big," Duncan added, just as an enormous form burst into the clearing.

It was a bear, dark brown, covered in shaggy winter fur. It was on Danny before he even had a chance to raise his sword. One swipe of a paw the size of a shovel blade sent the young Immortal flying across the clearing. His body hit a tree trunk with an audible crunch, then slid down. He lay sprawled, a stain of red spreading from the back of his head.

Fitzcairn had a scant few seconds to take a stand. His sword was at hand, and he used it, slashing at the beast. But he succeeded only in driving it to a further frenzy. With a terrible roar, it stood on its back legs, towering over Fitz. Face-to-face with such fury, he faltered for an instant. Daggerlike claws raked down his sword arm. He screamed and fell to his knees.

Duncan was there behind him. He swung the *katana* with all the force he could muster. It was the stroke that he would use to take an opponent's head, when the fight was over and the Challenge answered. But the angle was a difficult one—his sword bit deep into the bear's chest, missing the throat by a foot or more.

The beast dropped to all fours and charged Duncan, knocking Fitz aside in its wake. For all of its size, it was unbelievably swift. Duncan dodged to the right, the huge bulk brushing by him. It smelled of blood and decay. He wheeled and slashed again, cutting the shoulder to the bone.

With a howl that was echoed by Vixen, who had nearly strangled herself trying to get free, the bear turned. Claws ripped out, catching Duncan across one thigh. He felt a firestorm of pain, like four trails of flame laid on his bare skin. But he'd known worse, from rack and rope, and the swords of other Immortals.

He and the others would survive this, he knew. The beast could not kill them. But it could maim and mutilate. There were many theories among his kind about the limits of their healing powers. Duncan had never had any desire to test them.

Fitz's movements, as he struggled to his feet, caught the bear's attention. Duncan seized the opportunity. This time his killing stroke was downward, and his aim was true. The blow severed the beast's spine and passed half through the massive neck. Blood fountained from the torn throat, spraying across the clearing. The *katana* was pulled from Duncan's hands as the bear thrashed to its knees, shuddering violently. Finally it fell to one side and lay still.

The clearing seemed somehow smaller. Vixen was on her belly, whining softly. Fitzcairn got to his feet, and took an unsteady step forward.

"Exit," he said shakily, "pursued by a bear."

Duncan smiled, briefly. No Quickening marked the end of this fight. But somehow he still felt the exhaustion that followed that moment when the Immortal who was left standing received all his vanquished foe's power. What he wanted to do was collapse on the soft pine needles of the forest floor. What he actually did was direct Fitz's attention to Danny, who was just beginning to stir, coughing feebly.

While Fitz saw to his student, Duncan approached the carcass. He pulled the *katana* free. A spurt of blood followed. He prodded the beast with his foot. The yellow eyes were glassy, the tongue hung out, and a foul-smelling fluid was spreading beneath it. It was most definitely dead.

Fitzcairn and Danny joined him. The young Immortal still seemed dazed.

"This would be a bear then?" he asked.

"Aye, lad," Fitzcairn said, putting a steadying hand on his shoulder.

"I've only seen the heads of them before," Danny continued, "hanging on walls. And the madam—she kept a creature that was said to be a bear. It rode a ball. And juggled. But it was—smaller."

"We shouldn't have seen this fellow either," Fitzcairn said. "Not at this time of the year. If he'd been napping the winter away in some cozy den, he'd have lived to see his cubs in the spring."

Duncan knelt by the carcass, examining it. "This animal was sick, I think. It's a good deal thinner than it should be.

And look at the fur." He ran his hand along the beast's side. "It's coming out in clumps."

Fitz bent to look closer. Duncan hesitated, then ruffled through the dense fur again.

"Fitzcairn, see here," he said.

A knife was buried, up to the hilt, in the bear's side.

The two Immortals exchanged a glance.

"That's not an old wound, is it laddie?" Fitz asked softly.

Duncan shook his head. He rose. "The bear came through the trees over there." He pointed. "Let's see if we can follow the back trail."

What might have been a task to test Duncan's tracking skills was made simple for them. The moment they released Vixen, she shot off into the woods. Her high-pitched barks were easy to follow.

In perhaps a quarter of an hour, they came upon the first dead dog. It lay at the base of a tree, head at an odd angle, claw marks clearly visible on one side. Duncan paused briefly. The dog, a brown-spotted bitch, was one of those they had bought in the village. She'd been made the swing dog on the team driven by Sam's brother. The blood matting the fur was still wet.

Ahead, Vixen had fallen silent. The three Immortals moved as quickly as they could through the trees, following the path of destruction made by the passage of the bear.

Pushing through a shoulder-high stand of bushes, Duncan nearly tripped over the second dog. It had been ripped apart. What lay at his feet was the head and front quarters. Fitz, brought up short behind him, muttered softly.

"Poor beastie. Is it the one called Nishka?"

But Duncan hardly heard him. Past the bushes, he could see Vixen, pawing at a figure lying on the ground. A few steps farther, and he could tell that the figure was human.

The ground underfoot was soaked in blood. The place

reeked of it, and of the stench that comes with violent death. That was a smell that Duncan knew well. Any man, Immortal or not, who had been in battle knew it.

He walked the last few paces. The body lay on its back. The face was nothing more than a hollow of blood and bits of bone. One arm was missing, and the guts spilled out through a terrible wound that extended from stomach to thigh.

The bear, perhaps driven mad by sickness, had turned whatever crossed its path into so much unrecognizable meat. Two dogs, at least. And one man, whose felt hat, stained an even darker red, lay beside him.

Siwash Sam was not surprised when the three cheechakos brought his brother's body back to the camp.

This day they had decided to rest from the work of digging the gold, though the Irishman had not liked the idea. The three went off together to do white man's business. Sam had his own work to do—traces to mend, newly caught fish to salt. And before the day had even begun, his brother had been gone, taking his rifle and four of the dogs with him. There were elk in the forest, higher up.

One dog had returned hours later, marked by the claw of a bear. Sam had known then.

The Scotsman had given Sam his brother's hat. He said that his brother had fought the bear bravely, that he had wounded it deeply with his knife. The rifle they had found broken on the ground. It had not been fired.

They had killed the bear, he said, the three of them. They had been able to do this because of how weak it had been after the fight with Sam's brother.

Their clothes were bloody and torn. But they did not walk as men who were hurt. Yet the truth of what they said could not be doubted, for they had brought the head of the bear back with them.

All the next day, Sam prepared to send his brother to his rest. The Scotsman offered his help. Sam hesitated. This was not a thing for those who were not Siwash. But he had come to believe that the Scotsman truly had lived with a Southland tribe. He knew things, in his head. And in his heart. For Sam had overheard the Englishman and the Irishman talking, marveling still at how the Scotsman had insisted that they bring the head of the bear to him.

It had been the right thing to do. The bear was not to be killed lightly, and his spirit was to be given respect. Though Sam ached for the loss of his brother, to die as he had was a noble thing.

So while Sam cleaned his brother's body in the clear waters of the lake, wrapping it in soft blankets, the Scotsman made preparations for the meal that would be eaten in his memory.

And when darkness had fallen, the two of them sat beside the lake. A small fire burned before them, a rabbit on a spit suspended above it. The body lay on a bed of kindling not far away. The bear's head, decorated with feathers, lay with it. The eagle feather from the red felt hat rested in its mouth.

As they ate and drank, Sam spoke of his brother, and of the hope that he was already born anew in the belly of one of the women of the tribe. He praised the bear for its courage in facing so many men. He wished its spirit well.

He rose then and took a blazing brand from the fire. The Scotsman walked beside him. He lit the branches beneath the remains of his brother.

They watched as the loose wood caught fire. Sam searched the night sky, but he could see no eagle in flight. That was not a bad thing, but it would have been better were one to appear.

The Scotsman asked if he could know the true name of Sam's brother that he might use it when he said his farewell. But Sam had to deny him that.

The body burned brightly for some time. Sam stayed by it, as the smoke rose into the chill air. The next day, when the ashes had cooled, he gathered them and cast them out into the water of the lake. The skull of the bear, burned clean of flesh and fur, he buried.

The Scotsman stood with him through it all.

"Fitzcairn Manor," Fitz said as he walked toward the lake shore. He had just stowed away a fifth bag of gold. "Stately Fitzcairn Manor. Less intimidating than Fitzcairn Castle, don't you think?"

Vixen yipped and wagged her tail. Fitz held out a bit of dried salmon, which she took daintily from his fingers.

He shivered, and pulled down the earflaps on his hat. An odd-looking thing it was, sitting on his head like some small furry creature, whole and entire. In color, it almost matched his hair, so that at first glance, it looked as though he had grown his own shaggy winter coat. He'd gotten it in the Indian village. A young woman—he supposed they were called squaws—had been selling them. Dark-haired, with the blackest eyes he'd ever seen, and skin the color of a new-minted coin. MacLeod had raised an eyebrow, but Fitz had been enchanted—with the hat, of course.

Which was proving its worth, as the weather began to turn. Yesterday it had snowed, two inches or more. The tops of the mountains were lost in thick clouds.

This morning, they'd heard a rumbling from above. They stood and watched as what seemed to be half the side of one of the lower peaks sloughed off. The snow thundered down, picking up speed as it went. It made a noise like cannon on a battlefield, or distant thunder, coming ever closer. The Indian turned away, but Fitz and the other two Immortals stood and watched as the white mass rolled on. He had never seen the like of it, and he was fairly certain that the same was true of Danny and MacLeod.

The avalanche broke up finally at the tree line, leveling dozens of the dark spruce in its wake. But all through the day, the sound of thunder echoed through the valley. The first and last big snows of winter were heavy and wet, the Indian said. Such disturbances were to be expected. In fact, they were very late this year. Usually, such snows came well before the end of November.

"What's a ton or two of snow coming at you like a runaway train?" Fitz asked Vixen, who trotted along beside him. "Not to worry. Business as usual!" The sun, a distant murky speck in the sky, cast no heat. Yesterday's snow was still underfoot. Fitz had brought a leather tarp with him. He spread it on the ground and sat down cross-legged to smoke his evening pipe.

He'd not taken a lantern along, and the darkness was complete, save for the glow of his pipe. The canopy of stars, usually a sight to take a man's breath away, was obscured by clouds. He wondered if they would ever see the fabled Northern Lights. He smiled. For all the gold that they had found, he knew that MacLeod would leave a disappointed man if they did not.

Vixen crept close, leaning against his thigh. He pulled on his pipe.

"Aye, beastie. Here I sit, a rich, rich man. Behind me sit another three. And are we capering about in merriment? Dancing on our hind legs, as you might if you were to find a cache of bones?" His breath blew out like a stream of smoke. "No, we are not. Not at all." Fitz sighed.

He'd been particularly concerned about Danny. The lad was working as hard as ever. But he went through the days silent and abstracted. Finally, under Fitz's prodding, he'd reluctantly admitted that he was building in his mind the house that he would soon build for real. He'd seemed embarrassed by the admission. So, for the promise of a guest room set aside, with a four-poster bed more than big enough for two, Fitz agreed to keep it between them. Danny had laughed, and said that the room had been furnished days before.

And MacLeod—the death of Siwash Sam's brother had sent him into one of his blackest moods. Fitz had tried everything. Sense. (Pointing out that they would not even be in this valley were it not for the Indians. So any logic that held them responsible for what had happened was suspect.) And nonsense. (An evening spent trying to goad him into an argument about tartans versus tweed.)

Neither had worked.

Only Siwash Sam seemed unchanged. His brother's fate surely must have affected him. But as he hardly ever spoke, it was difficult to discern his mood at any given moment.

A few flakes of snow settled on the dog's fur. Fitz brushed at them gently. He was reminded of a time before he was Immortal, when he'd first seen snow. It had seemed a wonder then. Now, as the few flakes rapidly became a thick fall, he groaned and headed back toward the warmth of the fire, where Danny, the Highlander, and the Indian all sat, each lost in his own thoughts.

The plain truth of it was that Danny just did not trust Siwash Sam.

The Indian said that they should have left the valley two weeks ago. The time of the snows was upon them, he said. Soon, the passes would be blocked. The way would be dangerous. They must go now, to the fort called McPherson. Closer than Dawson City, it was a place where they could stake their claim and wait out the long winter.

Danny wanted no part of that. He said so. And, in private, he'd told Hugh the why of it. The moment they were gone, more of the heathens would come and take what they had found. He was that certain. Why else would Sam be so eager to leave? Men *did* stay the winter on the land—hadn't they passed at least one cabin on their way to the valley? Well, then, he could stay, too, and that was the end of it.

Though his teacher did not agree, he stood by Danny. They argued it for several days. Finally, MacLeod gave in. Though it was clear to Danny that the heathen still objected, they decided that a shelter could be built, to keep him secure through the winter. There was food a plenty, and they would leave him with more than enough firewood.

It was settled then. Afterward, Hugh was distant with him. It grieved Danny to disappoint his teacher. But they had worked too hard to see their efforts stolen from them.

He'd thought it best to leave the camp for a space of time this morning. Tomorrow they would start the building of the cabin. Today, MacLeod and Hugh were planning to check the snares set in the woods, while the heathen began the organizing of their supplies.

He climbed the mountainside to the place where they had last been working. It was fair cold up there. The ground was already half-frozen. Danny had brought pick, pan, and pail with him. But he was getting no use of them. Instead, he sat quiet on a rock, and lost himself for a wee bit in the halls of his grand house.

A scrabbling noise from below caught his attention. Hugh was coming up the hill, followed as usual by the brown dog. He'd pulled his furry hat far down on his head, and wound a long scarf 'round his neck. He was picking his way carefully, mindful of the icy patches that dotted the hill.

"Have you left off hunting rabbits, then?" Danny asked. "And come to join me in some prospecting?"

The greeting brought a smile to Hugh's face, as Danny had hoped. "Six bags of gold is enough for now, lad," he replied. "That's the ransom of at least one or two kings I've known."

He sat down beside Danny. His face was red from the cold. It made his eyes seem an even brighter blue.

"I left the bunnies to MacLeod." he said. "I thought we might have a word or two." Danny turned to face him squarely.

"You're wrong, you know," he continued, quietly. "The winter will be fierce. And you'll be alone. There won't be any strangers, friend or foe, dropping by for tea and jerky."

Ah, if only he could make his teacher understand! "The cold and snow won't be killing me, Hugh," he said. "I'll have my sword to hand, though I doubt I'll have the need of it. And a rifle. If it should be that I'm not wrong—if company does come to call."

Hugh shook his head. "Daniel Patrick O'Donal, you're as stubborn—well, as MacLeod himself. If I truly thought I was leaving you to danger, I'd stay behind." He rubbed his gloved hands together briskly.

"I'd not be asking that of you," Danny said. Then he grinned. "Sure and I know that you have to be going. You must be greatly in need of the sight of a face that's not covered with whiskers."

His teacher laughed. "Even the sight of my own face clean-shaven would be welcome, in point of fact."

A loud rumble filled the air.

"It's to be expected," Hugh muttered. The dog got to her feet, whining.

A second, louder sound came from above, then another and another. Like the explosions from the big guns on the line, Danny thought. He could see his teacher's face. He was looking over Danny's shoulder, up the mountain. His eyes widened.

"Bloody hell," he whispered.

Danny turned. For a bit of a second, he didn't understand what it was he saw. Then it came clear.

From out of the clouds that covered the peak, a moving wall of white was sweeping down. He remembered the stories that he'd heard in Skagway of the great disaster at Chilkoot. Had it happened so quickly there, too? A day cold but dry, and then death coming from above, so sudden?

Hugh grabbed his arm and hurried him away. The dog raced ahead. Though they were in no danger so far below, still it was best to be off the slope.

They slipped and slid their way toward the lake. The whole of the time, the cannon sound rolled on. Hugh fell, landing on his bottom. Danny helped him to his feet. As he did, he chanced a look back. The mass of snow had reached the tree line. It would be stopped there, Danny thought.

But on this side of the lake the trees were sparse. The ground—the rocky ground that had given up its treasure to them—was not hospitable to growth.

"Sweet Jaysus," Danny said, as the white wave crashed on. It uprooted trees, sweeping them along. Then it came to the edge of the rocky slope, dislodging boulders, sending them careening downward.

There were times when Danny thought that Mother Kelly still watched over her changeling child. This was one of them. It was only by the merest fraction that he and Hugh missed being buried beneath the mingled rock and snow. Knocked from their feet they were, and tumbled about. But the bulk of the terrible slide swept by them, down upon the camp below.

The cheechakos did not know how lucky they were. But Sam did. The rockslide had taken the tents and one of the sheds. It was the one where they kept the gold-hunting tools and the fresher stores of food.

A sled and four of the dogs who had been staked out, because they could not be trusted to roam free, had also been caught. Sam felt that loss the most. But the second shed, with the store of blankets and the food supplies that they had brought with them, had been spared.

And it was in this shed that they had kept the gold. So that, too, was spared. Though Sam would have gladly traded a pouch or two for more meat.

Sam would not have wished this thing to happen. And he took no joy in it. But it did put an end to the crazy plan of leaving the Irishman behind. It had surprised Sam greatly that the Scotsman had agreed to it. He knew that when the snows melted, they would have returned to find the young fool's body frozen where it lay. He told the Scotsman this. But it had not seemed to concern him. Sam thought that strange.

Now it did not matter. There was no more of such talk. They must all leave, and leave at once. The fort was many miles distant. Much time had been wasted.

His fault, his responsibility. He had been distracted by his grief. And his burden of worry—had they waited too long?

This he had not told the Scotsman.

Sam stood in the dying light of day at the waters edge. He spoke a word to the spirit of the bear, asking it to guard the valley, until the time when he and the three white men might once more walk by the lake.

Tomorrow, before the dawn, they would be gone. And when the snows came, Sam knew, it would be as though they had never been there.

Chapter 8

We left the valley in the first week of December, Duncan thought to himself, composing his next Argonaut's report as the two sleds raced through the snow-covered emptiness. He had the team led by Vixen. She was full of energy today, leaping through the fresh powder, pulling the other dogs along in her wake. They'd been running beside Sam and his sled, but now they had drawn ahead.

We were fortunate, he continued, *to find that the passes were not yet blocked. We made excellent time through the mountains. We are now well on our way north and a bit west toward Fort McPherson.*

He whistled and pulled on the traces. Ahead, the ground sloped slightly. At the bottom of the slope lay the frozen surface of a narrow river. The smooth ice was dusted with snow.

Duncan guided the sled to the place where the snow was disturbed by the tracks of several deerlike animals. Vixen barely slowed her pace as they skimmed across.

He was just calculating that they might well reach McPherson by December 25, when he heard a terrible chilling sound. Thunder, muted rolling thunder, mixed with a sharp snap/crack. It was ice breaking, he knew. Yet it sounded like wood in the fireplace, green wood popping and sparking as it burned.

He braked the sled, pulling the dogs to a stop. But they were still moving as Danny threw himself off to the side, and rolled clumsily to his feet. He gave a strangled cry as he rose.

"Hugh! Sweet Jaysus, Hugh!"

As he turned and began running through the snow, back toward the river they had just crossed, Duncan had a fleeting thought that he had never heard the young Immortal swear before.

Danny was flailing in the deeper snow, but Duncan kept to the path just broken by the sled's passage. Without snowshoes, it was a heavy task, but he had no time to strap them on.

The white world was full of other sounds now: Danny behind him screaming Fitzcairn's name over and over; the yelps of the dogs that had been pulling the second sled, as they struggled vainly to break free of their traces; Sam's guttural voice, crying for help in a mixture of Siwash and English.

He did not hear the familiar tones of the man he had known for three centuries, the still-detectable British accent that grew more clipped in times of excitement.

As Duncan got closer, he slowed. If you examined the seemingly solid expanse of ice closely, you could just tell where the water ended and the land began. The sled had fallen through a good fifteen feet out, the ice beneath breaking up like spun glass. The flailing of dogs and men had widened the hole, and the rushing torrent of water beneath could now be seen clearly. And heard.

Cracks extended out in all directions. Even as Duncan

watched, another ragged chunk of ice broke off and was swept away, sucked under the surface and borne downstream.

The ice held for the deer, he thought. *It held for me. It's December. The rivers should be frozen solid.*

But *this* river most certainly was not. And by a stroke of ill fate, the ice had not held for the second sled.

He saw one dog disappear. He saw Sam clinging to the sled. He did not see Fitz.

Danny caught up to him then. He didn't stop, but stumbled on toward the frozen river.

"Danny." Duncan grabbed him by the arm. "No. Wait."

The young Immortal struggled to pull free.

"Wait? Are you daft? Look there, MacLeod." He gestured wildly toward the still-widening hole in the ice. *"Where is Hugh?"*

"You look." With some difficulty, Duncan held him back. Fitz had told him truly—Danny was strong. "The ice is breaking up all over. We must go carefully or we'll all be lost."

Duncan kept his grip, until he could see the young man calming himself. Only then did he release his hold. Danny stood statue-still.

"Hugh does not swim well, you know," he said in a hollow tone. "What shall we do then, MacLeod? How shall we reach them?"

Duncan looked around. There was no time to go back to the sled for the rope that was in the gear. And no place near to the river bank to anchor it, even if it were to hand.

But they had their belts. And the whip, which had been frozen to Duncan's glove, had dropped just a few paces back. Danny fetched it. Then the two men unfastened layers of fur and thick wool to reach the wide strips of leather around their waists.

As quickly as his fingers, made clumsy by the heavy gloves

he dare not remove, would work, Duncan joined the two belts together.

Sam's cries were becoming more feeble, and the yelping of the dogs was abruptly cut off . "Another poor beast has just gone under," Danny said flatly.

Duncan knelt in front of Danny, and attached one end of the joined belts to his ankle. "Danny. Listen to me. You're lighter than I am so you must go out first. Take the whip and lie down flat. Spread out as much as you can." He measured the distance to the hole with his eyes. "Here." He handed the whip to Danny. "I'll hold on to the belts. You get as close as you can—if Sam can get a grip on the whip, I can pull you back and him out."

The young Immortal took a deep breath and turned toward the river. Two of the dogs that had been harnessed to the lost sled had somehow gotten free of their traces and pulled themselves out onto the ice. They'd crawled a few feet away, where they lay, whimpering and twitching. Duncan did not want to give a thought to how cold the water must be.

Danny knelt then, and slowly, so slowly, inched his way toward the Indian. Duncan stretched out behind him.

They did not speak of Fitzcairn.

Often before, in situations of great danger, Duncan had noted how time ran differently. He had fought in battles that were over in an eyeblink or went on for hours, though by the clock both had lasted the same number of seconds. He had faced other Immortals, had crossed swords for what had to be many minutes but felt like a few heartbeats.

The sled had gone through the ice perhaps five minutes ago. Now, as Danny crawled across the ice, lifetimes were passing.

"Softly, that's it. A bit more." Duncan murmured encouragement. A sharp cracking sound, and Danny went still. But no more ice broke, and he was able to get near enough to extend the whip to Sam.

The Indian grasped it. He was very weak, Duncan could tell. But he was also wiser than any of them in the ways of survival in this land. So he wound the whip around his wrist and held on with both hands.

Duncan pulled back, slowly, steadily, hand over hand, backing up himself, until he had solid ground beneath him. There he rose to his knees. He closed his mind to everything else—the churn of the water, the cries of the dying dogs, Sam's grunts of pain as he was hauled across the ice. There was a thing to be done here, and he would do it.

And then they would talk of Fitzcairn.

There was one bad moment when another foot of ice gave way, and Sam and Danny both nearly went into the frigid water. But Duncan struggled to his feet and tugged sharply. He reached down and grabbed Danny, nearly lifting him and Sam, who still had a devil's grip on the whip, into the air.

The three men lay then, in the brittle snow on the bank of the treacherous river. Danny was panting as though he had run a long, difficult race. Every muscle that Duncan could feel was a knot of tension. Yet they knew they could not rest.

"Scotsman," Siwash Sam said. His voice was a harsh whisper. "You must build fire. Big fire. Warm me. Dry me. Or I freeze." He coughed. "And leg—right leg. It is broken, I think. It is hard to tell."

"Yes. All right then." Duncan rose, stumbling upright. The sled was where they had left it, more or less. The dogs had simply dropped down in their traces. "Danny, bring the sled. We'll head—that's a stand of trees up ahead. There." He pointed, as the young Immortal slowly got to his feet. Sam grunted. Duncan took it for assent.

Danny faced Duncan. His face was white and set, his blue

eyes dangerous. "Are you not forgetting something, High-lander?"

Duncan glanced at Sam. The Indian's eyes were closed, and he seemed only half-conscious. "Fitzcairn will survive this, Danny. You know that. But if we don't tend to him immediately, Sam won't."

"Englishman dead." Siwash Sam spoke without opening his eyes. "No chance he survive." He coughed again. A bit of blood clotted his lips.

Danny glared at Duncan a moment and went to get the sled.

Fitz will survive, Duncan thought as he watched the sled itself finally vanish, swept into the river. But at what cost? For a moment, his vision blurred and dimmed. But it was too cold for his tears to fall.

Drowning. Why did it always have to be drowning? As the sled crashed through the ice, Fitz, who had been riding, was thrown off. Almost at once, he was trapped underneath.

He fought to get free, but the tangle of panicky dogs, Sam's flailing legs, and the spilled contents of the sled confounded him. In a short time he gave up.

Icy water filled his lungs. His body was carried by the current beneath the ice, banging from rock to rock. Once, as he rolled on his back, he could see up through a clear patch. The sky was white, too, he thought, like everything else in this blasted land.

It was his last thought for a while.

When he choked back to life, he found that he was no longer in motion. He'd become wedged between two rocks, faceup, his head pointed downstream. He held his breath for as long as he could and tried to push upward to break through from beneath.

Bloody freezing, bloody water, chunks of ice hitting his face, bloody cold, bloody—

He drowned, again.

The next time he revived, it was dark. He sputtered, coughed, and began to feel the first faint stirrings of worry. What was the possibility that Duncan or Danny could find him in the dark? None.

It was going to be a long, cold night. Already, it felt as though every spark of warmth he had ever had in his life had been damped out and then whatever was left chilled to crystal. As he lay in the water, drifting back and forth between life and death, he tried to kindle some heat with memories of past loves.

There was Arianna, the "virgin" daughter of the duke of Verona. She'd taught him a thing or two as they rolled about on sweaty sheets, beneath a satin-covered, down-filled duvet. Until MacLeod had come to save her honor.

That memory made him laugh. Icy water burned inside his nose. *Forget the Highlander, Hugh Fitzcairn,* he chided himself. *There are far lovelier thoughts to think.*

Remember Ashley, brown-haired, brown-eyed Ashley. They'd dallied a hot summer away. She'd been a fiery-tempered wench, and brighter by far than any woman should be.

And pretty Nan, a blue-eyed blond, with a sunny smile that could light up the day and night. She'd giggled when he kissed her soft neck as she sat at his feet while he smoked his pipe.

Ah, the glow of that smoldering tobacco!

He thought of jolly Kath, who rolled with him in the new grass of a secret spring meadow, while the sun poured down on them like warm honey.

When London was burning in 1666, he'd been in bed with Mrs. Mitchell, the king's current favorite. He'd risked his head for her since Charles was sometimes a jealous lover, but she had been worth it!

So it went through the long, long night. When dawn came,

Fitz was revived once more by a sight he'd wager no man had ever seen from a position such as his.

From under the ice, he watched the sky shade from pale lavender to soft amethyst to petal pink as the distant sun climbed in the sky. This time he held his breath not just for the sake of the few minutes of life, but in awe.

His last thought as he drowned again, was that if worse came to worst, the ice would thaw in spring. Now wasn't it good that he'd had so many fine memories to entertain him until then?

"How bad is it, then?" Danny asked as he handed Duncan the second of the slender tree branches. Duncan positioned it and tied the splint securely in three places with leather cut from extra traces.

Siwash Sam was conscious through it all but, even at the worst points, he barely groaned.

"It's bad," Duncan replied. He didn't lower his voice. The Indian knew better than he, probably, the nature of his injury. "The big bone in his thigh shattered and came out through the skin. The wound—it's an ugly one. And," he hesitated, "I don't know—the freezing water and the cold—how it will affect the healing."

Danny shook his head. "Not the leg. I've seen far worse, after the fighting." He regarded Sam with a curious detachment. "Most times the doctors were quick to take the limb."

Sam stared at the young man. Duncan narrowed his eyes. "Well, this isn't war, and I'm no battlefield surgeon. The wound was clean at least, and I used sulfa powder under the dressing. We'll keep him warm and—"

"What I meant, MacLeod," Danny interrupted, "is how bad is it for us, do you think?"

Duncan considered. They'd lost the sled, all the supplies and gear on it, and four of the five dogs. The fifth, Sam's lead dog Rip, was one of the two that had gotten clear of the river. He was not in the best of shape. But they had wrapped him in a fur robe and moved him close to the fire, away from the second team. Through his own pain, Sam had directed them to do so. The injured dog, he explained, was at risk from the healthy. They were running on short rations—the dogs were hungry. They might well turn on the weakened one and tear him apart.

"I've no good answer, Danny." Duncan replied. "We can't stay here long. These trees aren't much of a shelter. And the weather could change in a moment. Sam has said that all along." Duncan rearranged the blankets covering the Indian. "A night, no more. Then we lash him to the sled and go on." He paused, rose to his feet, and walked a short distance away. Danny followed. They both stood looking back at the frozen river.

"If the dog can pull, we'll harness him. If not, we'll have to leave him. We've got over half the gear and food left and we'll be moving at a slower pace. You and I will be walking for the most part." He stared around at the unbroken stretch of white that never seemed to meet the sky no matter how far distant you looked.

"And Hugh." Danny said in a low tone. "We leave him like the poor dog?"

"Danny, we've been over this. Fitzcairn will be all right. He'll come up through another hole in the ice, or be carried downstream to a larger river." Duncan turned to face the young Immortal. "In fact, he might even reach a place of safety before us. There are cabins built by these rivers. And," he added with a twisted smile, "his head is safe. The Game is not meant to be played in a land where a man's breath freezes in his beard."

"That had best be true," Danny said, bleakly, "for his sword was on the sled."

Duncan was silent. Fitz had carried that bright blade since before they had met. A cavalier's sword, with a well-polished guard and a keen edge. It was not fancy, but it suited him and had served him well for centuries. Still, though a swordless Immortal could usually be judged an Immortal at great risk, Duncan thought that, at this moment, in this hostile place, it was not any of their kind that Fitzcairn need fear.

"Consider this," Danny continued, "might Hugh not be just around the bend there"—he gestured downstream—"freezing to his death, waiting for his *old friend* to come to his aid?"

"He might at that," Duncan conceded softly, "but we can't leave Sam and the dogs. We must stay together. To separate is foolish. And dangerous."

"*We* can't. But I can. And I will, MacLeod. You'll not stop me, except with your own sword."

Duncan saw that Danny was determined, so it was agreed then—the young Immortal donned snowshoes, took a pickax, rope, a fur blanket, extra snowshoes, a kerosene lantern, and a bit of food and set off downstream. Darkness was already falling. He had, Duncan told him, until three hours after dawn the next day to return with Fitzcairn or not.

And what will you do, Duncan MacLeod, if he does not come back?

As though he had heard the thought, Siwash Sam spoke from his nest of fur, "Irishman dead now, too. Next day come, we go on, Scotsman."

Duncan glanced down at him, then back at Danny, a figure vanishing in the gathering gloom. He was going slowly, following the course of the river. Not dead, not really, Duncan thought. And yet—it was something he rarely talked about, only a bit with Connor.

When their kind died, it did not last. But for a time—sometimes seconds, sometimes hours—they *were* dead. And when that brief death touched a friend, Duncan felt it. He had seen

Fitz die before—in fact, when they had first met, he had run him through with his own rapier, to save him from the wrath of a mortal. He knew that whatever fate befell Fitz—and Danny—in this cruel whiteness, would not be a permanent one. But that knowledge did not ease the small sting of grief.

Duncan moved toward the fire. It was important to keep it blazing, to keep a circle of warmth and light around men and dogs alike. He must eat and heat soup to feed Sam.

It was going to be a very long night.

Lift one foot carefully, put it down, and shift your weight before lifting the other. Sometimes the snow held, sometimes it didn't.

The moon was near full, though. That was a help. Holding the lantern out had been a wearisome strain on the arm and wrist. Danny soon realized he didn't need it. He could see plainly and needed only bring the light into play if something caught his eye.

Lift. Place. Shift.

The ice was thick in places, solid white, hiding the rushing water beneath. In others, it looked so clear and thin that Danny imagined he could thrust through with one hand.

He was reminded of the glass that came from the factory in Temperanceville. Some was heavy, plain stuff made for the kitchens of the likes of Mother Kelly. But some had been fine and delicate, thin-stemmed pieces Danny had loved to handle, happy to touch them before they left Temperanceville for the more splendid neighborhoods of Pittsburgh. Neighborhoods he would wander through himself on nights like this when the moon shone full.

Lift. Place. Shift.

He saw the ruined sled caught up in the shallows. He got as close as he dared to see if Hugh's sword remained with it. But only a piece of heavy canvas still clung to one runner, moving like a live thing, back and forth with the current.

The gold, Danny thought. Gone. All three of the moosehide packs, filled with nuggets, washed away. It seemed not right to fret about that, with Hugh still missing. But Danny could not help it. He stopped for a time and swallowed a lump that came, it seemed, up from his gut.

Half of the gold—gone.

Nothing to be done, though. And half still remained. It would be enough. Get on, now.

Lift. Place. Shift.

It was a long night. The going was slow and several times Danny was fooled by a trick of light and shadow. Once, investigating such an illusion, he felt the ice beneath him begin to shift. He narrowly managed to reach solid land before a crack a foot wide opened up where he had been mere seconds before.

After that, he proceeded with even more caution.

He stopped only once, to eat some of the dried beef he had with him. He was numb with the cold, and exhausted. But he would not, could not, give up.

Lift. Place. Shift.

Hugh had not given up on him, though he had tried his teacher's patience often, he was sure. He had kept Danny with him, and in the past few years had taught him well. Not just about being an Immortal but about life and the world and the infinite possibilities that it offered. Danny could read now, and write a good hand and ride a horse, and tell good wine from bad, and—

The moon went down. Danny relit the lantern and went on.

A hint of gray. The weak sun was struggling to rise. Danny wondered, if he didn't return, would MacLeod really leave him? He had to turn back, he had to go on. He *knew* Hugh was somewhere near.

And then, like a blessing, the feeling came. Hugh *was* somewhere near! Danny stopped and peered through the dim brightness. There! About five feet from the riverbank. Like the sled, Fitzcairn had become wedged in the rocks where the water ran less deep.

Conscious of the minutes passing, Danny moved quickly, but with great care. Full dawn lit his efforts as he stepped out onto the ice. It was thin and clear beneath him. He could see Hugh as if he were trapped on the other side of a mirror. His eyes were closed and his hair moved gently in the eddies. Danny removed his snowshoes and crawled to a place just behind him. A sharp blow, then, with the pickax. A small hole appeared and a spiderweb crack that Danny widened with more careful blows. It would not do for him to join Hugh in the icy water.

Finally, the hole was large enough. The rope now. He plunged his hands into the river. Even through the thick leather and fur gloves, he felt the sting of the water.

Quickly, he passed the rope around Fitzcairn's torso, under his arms. Once he lost an end in the current and had to start again.

But it was done, and Danny backed up slowly 'til he reached the bank. Then, rising to his feet, he put his whole strength of body and mind into it and pulled Fitzcairn from the river.

"Hugh," Danny said, leaning over the sodden body. *Could you rouse an Immortal more quickly than their nature intended?* Danny didn't know. But he did know that, upriver, Duncan MacLeod was no doubt also awake with the dawn. "Hugh," he shouted. And slapped the ice-cold face.

Whether the shout and the slap had to do with it or not, Danny did not know. But Fitzcairn groaned then, and gasped. He sputtered water from his mouth and nose, and finally he opened his eyes. Stark in his white face, they looked like the blue marbles Danny had played with as a lad.

Fitzcairn's lips were blue, too, but he still managed a whisper of a smile.

"Ah, I was having a lovely dream, Danny my boy. But I think I'll forgive you for waking me."

The sled was packed. Duncan had seen to Sam's leg, sprinkling more sulfa powder into the ragged wound. He lifted the Indian as gently as he could and carried him to the sled. He was secured there now, resting among the gear, swathed in fur.

Both men had eaten; Duncan some hardened biscuits and the Indian more soup. The fire still burned—damping it would be the final task—and Duncan had turned to harnessing the dogs.

He was, every move he made, every step he took, painfully aware of the passage of time. He and the Indian had exchanged only a handful of words since dawn, but in Sam's dark eyes, Duncan read the words: Englishman dead, Irishman dead.

Rip had survived the night and seemed to be fit. A six-dog sled team could be a problem, if the two lead dogs would not work together. But six dogs was what they had. And if there were only the two of them, he and Sam, they would make excellent time.

Blast you, Danny O'Donal! Duncan thought. *If—when—I see Fitz again, he'll na forgive me if you are lost.*

The traces had to be lengthened to accommodate the extra dog—that would take a few minutes—and getting the dogs to their feet and into their harnesses a few more.

The cold, the blasted cold! He reached for the pieces of leather just as Vixen leapt up and began yipping furiously. She was fairly dancing with excitement.

Duncan felt it then, and turned to see two figures rounding the river bend, walking one behind the other, moving quickly back over the trail Danny had broken the night before.

Siwash Sam lay on the sled watching the three men gathered around the fire. *Englishman dead,* he thought, *under the ice.*

But the Englishman was not dead. He sat with the others. He was drinking the hot tea that he had demanded immediately and eating smoked fish.

The young Irishman had said that he had found the other on the riverbank, where he had crawled after pulling himself out through another hole in the ice.

Sam did not believe this. He was, in fact, fairly sure that the account was for his benefit. And even if it were true, soaked in icy water, lying in the snow overnight, the Englishman would be frozen as solid as the land around them.

Sam had seen men die so.

But these men—they were not ordinary men. The Englishman had been shot at the White Pass. And he had lived. All three had fought the bear. And lived. There was something in their eyes, the Scotsman's particularly. It should have frightened Sam, but it did not.

Instead, it gave him hope that even if the land played more tricks on them, they might all survive, they might all live to see the wooden walls of Fort McPherson.

Now, though, he was tired and needed to rest. Let the three—whatever they were—argue among themselves.

Sam closed his eyes and slept.

"Look, Highlander," Fitz said, taking off his glove and wiggling his fingers, "all the important bits are still attached." He put the glove back on, hastily. "I will admit that many of them, including one in particular about which I am somewhat concerned, are still numb. But"—he swallowed a huge gulp of steaming tea—"I can walk, thank-you-very-much. Six dogs may be a full team. But they're bone-tired, the poor beasties."

"They can carry two men, Fitzcairn." Duncan insisted. He lowered his voice. "You may be Immortal, but you're not made of iron."

Fitz snorted. He held his cup out to Danny, who took it and filled it again.

"If I were, I'd be bloody rusty by now." He drank. "The dogs can carry two, yes. But they needn't."

"Ye need sun for rust, which you may have noticed we hardly have," Duncan replied. "But what we do have is miles and miles of nothing. Now, I don't know about the two of you, but I want to get across this white wilderness. Back to somewhere where there is something that is warm and dry and some other color besides white or gray"—Duncan took a breath—"as quickly as possible. So if ye don't mind, finish your tea, and move your English arse onto the sled."

Fitz blinked, considering a retort. Then Danny spoke.

"MacLeod is right, Hugh. You were faltering behind me, you know. By this time tomorrow, you'll be fine, no doubt. But now—"

"Well," Fitzcairn said, draining the cup, "I can't be arguing with the both of you." He rose slowly and made a show of looking over his shoulder. "My English arse is one of the numb parts, as it happens. So be sure to treat it with respect."

As he began walking, Duncan drew him aside.

"A moment, Fitz," he said, quietly. "There's something you should know." He hesitated. "I didn't send Danny to search for you—"

"I should think not," Fitzcairn interrupted. "In fact, I'll wager you argued against it."

"He told you?"

"Give me a bit of credit, MacLeod," Fitzcairn said. "I figured it out for myself." He glanced toward the sled.

"The Indian—you need to get him to that fort as quickly as possible, I'd say. You had no time to fritter away looking for stray Immortals." He shrugged, then shivered.

Duncan frowned. "What you say is true enough, Fitz. But I might have—"

"Come now, laddie." Fitz shook his head. "You've nothing to be glum about. I might have gotten a wee bit pruney after a while. But I wouldn't have melted away, you know."

Duncan felt an enormous sense of relief. "All right, then. Be reasonable. I'll not try to apologize to you anymore." He put his arm over his friend's shoulders. "You're chilled to the bone still, Fitz. Let's get you settled in."

"Of course," Fitz added, "you'll never hear the end of it. And the next time *you're* trapped under a frozen stream, I most certainly won't stir myself any too quickly—"

"I'll be sure to keep that in mind." Duncan gave him a small shove forward.

In a short time, he and Danny working together had Fitz bundled next to Siwash Sam, the dogs harnessed, and the camp broken. Duncan released the gee pole, cracked the whip, and the sled moved forward. Danny walked behind carrying the three remaining pouches of gold which had been removed to make space for a second rider.

The miles and miles of nothing, white and gray as far distant as could be seen, stretched before them as they moved on. And behind them, the only traces of their disaster were a small hole in the ice rapidly freezing over, the stiff body of one of the luckless dogs sprawled next to it, and a cavalier's sword gleaming in the ripples on the river bottom.

Chapter 9

"MacLeod," Fitz grumbled, only half-awake. He nudged the form next to him. "Turn yourself over. You're snoring like the devil him—" He stopped and opened his eyes. The fire still burned brightly. He could clearly see his three companions, sleeping soundly, wrapped snugly in blankets and fur robes.

It wasn't MacLeod who had disturbed him. It was Vixen, lying by his side. She was growling softly. Her head was up, her attention directed beyond the fire's glow.

"What is it, beastie?" he whispered. He raised himself on one elbow and reached out toward the dog. Under his hand, he could feel her neck fur bristling.

Vixen slowly got to her feet and walked a few stiff-legged paces forward, growling all the while. The other dogs, staked out in a group at one side of the night's camp, began to stir. Rip rose from his place next to the Indian. His teeth were bared, and the fur along his spine stood straight up.

Fitz peered into the frozen darkness. There! Wait—was it his imagination? No, there was something moving just beyond the circle of light and warmth cast by the fire.

Then he saw the eyes. One pair. Two. Three. Gleaming red.

He blinked and shook his head. They were still there.

Not an illusion or a dream, then—quite, quite real.

One of the creatures came closer still. Fitz could clearly see the head and shoulders. It looked directly at him, then lolled out a long tongue and licked its lips.

Rip exploded into loud barking. He rushed forward, stopping short at the edge of the firelight. Vixen stayed where she was, but she, too, began to bark.

All the dogs were up now. The burly gray male the Indian called Klute joined in the chorus, straining at his tether. But the others whimpered in fear, cowering behind him.

The noise woke the three men. MacLeod was on his feet in an instant, his *katana* ready. Fitz saw the Indian's eyes widen at the sight. Danny rolled to his knees, fumbling for his rifle.

But the flurry of activity drove the wolves away, back into the night.

Afterward, they all huddled close to the fire. Danny melted snow—whatever else they might be lacking, there was certainly enough of that around—and made coffee. Though he could tell that the Indian objected to it, Fitz tossed a bit of salmon to Vixen and Rip, who were both still pacing about, whining.

The Indian said that the wolves might indeed be back. They would lurk nearby. But they were not likely to attack. Unless, he added in that infuriatingly stoic way, they were hungry.

Well, of course, there was no bloody way to ask them when they had last had a satisfying dining experience. So MacLeod declared that they'd have to stand guard, for as long as their unwanted four-legged company was threatening to drop in.

Danny volunteered to take the first watch. *Time alone to*

work on the dream house, I'll wager, Fitz thought. *The lad must be up to the attic by now.*

MacLeod lay back down, the *katana* unsheathed by his side. The Indian groaned but was soon silent. Fitz tossed restlessly, his mind filled with images of burning eyes and dripping saliva.

He fell asleep finally to the sound of a long drawn-out howl that seemed to linger forever in the still air.

"They're following us still, MacLeod." Fitzcairn called. He was walking a few paces behind the sled, carrying the bags of gold.

The wolves had been with them for three days now. Duncan narrowed his eyes against the glare. He could just make out a scatter of burly gray shapes, moving like shadows across the landscape.

"They're still keeping their distance, Fitz." he said, cracking the whip at the yellow mixed-breed named Bigfoot. Placid, but somewhat lazy, he had a tendency to lag.

Danny turned at the sound. Duncan waved him on. Today, the young Immortal was breaking the trail. Though there hadn't been any fresh snow for a while, his was still the hardest going.

"Bloody beasts," Fitz grumbled. "They're waiting for someone or something to die. Then we'll see what distance they keep."

Siwash Sam spoke up from the sled. His voice was tight with pain. "Wolves not eat things already dead. Wolves kill for themselves. Wolves like blood warm and fresh."

"Thank. You. Very. Much," Fitzcairn said.

Duncan smiled, then winced as his cracked lips bled anew. Sam had given them a salve, a greasy concoction of animal fat and herbs. It helped some.

And, of course, they healed quickly. But Immortality could

not keep away the cold, could not keep a man's lips from drying up, could not protect his nose and cheeks from growing numb, could not prevent frost from forming on his beard and mustache.

He took some comfort in the thought that it would soon be over. They'd been on the trail for over a week. The going had been slower since the sled went through the ice, but they were making steady progress. North and a bit west, over terrain that was difficult to be sure, but not impossible. Perhaps another two hundred miles lay ahead. At their current pace, they would reach Fort McPherson in another ten days, after Christmas but before the turn of the year.

The night before, he and Sam had talked it through, while he changed the dressing on the Indian's leg. Duncan was concerned. Whether it was because of the cold or the lack of proper diet, the leg did not appear to be healing well. And the man was in pain though he tried not to show it. Duncan could only hope that there was some sort of doctor at the fort. And that the ten days' estimate was an accurate one. It was enough—more than enough—that one good man had lost his life already on this adventure.

Was it worth it? Duncan wondered, as he trudged behind the sled. When he'd stood with Sam and watched his brother's body fall into ash, he'd thought then that he would give all his share of the gold to have him alive again.

But the truth of it had come back to him over the past days. As they made their way through this phantom land, the only sounds to be heard were the crystalline crunch of the snow under the snowshoes of whoever was in the lead, the panting of the dogs as they strained in their traces, and the sometimes snap of the whip. Conversation was difficult at best when your breath froze as it left your lips. It gave a man time to think.

He remembered what Connor had told him, what he had

then learned for himself as the span of his life lengthened far beyond that of ordinary men. They were fragile, all the mortals. They had only so much time. And if you cared for one of them, as a friend or a lover, there was no denying the simple fact that you would lose them. Sooner. Later. It came to the same thing. There was nothing that could be done about it. Except to protect those who were important to you, as any man might do.

He thought of Little Deer. Sometimes, even doing that, even protecting those you loved, was not possible.

There were those among his kind who tried rather to protect themselves. They kept apart from mortal entanglements, choosing the company of other Immortals—those few they hoped could be trusted—willing to risk their heads before their hearts. That wasn't Duncan's way. It had never been.

Sam's brother had been a good man, and his death was a terrible thing. But the gold they still had with them, the gold that waited for them back in the valley, had been important to him. He had judged it worth taking risks for. That was his decision, that was his life. Duncan might mourn him, but it was not his place either to bear any burden for what had happened or to bargain with fate.

So he would keep his gold without regrets. He wasn't driven with lust for it like Danny. He didn't need it as much as Fitz, who had managed to live for centuries without saving a farthing. But it would pay a few years' rental on the warehouse in Paris. It would allow him to travel, preferably to a country where the temperature never got below freezing.

And it would make Amanda *so* happy.

Sam shivered under the blankets the covered him. His leg throbbed, a dull ache that never stopped. Though he was lashed securely to the sled, he felt uneasy.

The Scotsman knew, he thought. He was breaking the trail

today. Sam could see him walking ahead. He stopped more than once to look up at the sky.

It was a strange color, a misty gray that merged with the snowy land. The wind had picked up, and there was a chill edge to it.

Sam had known since first light. But there was nothing to be done. He had hoped that they would be able to stay ahead of what was coming. But as the feeble sun moved through the sky, it became clear to Sam that was not to be.

The Englishman was driving the sled. He was not as good at it as either of the others. But the dog Vixen worked hard for him, and that made up for his lack of skill. Today, though, the dogs were skittish. They yipped nervously, dancing in their traces. The Englishman was having trouble controlling them. He cracked the whip, and called to them by name. But they did not settle down.

The Englishman shouted to the Scotsman, asking if it was the wolves that were bothering the dogs so.

It was not the wolves, Sam knew. The wolves were gone, vanished into hidden places in the hills.

Vanished—because of the storm that was coming.

White. The whole world—what Duncan could see of it— was white. His eyes were nearly frozen shut, his beard was thick with snow. Icicles hung from the edge of his fur-lined hood. As quickly as he swept them away, they re-formed.

The blizzard had come on them suddenly. One minute, they were making their way across the vast untouched wilderness. The next, they were caught in a seething swirl of ice and snow.

There was no escaping the howling fury. Sam had said to keep going as long as it was daylight. So they would.

But daylight seemed a fanciful concept. There was no such thing. There was only the white blur surrounding them, the endless turmoil of wind-driven white, the stinging white that numbed his face and left him gasping.

He had felt the sting of wind-whipped snow before, of course. In the wilds of Mongolia, he had fought his way through a storm that swept down from the north, trusting his shaggy pony to bear him to the safety of the camp. And once in Montana, he had volunteered to help a rancher bring his herd farther down and closer in before a storm hit. They had not moved quickly enough, and he had spent a night trapped on a cold hillside before the weather cleared. Only the Lakota trick of climbing inside a fresh-killed animal carcass had kept him from freezing.

Mongolia. Montana. Both had been a walk in the spring heather of the Highlands compared to this raging white monster that bit at him with teeth of ice as he struggled on.

"Bloody blizzard," Fitzcairn muttered. Would the foul thing never end? The day was done, the blinding turmoil now invisible as the milky light faded, dimmed and vanished. They were all huddled around the sled, men and dogs, wrapped in fur blankets, pressed close together. There was no thought of a fire. Not in this fiercely erratic wind. So spoke the Indian. Well, it didn't take years of wilderness experience to reason that one out. Besides which, in the gathering of firewood, it was best if a man could see beyond the end of his frozen nose.

Danny was to one side of him, Vixen to the other. Both whined and twitched as they slept. He burrowed farther down between them, pulling the heavy fur up over his head. But the air grew stale, rich with the odor of wet dog and long-unwashed human. He pulled the robe away, just at the right moment to catch a writhing blast of snow full in the face. His eyes stung and watered, icy tracks trailing down his cheeks. He blinked, and stared into—nothingness.

He had thought the nights by the lake in the Mackenzie Mountains dark. This dark was something beyond that. He knew this dark; he had seen it before.

He shuddered. It was not from the cold.

Most often when he died, he revived quickly. That seemed to be the way of it with all Immortals.

But now and then the coming back took longer. No one knew why. The circumstances were not predictable.

Once Fitz had wakened wrapped in shroud cloth, lying on the ground next to a freshly dug grave. Two women, dear girls the both of them, were having a remarkable fight over his dead body. When he opened his eyes and struggled to sit up, the priest had pronounced it a miracle.

At another time, in another place, he had not opened his eyes until the grave was filled. So total was the darkness before him that he thought at first he had somehow lost his vision. He raised a hand to feel his face—and rapped his knuckles sharply on the bottom of the casket lid. He had not felt such fear since the second time he had been killed.

Had the wooden box been sturdier, had the grave been deeper, he did not care to think how long it might have taken him to work his way to the surface. As it was, the lass who had come to lay flowers by his stone must have nearly died herself from fright when he clawed one hand free.

Her name was Aisleen, and she was a resourceful girl. Instead of fleeing in terror, she stayed and dug into the soft earth, pulling him forth like a veritable Lazarus.

She'd also been too practical to believe in miracles. So he had told her the truth of it and kept her with him for a time. Until she fell victim to one of those diseases that periodically killed thousands of mortals. A cough, a fever, then a terrible swift wasting away. He laid her to rest, in a fine heavy casket, lined in pale green silk. Afterward, as he knelt to lay a sprig of lilac on her grave, he could not help but remember how it had been to wake where she was now, blinded by the darkness.

He'd not avoided death since then, but he had avoided the grave. Still, though it was centuries ago, it was not something that a man ever forgot. And as he stared into the terrible blackness, the memory swept over him, like another blast of icy wind.

He tried to sleep, but the whole of the endless night he could only doze fitfully. Again and again, he would start awake, flailing out, fighting back the shadows that seemed to press in on him from above.

So still it was. Not the quiet of a mother sitting peaceful by the fire rocking her wee babe. Not even the stillness that came over the battlefield and the men who stood ready there, just before the fighting was joined.

No, this was like the silence afterward, the next afternoon when the wounded no longer cried in pain and the field was left to the dead.

He had heard such silences before, at Gettysburg where he had first died. And at Cold Harbor just before dawn, as he lay among the thousand of corpses.

Still, in time those silences would be broken. The woodland creatures frightened away by the fury of the fighting would return. Birds would sing in the trees again. Cows would low in the bloody grass. The flies would buzz at their feedings.

And the ones that came to claim the dead would call out, when they found a brother or a friend, or stumbled across a body still clinging to life.

But this silence went on without end. Oh, they made noise themselves, as they struggled through three feet or more of heavy new snow. MacLeod and the heathen spoke in hushed, secret tones. Hugh swore as he fell into a deep drift, sunk up

to his waist in white. The dogs fussed more than usual as they
pulled the sled along, the crack of the whip was more fre-
quent.

But if they stopped, for a rest or a morsel of food, the silence was complete, solid almost, like a thing you could see.

And the weight of that silence was all that there was. No
bird nor beast moved across the land. No wolf howl or owl
screech broke the stillness.

To Danny it became like one of his silent dreams, a day
only half-remembered at night, a night forgotten in the day.

Siwash Sam was worried. After the great storm, the great
cold would come. He needed no sticks of glass to tell him this.

Already it had begun. He could feel it himself, feel the bite
of the frost on his nose and cheeks. And he could feel it in the
tips of his fingers when he took off his gloves to cover his face
with a layer of grease.

A man alone would be in grave danger in such weather. If
he foundered in the deepest snow, if he broke through ice into
even the shallowest of water, if he could not make his hands
move to build a fire, he would be dead.

Four men together should be safe, if they took care. He had
warned the Scotsman of what was to come. They must keep
moving for as long as they could, even past the dying of the
light. And when they stopped, they must build a fire big
enough to last the night through. Watch must be kept, so that
this fire never fell to smoldering coals.

He had passed the pot of grease around to them all. The
Englishman sniffed at it and made a face. The Scotsman and
the Irishman used it without a word.

Sam grunted in pain as the sled jerked forward. With the
cold also came the ice, crusting on the surface of the snow.
The dogs slipped and slid on it, their claws chittering like the
small mice that hid in the walls of the hogan. Behind him the

Irishman stumbled. The ice was thick enough in some places to hold the weight of the sled—and not in others.

Sam knew this would make the going harder. That was the way of the land—it did not easily give up anything, to man or animal. Not the gold beneath the earth, to be sure. But not such simple things as food or shelter—or a safe passage through the wild.

"Blecch." Fitzcairn said.

Duncan turned from the fire. His friend sat a few feet away. He was wiping furiously at his mouth with the back of his mittened hand.

"Got a taste of that infernal stuff we're covered with," he mumbled. Then he spit to one side. A sharp crackle sounded as the spittle hit the snow. The dog Vixen was lying to one side, biting the ice balls from the pads of her feet. She cocked her head at the sound.

"Hah. Fancy that!" he exclaimed. Then he spit again. "Did you hear that MacLeod? How cold must it truly be, do you think, that such a thing would be?" Vixen got up and nosed the two stains on the snow.

"Here, let me show you—"

"I saw it the first time, Fitzcairn. And the second," Duncan said. "Further demonstrations aren't necessary."

"Where's your spirit of scientific inquiry, man?" Fitzcairn demanded. "Does it not make you wonder what other bodily fluids might be likely to freeze if they were cast upon the bosom of the snow?"

Duncan threw another branch on the fire. "Go spit for Danny, Fitz. Maybe it will impress him."

Fitz sighed. "What you mean, Highlander, is that maybe it will bring him out of the fog he's in."

"He's not said a word in days, I think." Duncan hesitated.

"I'll admit that I've not had that much experience as a teacher. But even as his friend—are you not worried?"

Fitz rose and looked around. Danny was nowhere to be seen. He had gone off to gather even more fuel for the fire that had to last the night through.

"Tell me, MacLeod." He gestured into the somber twilight. "What do you see?"

Duncan frowned. "I see snow, Fitz. A goodly lot of it."

"And do you recall the lovely Miz Benét, when she was trying to discourage us from continuing our quest, saying that some tribe native to this place had two hundred different words to describe snow?"

Duncan nodded. "I thought then that she was—embellishing."

"Well, for myself, I've no interest in learning a one of them. Although I could add a few, none of which could be shared with a lady." He spit again, emphasizing his words.

"Now, you'll have to concede that what we have around us is, as you put it, a goodly amount of nothing but snow. And you must further concede that language lessons are not on our agenda, even if conversation were possible, as we make our way, step after interminable step, through this godforsaken land."

"How cold does it have to be, I wonder, before a man's mouth freezes shut?" Duncan said.

Fitzcairn ignored him. "But we must somehow occupy our minds along the way. You and I have centuries of memories to sort through. Wine. Women. The odd song here and there."

"More wine? More women?" Duncan suggested. But Fitz was unstoppable.

"Danny's not even lived a mortal lifetime yet. So he's found another way to pass the time." He paused. "I've a good idea what's occupying him. Trust me, Highlander. It's nothing to cause concern."

The young Immortal came into view then, his arms loaded with broken branches. Fitzcairn grinned, blue eyes bright beneath the fur of his ridiculous hat. "Danny, lad," he called, "I've something to show you." He set off to join him.

"Fifty below," Siwash Sam said.

Duncan was startled. He'd thought the Indian was sleeping. How much of Fitzcairn's rant had he heard? How much sense had he made of it?

"What?"

"The water from a man's mouth freezes when it is fifty below. I have heard the redcoats say that," Sam answered.

Fifty degrees below zero. That did not bear thinking about. Duncan thought it best not to tell the other two Immortals.

Since the blizzard, their pace had slowed. The ten days that he had estimated were going to stretch into two weeks. Still, if they went on, taking all the cautions that Sam had advised to guard against the bitter cold, they should still reach the fort before food became a serious problem.

Duncan turned back to the fire, warming his hands. He felt a creeping numbness, even through two pairs of gloves. He thought of Claire—he'd not put words on paper since they had left the valley where they had made their strike.

And if he were to do so, if he could take off both pairs of gloves and write a note before his fingers grew stiff and clumsy, what could he say?

He could ask her if one of the two hundred words for snow was "frozen hell." Or he could write in his argonaut's report that when it grew colder than could possibly be imagined, spittle turned to ice. No doubt the readers of Silas Witherspoon's paper, sitting at their breakfast tables in their dressing gowns with their pots of tea and buttered toast would find that fascinating!

He smiled, thinking of her silvery laugh. He would write to her, he determined, in just a few days, when they reached

McPherson. Tonight, he would take his turn watching the fire, and try to forget that he could, in fact, tell Fitzcairn how cold it truly was.

Ah, Fitz thought, *I swear I'd give half my share of the gold for a good smoke!*

It was the hour before dawn, the last watch. He sat close to the still-blazing fire, waiting for the first glimmer of light to edge over the horizon.

He considered attempting once more to fill his pipe, then thought better of it. Tobacco was a pleasurable vice. Fingers were a necessity. Two previous attempts had left his bared hands frighteningly numb in the space of seconds.

Instead, he sat quietly and watched the rolling hills and shallow valleys stretching away into the distance become visible bit by bit. The whole of the land changed color as the sun slowly rose. Indigo-blue, then a wash of purple, then a deep pearly pink. And, eventually, stark white.

The day was going to be as clear as any they had seen since they'd left the valley. To the south and a bit east, the Mackenzies seemed only a brief walk away. The pinnacles stood out against the morning sky like a drawing made by a child, black and white against the deep, cloudless blue. North and a bit west, where they were bound—from where he sat, north and a bit west there was only a great deal of nothing.

Well, he shrugged, if not the pipe, a mug of tea then! It would be a kindness to the others, would it not, to have water cheerfully aboil before he roused them for the day? He rose, strapped on snowshoes, took up the battered pot, and walked a short distance from the camp to gather snow. Vixen trotted by his side, then disappeared off into the trees, intent upon her canine business. In the early hours of the day, she and Rip often vanished for a time. They would return before camp was broken, muzzles sometimes stained red.

Beyond the warmth of the fire, the cold was vicious. It snapped at his cheeks and nose. Blast! The icy crust on the snow had frozen solid. He whacked at it with the pot, to no avail. Nothing for it then but to go back for the hand ax.

His way took him by the team, piled all together noses to tails. They were still being staked down at night, the wretched creatures. Not that they'd be likely to stray—after the wolves and the snows, they were content to stay where it was warm and safe. But the Indian was cautious about the food supplies.

Fitz was sure that Vixen—and Rip—would keep the others in line. But there was nothing to be gained by arguing.

Three of them were on their feet, he saw. The fourth, a black-and-white spotted bitch, the last of the dogs they had bought in the village, still lay sprawled on the snow. The dog called Klute was pawing at her.

As he came nearer, Klute raised his head, growling low in his throat. The other two dogs whined. One shouldered past Klute, who snarled and nipped.

The black-and-white bitch did not move.

Fitz shouted, and threw the pot. The dogs backed off far enough for him to kneel in the snow next to the bitch. She was as cold and stiff as the ground beneath, he could see. There was no mark on her, nor blood around her.

A crunch of snow. MacLeod was beside him, a sharp knife in his hand.

"Frozen, laddie," he said softly. "The poor beastie froze to death while she slept."

MacLeod reached down and cut the leather traces binding the dead dog. "Pull her clear, Fitz. We can't let the others at her."

Fitz looked up. His eyes were level with the dog Klute's. The animal stared at him, not dropping his gaze, lips curled in a snarl. "Aye," he said. "This one here looks ready for a bit of a snack."

Together, the two of them carried the stiff carcass across the snow to the edge of the trees.

As they walked back toward the fire, Fitz stopped to fetch the pot. Klute snapped at him as he bent to retrieve it.

"He's going to be trouble, I'll wager," Fitz said to Duncan.

"Dogs hungry," Sam said, in a harsh whisper.

"Should we let them—eat?" Duncan asked, looking back at the body of the dead dog.

Sam shook his head, weakly. "No. They get taste, they turn on one another." He paused for breath. "Man try to stop them and fail. They lose the fear of the whip. They turn on man next."

Fitz sighed.

It had been *such* a beautiful dawn . . .

Carefully, oh so carefully.

Duncan held on to the sled, wary of his footing. Though it was bright and clear, the weak sun low in the sky did nothing to melt the thick ice covering the snow. It cast light, but no warmth.

That morning, Sam had said that the wind was coming from the south, bringing with it a rise in the temperature. If that were so—and Duncan trusted that Sam knew such things—it wasn't yet obvious. He could still feel the sting of the cold in his fingers and face, his eyes teared from staring at the bright whiteness, the tears froze on his cheeks.

Under these circumstances, a man ahead breaking the trail was of no use. So both Fitzcairn and Danny followed behind. Even on snowshoes, the way was treacherous. Their progress was slow, their every movement cautious.

For hours, Duncan had struggled with the sled. The dogs, their claws chipping small pieces from the frozen surface, had the best purchase. And the runnered sled glided along with ease. After days of laborious progress, foundering through old and new snow, now he had to fight to hold the team back.

Vixen was as steady as ever, but the dogs Klute and Rip—never on the best of terms—were now harnessed much too close to one another. Again and again, Klute nipped at Rip's flanks. When Rip tried to turn and retaliate, the sled skidded sideways.

The fourth time it happened, Duncan was forced to use the whip.

"Sam?" he said. The Indian more often than not spent his days and nights both in a pain-wracked half sleep.

"We stop soon." A whispered response. "I tell you new way to harness dogs."

Duncan nodded, though Sam couldn't see him.

Ahead lay a steeply sloping hill. A few days past, plowing upward would have been exhausting for men and dogs alike. Today, Duncan stepped on the back of the sled and whistled to the dogs. Vixen barked, and the team dug in with their claws. In an eyeblink, they had skimmed to the top, gliding easily over the ice.

Duncan turned the sled and set the brake. The dogs dropped to their bellies, as they were trained to do. Rip growled and twisted his head to snarl at the burly gray male. The small brown bitch next to him, called Pie by Sam's brother, whined nervously.

Duncan spoke sharply to them. He turned to look down the far side of the slope. It was much steeper and just as icy. The going up may have been easy. The coming down would not be.

"MacLeod," Fitzcairn called. Duncan looked back down the hill. Fitz stood at the bottom, hands on his hips. Danny was a few feet behind him.

"As we've neither wings nor claws," he shouted, his breath

steaming in the air. "Have you any thoughts on how we might join you?"

"Hot air rises, doesn't it?" Duncan yelled back. "That should work for you at least."

"It's cream that rises, Highlander," Fitz retorted, kicking at the snow, "but not when it's frozen."

Duncan laughed. He was tempted for a brief moment simply to stand and watch his friend attempt to climb the glassy slope. But that would be time wasted. With one less dog, and the going made even slower by the precarious footing, they had no time at all to spare.

There was a length of rope packed among the gear stowed at Sam's feet. In short order, Duncan had secured one end to the sled and thrown the other to Fitz and Danny.

"One at a time," he cautioned. The sled, with Sam aboard and the dogs in harness, far outweighed the two Immortals. But Duncan had learned not to trust anything in this harsh land.

Danny made the climb first, hand over hand on the rope, each foot carefully placed. In a few moments he stood beside Duncan.

"Mind the dogs," Duncan said. "They're in a state."

The young Immortal looked at him blankly, then stepped to one side.

Duncan waved his hand, and Fitzcairn began his ascent, awkward in his snowshoes.

"Pretend you're climbing a tower to your lady fair," Duncan suggested. "You've had some experience at that, I believe?"

Just as Fitz stopped, doubtless to offer a response, a muffled shout caught Duncan's attention. He turned.

"Scotsman!" It was Sam, his voice strained, calling to him from the sled. "The Irishman—look!"

Duncan looked. Danny was nowhere to be seen.

Sam gestured, weakly.

The young Immortal, Duncan saw then, was tumbling down the hill—silently—his arms and legs flailing.

Quickly Duncan turned back. Too quickly. He lost his footing and fell heavily against the sled. The impact brought the dogs to their feet. Vixen stood in place, but Rip leaped in his traces. Then Klute bit Pie, drawing blood. She yelped and flinched, jerking sharply to the right.

That was enough. Even with the brake still set, the sled began to move, sliding sideways. The dogs, feeling the weight pulling on them, became confused and panicky. They lurched forward, then began to slide, too, losing their footing on the downward slope.

Frantically, Duncan grabbed for the rope. But his efforts were for naught—once enough of the weight of the sled cleared the top, gravity took over.

He was able to catch Fitzcairn, pulled off his feet and up the hill, just as he reached the crest. The two of them lay on the snow watching as sled, dogs, and—some yards distant—Danny O'Donal, all came to rest below.

"Bloody, bloody hell," Fitz murmured.

"For once, Fitz, I can't disagree."

"How do we get down?"

"The quickest way possible." Duncan replied, rolling to the edge.

He sat and slid, controlling his descent as best he could with hands and feet. Fitzcairn went rolling past him, whooping aloud.

He checked the sled first. It lay intact on one side. Fitz joined him and they righted it with ease.

Sam had been strapped in well. But the wild ride down the slope must have been painful. Duncan leaned over him, risking his hands to the frigid air as he checked the Indian's pulse.

At the touch of Duncan's fingers on his neck, Sam's dark eyes opened.

"See to dogs," he grunted as he handed Duncan his hunting knife. "I live."

"Fitz," Duncan said, turning to the tangled heap of yelping fur and twisted leather, "go. I'll do this. You find Danny."

Fitzcairn started across the snow toward his student. Duncan took the knife, cutting the traces where they joined the sled. Then he pulled at the loose ends, separating the dogs.

When they were all free, he assessed the damage. Four of the five were fine. Vixen shook herself, and trotted after Fitz. Rip went to Sam, nosing at him and whimpering. Klute stood stiff-legged, some distance away. Bigfoot, the sometimes lazy male, simply lay down, his head between his paws.

But Pie, the little brown bitch, was not fine. She cried as she tried to get to her feet. Her right front leg would not hold her. It dangled limply, obviously broken.

Duncan knelt on the snow, watching as the dog struggled feebly. What had to be done had to be done. But he felt a wave of sadness.

And then the close presence of another Immortal.

"Would you get me the rifle, Fitz?" he asked softly. "I'd best end her suffering."

"MacLeod—yes, of course—" Fitzcairn replied. "But, Duncan, I—"

Duncan glanced over his shoulder. Danny was standing by the sled, holding on as though he were about to fall again. His face was white as the snow all around them.

"Fitz?" Duncan asked. In the hundreds of years he'd known him, he had never seen his friend look so sick at heart.

"Danny—he walked off the hilltop because he can't see a thing in front of him. Duncan, he's gone blind."

* * *

Danny frowned. "The heathen is sure of that then, he is?" His voice trembled.

"Have you not noticed, lad," his teacher said, "that the Indian is right about things even more often than MacLeod here?"

"Sam says you'll be fine, Danny," MacLeod repeated. "The sun's glare on the snow is what does it." Danny could hear a touch of impatience in his voice. "You'll need to keep your eyes covered the rest of the day, and maybe tomorrow, too."

"Come now," Hugh said. "I'll be driving the sled. You walk right behind." He helped Danny to his feet.

For the next few hours, he stumbled along, tethered to the back of the sled like one of the dogs, a strip of flannel torn from a shirt over his eyes. Strange, he would have thought that being blind was a thing of darkness. But what he saw, eyes closed or opened, was white, a bright, shining white.

The going was slower even than before, since they'd left another of the team dead at the bottom of the hill. He'd not seen it die, but he'd heard the rifle shot echo and echo in the silence.

And he heard the awful sounds that followed, when MacLeod, on the order of the heathen, had cut up the sorry beast and fed it to the dogs that were left. It had made him near as ill for a brief time as he had been on the sea voyage from San Francisco.

How long ago that seemed! Yet it was only a matter of a few months, no time at all, if you were one of those who would live forever.

They stopped at last for the night, and Danny sat close by the fire that he could feel and hear but not see, lost in the whiteness and the memory of the day just gone by.

He had walked, hour after hour across the ice-covered snow.

One foot, then another. After a bit of time, he'd had to squint even to see his teacher's back, but a few feet away.

Hour after hour, and he'd begun to see things at the edge of his vision. A sparkle, like sun shining through fine crystal. Rainbow colors, shimmering just above the snow, a golden glow right under his feet.

Were there figures there, dancing in that rainbow? The angel women from his dream house, they might be. Or the faery folk, his true parents, come to claim him at last.

He'd thought he might be asking Hugh if he saw them, too. But when they broke their journey for a bite to eat, his teacher and MacLeod had gotten caught up in a worry about the big brute of a dog that had nipped him that morning.

Danny had sat with his cup of tea and a bit of bread, paying no mind. He'd stared out, past the fire, past the dogs, past the Indian lying in the sled, past the other two of his kind.

On the horizon, he could have sworn that he saw a ship, all sails rigged, cresting the pure white waves. He'd recognized it, though that could not possibly be—it was the very ship that had brought him across the great ocean when he was a wee child. He'd narrowed his gaze, and it was gone, vanished into the sunlight.

Hour after hour, one foot at a time. Danny had searched and searched for another glimpse of the vessel. He'd seen the dancing figures again. He'd seen the wolves, loping in a perfectly straight line not more than five hundred feet away. They turned their heads, and their eyes were washed with rainbow hues. He'd seen other eyes, laughing eyes, green, blue, floating before him.

But he hadn't seen the ship, until he stood at the top of the hill. There it had been, all of a sudden, right before him! The gangplank lowered, and a voice bade him come aboard. He had stepped forward—and found himself falling, falling through a silent space of brightness.

He'd lain stunned on the snow. Behind his closed eyes, rainbow colors flashed and flashed again. Like fireworks they were, exploding in his head.

Then Hugh was there, bending over him. Danny had heard the worry in his voice.

And when he'd opened his eyes, all he'd seen was—white.

Siwash Sam had decided. The cheechakos must all hear what he had to say. By now he knew that they took their lead from the Scotsman. But this must be said to all, not one.

He asked to be brought closer to the fire. Then he began to speak.

"Four dogs we have left," he said. "One no good. He trouble. He should be shot." He doubted they would do that though, and he hadn't the strength.

"Even if he not, four dogs not enough for what is to come."

The Scotsman looked straight into Sam's eyes then. Sam could read a great worry there, but no fear.

"The wind from the south—it will bring more snow with it."

The Englishman swore under his breath.

"Maybe as much as before, maybe more."

"When will this be?" the Scotsman asked.

Sam shrugged, then winced at the pain.

"After the dark comes tomorrow. After the first light of the day after. Soon."

"Well, what can we bloody do about it?" the Englishman said. "It's not like there's some snug hotel nearby that we can check into until the storm is over."

"I will tell you. The fort of the redcoats is not far now. If a man were to travel light, it could be reached before the snows came again." He took a deep breath. That caused him to gasp and choke.

"Leave me. Leave the gold. Take only what you need for four days journey. Leave at first light, and do not stop."

"I'll not be a part of leaving the gold behind," the Irishman said. "Sighted or not, I'll fight the man who tries to do so."

Sam sighed. He had expected that. And what came next.

"And I'll not be a part of leaving Siwash Sam."

"My journey is about to end, Scotsman. You know that. I have seen the knowledge in your eyes."

The Scotsman shook his head, firmly. "We came through one storm. We can survive another. We'll make it to the fort, all of us. Together."

Sam could do no more. He thought of taking the knife and opening the big vein in his throat. Even the Scotsman would leave him if his spirit were no longer in his body. But that would not be a death with honor, worthy of his brother and of the bear.

In Skagway, he had made a pledge to these cheechakos. Though he needed them now far more then they needed him, he had given his word. So he must live on and see this through, whatever lay ahead.

Chapter 10

"Well," Fitzcairn said, as he pointed. A small log cabin lay ahead, nestled in a stand of winter-bare trees. "Do my eyes deceive me, or is that not a snug hotel!"

Duncan braked the sled. The four remaining dogs, harnessed now in a fan shape, dropped in the snow. They'd been on the move scarcely an hour, making decent time under the rapidly lowering sky.

"Shall we check in?" he added.

"Wait," Sam said weakly. "It always wise to knock before opening door."

"I'll go." Duncan said. He handed the leather leads to Fitz and drew the *katana* from the gear on the sled.

The one-room cabin, it turned out, was not occupied. From the doorway, Duncan quickly surveyed the interior. There was an iron cot on the right, a tangle of blankets thrown over it. The headless pelt of a white bear lay on the floor in front of the stone fireplace set in the middle of the back wall.

Duncan entered cautiously. He bent down by the fireplace. A poker lay on the rough hearth, amid a scattering of cold ashes.

Opposite the bed was a table, shoved against the wall. One leg was missing, and it only stood upright because it was propped on a protruding wood knot.

There was an unpleasant odor in the air, which he traced to a half-full chamber pot shoved under the bed and fresh mouse droppings on the floor.

Whoever had lived here had left sometime ago, he judged. The cabin seemed secure. And the wind was rising.

In a short time, they did indeed check in. Sam was made as comfortable as possible in the bed. Fitz, holding his nose dramatically, emptied the chamber pot some distance from the cabin. Danny, who'd wakened that morning with his vision restored, found a broken broom and set to work sweeping the floor.

Duncan inspected the immediate surroundings. He found a nearly empty woodpile, sheltered from the snow by a slanting roof, behind the cabin. Loading his arms, he carried the wood inside. Then he checked the two square holes cut in the front wall that served as windows. They were covered in heavy canvas, tied down by thick rope looped through iron rings driven into the wall.

He looked around. Everything, even the sled, had been brought inside. They could wait out the storm here, and be back on the trail by tomorrow.

The tension in his shoulders began to ease. He crossed the room to help Fitz and Danny stow the supplies out of reach of the dogs, on the high shelves by the table.

As he did, the first blast of wind-whipped snow rattled against the heavy canvas over the windows.

*　　*　　*

The snow stung his face, icy pins and needles, stitching a pattern of pain on his cheeks and forehead.

Around him, the cannon thundered, bright flashes of red, fire against the white, blood against the white.

Then a man came out of the whiteness. He felt him before he saw him, a black-robed figure, like Death itself, walking the battlefield.

But this man was not death, oh no—quite the opposite. He was life and hope. And he spoke to Duncan in a low voice, asking him questions, telling him things that would change his life forever.

Duncan reached out his hand to call Darius back—and the hand that held his was soft and delicate. The face before him was golden in the light of the low fire.

Outside the tent, the wind howled on. Gently he touched her face, then slowly unwrapped her from her layers of fur.

He was her student no longer, he was now just a man and she a woman. And the battle that they fought, naked body to naked body, was one that had no loser.

He kissed her then, and whispered good-bye May-ling, as the snow caught on her lashes, melting on her cheeks like icy tears. She opened her mouth, threw back her head and growled deep in her throat—

He opened his eyes, just as the guttural growls turned to furious barking.

In the darkest corner of the cabin, he could barely see two of the dogs, facing one another.

He rolled to his feet. Fitz had already found the lantern. He lit it and brightness filled the room.

The dogs were too intent on one another to notice. They had fallen silent. Heads lowered, they stood only feet apart, each waiting for the right moment to attack.

"Bloody damn brute!" Fitz muttered. "Vixen!" He spoke

sharply to the brown-and-white bitch who stood by him, growling softly. "Stay!"

The dog obeyed him, Duncan was glad to see. It was going to be hard enough to keep Rip and Klute apart without having a third animal to deal with. Bigfoot—well, Bigfoot was cowering under the table, whimpering.

The three Immortals approached warily. Rip seemed to take notice of them but Klute did not. Seeing that his adversary was distracted, he sprang at the other dog, all teeth and fury. But a sharp blow from the butt of Danny's rifle threw him to one side.

Fitz quickly grabbed Rip and dragged the dog across the cabin. Duncan and Danny turned their attention to Klute, who was back on his feet. He slunk into the corner and faced the two men, snarling defiantly.

"Should I not shoot the devil here and now, and be done with it?" Danny said as he raised the rifle to his shoulder.

"No." Duncan grabbed the barrel. He looked toward the iron cot where Sam lay in a desperately deep sleep.

"He's strong still, maybe even stronger than Rip. We'll need him when the storm is over."

For a long moment, Danny stood, rifle still aimed at the dog. Then he gave a small shrug. "What, then?" he asked.

Duncan considered. There was the whip. What had Sam said? If the dogs were hungry enough, they'd lose the fear of the whip and of the men.

If he tried the whip and it failed, there would be no answer other than Danny's.

Instead of the whip then, he'd use the hunger.

"Fetch me a bit of the dried fish, and a length of rope," he instructed Danny. "And my gloves," he added, as the dog lowered his head, teeth bared.

Danny and Fitz kept back as Duncan crouched down. He extended the food with his left hand. Klute sniffed suspiciously, then came forward slowly. He was still growling, but the fur on his neck lay smooth.

As the dog reached out to take the fish, Duncan quickly slipped the rope over his head. Klute jerked back, then lunged at Duncan, biting viciously, tearing through the glove to the flesh beneath.

Fitz grabbed the rope, pulling the dog off Duncan. The animal raged on, but it was done. They tied him to one of the iron rings that held down the canvas over the windows. As a precaution, Rip, too, was tied, to the leg of the bed.

By the lanternlight, Duncan examined his hand. The bite wasn't deep—the glove had taken the worst of it. There would be no sign of it by morning. He glanced at Sam. Best he had slept through it all. He would have noticed the hand healing, just as he had noticed how quickly Danny's snow blindness passed. He hadn't spoken of it, but Duncan knew.

"Do you need anything, laddie?" Fitzcairn asked.

"No," Duncan replied, blowing out the lantern.

As he was drifting back to sleep, he heard Fitz's voice in the darkness imploring all the saints and angels to stop the bloody howling of the bloody wind.

"How bloody long has it been?" Fitz asked.

"Three days," MacLeod replied.

"So says the heathen," Danny said. "How are we to know for a fact? We've not seen a thing but these four walls since this storm began."

"We can't know for certain," MacLeod answered. "But Sam—"

"The Indian's guess is as good as yours or mine," Fitz interrupted. "But if we don't get out of here in the very near future, we're all going to die from the stench." He took a deep breath, then blew it out.

"Or at least we may wish we were dead."

Four men, four dogs, three or four days—and no open windows. The Highlander had tried—once only—to open a flap of the canvas and empty the chamber pot.

The result had not been pleasant. Years from now, he would no doubt remind MacLeod of it relentlessly. At the moment, the humor in the situation was elusive.

For adding to the problem was the foul smell rising from the Indian's leg. MacLeod was deeply concerned about it, and rightly so.

Once or twice, Fitz helped him change the dressing on the wound. An infection had set in. It wasn't gangrene. All of them, Danny included, had seen that horror.

But it was serious enough. Pus seeped from the edges of the tear in the skin where the broken bone had protruded. Even if the bone itself was knitting, the wound would not heal.

They still had some sulfa powder left in the medical kit, and MacLeod used it carefully. He applied hot compresses, which seemed to ease the swelling somewhat. And he brewed a tea from what looked to Fitz like bits of twigs and bark that helped the pain.

Yet the wound wept still, and the Indian grew feverish. His moans filled the cabin, louder sometimes than the incessant sound of the storm that still raged outside.

Fitz sighed, lighting his pipe from a firebrand. Small blessing, that. Within these four walls, he could at least have his tobacco. And for a brief time, the aromatic smoke rising in the still air would mask the stronger scents of human and animal frailty.

Danny sat at the three-legged table, polishing his sword. Sure and there was no more need for him to keep his weapon out of sight, by his figuring. Hadn't the Highlander drawn his fancy sword more than a time or two in front of the heathen?

The man was dying, anyway. It was plain to see.

More gold for the three of them, then.

Daaa—

A whisper, under the wind.

Daa-nee

He looked around sharply. Hugh sat smoking by the fire. MacLeod was slumped on the floor by the bed, dozing.

Daaa-neeeee

Louder now, more of a scream. But not a one of the dogs even pricked up an ear.

Danny swallowed. His heart was racing, his hands shaking.

Danny-boy.

A voice, a clear voice. He turned his head, and caught a glimpse of white, fading like the sun sparking on the snow.

We're here, Danny-boy

"No! Bloody hell, no!" Fitz's face was flushed with anger. He stood toe-to-toe with Duncan in the center of the room.

Duncan glanced over at Sam. The Indian watched him impassively.

"The food was measured out when we left the valley, Fitz. For a certain number of days. We're past that time already. The storm may be over, but we're not going to be able to go on for a while. Have you looked outside? There's four feet or more of fresh snow out there. And it's still coming down."

"And we're to turn these poor beasties who have served us so well out into it, to die?" Fitz raged. "So that we can eat their few bits of fish for ourselves? No, I say! I went along with using that poor little bitch for dog food. But I'll not agree to this." He shook his head furiously. "We might as well just carve them up for stew and be done with it!"

Which was, in fact, exactly what Sam had first proposed to Duncan. The Indian was a practical man. If his dog had to die so that the men might live, he would bear it.

Duncan had once been forced to eat the horse that had been

shot out from under him. Still, though he might have been tempted to throttle the dog Klute with his bare hands, he found the idea of actually eating him afterward unpleasant. And he knew that there was no possibility that Hugh Fitzcairn would agree to any such notion.

But he had recognized the truth of what Sam had said about the food. So he had proposed instead that the animals be set free to fend for themselves—a suggestion that was no more acceptable to Fitz.

How far could he push his friend? What price would he pay for a few bits of fish?

Then help came from an unexpected source.

"It not sure they die," Sam said.

Fitz turned toward him. "This was your idea?" he asked sharply.

"No. I say we eat dogs. Scotsman not agree."

Fitz looked back at Duncan, who shrugged helplessly.

"Rip, Vixen—I know long time. Klute, I watch. Like dog that run away in the valley—the wild calls to them."

"And you will, of course, share with us exactly what that means?" Fitz said.

"Set them free. They go. They hunt. They maybe run with wolves." He stopped, catching his breath. "They not die for sure."

"And Bigfoot?" Duncan asked, curious.

The Indian did not reply.

Fitz looked around the cabin. Rip lay by the bed, alert as always. Bigfoot was sound asleep by the fire. Klute, still tied up, was on his feet, growling at nothing.

And Vixen sat by the table, her head cocked as though she were following the discussion.

"It's fond of the brown dog you are, Hugh," Danny said. "But would you be having us starve to death because of her?"

Reluctantly, Fitz gave in. But he would not be a part of it.

So Duncan and Danny gathered the dogs together. The door was opened, then closed.

And in time the sound of the wind drowned out Bigfoot's cries, as he whined to be let back in.

There were three then. The singer, the silent one, and the one who whispered. On and on, she whispered, 'til he could hardly hear MacLeod giving him orders or Hugh questioning him or the heathen dying in the bed.

He could still not see them clearly, but he had no doubt they were here in the cabin, with him all the while.

They'd followed him back from the woods, from the red-stained killing ground where he'd found what was left of the yellow dog.

The nasty gray brute had probably done him in, the heathen said.

Hugh had turned away at that.

Should have shot him when you had the chance, Danny-boy.

That was the brown-eyed one, whispering.

They'd come back with him because he'd finally, alone in the woods with no one to hear, spoken aloud to them.

If angels you are, he'd said, then help us. We can't go on. We can't stay back. We need to find food. We need the cold to break. We need the snow to stop.

Oh, we'll be here, in sunshine, in shadow, the singer sang.

That was no good answer. But it was all they had to give him, save laughter that shimmered like crystal in the air.

The green-eyed silent one had led him from the forest, shyly peering back over a cloudlike wing, melting through the cabin wall.

He'd found her inside, hovering above the crooked table. They'd been there since, all three of them.

* * *

Blasted snowshoes! An abomination, that's what they were. Webbed feet were the proper state of ducks or geese. Not Englishmen.

Fitz lay spread-eagled, flat on his back in five feet of snow.

The thought of resting there for a while gazing at the clear blue of the sky was mightily tempting. It had stopped snowing at long last. The weak sun was shining, and the air was crisp and still.

But his hat had come off when he fell, and quite a bit of snow had worked its way down his neck. It was wet. And cold.

He sighed.

Duty, in the form of the hand ax and the surrounding trees, called.

He rolled over awkwardly. The well-worn piece of fur lay on the snow, just out of reach.

As he flailed toward the hat, a brown-and-white shape darted out of the woods and snatched it up.

Fitz laughed. Vixen backed up, wagging her tail.

"Well now, beastie. Tag, I'm it, then?" He lunged at the dog, who narrowly avoided him.

Siwash Sam had been right—again. Fitz was glad of it.

Vixen seemed to be faring well on her own. She came around at least once a day, and he slipped her bits of food. But he had no sense that she was in dire need of it.

MacLeod had seen Rip once or twice. Klute had vanished, after apparently making a meal of poor Bigfoot.

Good riddance, there.

Blasted snowshoes! He struggled to his feet and dived once more at the dog. This time, she allowed herself to be caught.

Man and dog wrestled in the snow over the prize of the fur hat.

"To the victor," Fitz shouted, as he pried the soggy fur from her jaws, "go the spoils!" She barked and butted him with her head, nosing at his pocket.

He thumped her soundly on her side, then took out a sliver of dried meat.

Vixen ate it delicately, gave a muffled woof, and bounded away. He stood watching her.

"Take care, beastie," he murmured. The notion that the dog Klute might still be about weighed on his mind.

Then he turned back to the task at hand.

There now—off to the right. A tree, already downed. It was but a few minutes' work to cut it into manageable lengths. Leaving the ax behind, he loaded his arms with wood, and started back to the cabin.

A few steps, and he stumbled. Something under the snow held his right leg fast. He pitched forward. The wood went flying, as he landed full on his face.

Had there ever been a time when he had thought snow pleasing to the eye? He remembered a sunset on Salisbury Plain, after a snowfall that left the great henge iced with white. It had been glorious.

So young. So foolish, he thought, as freezing water dripped from the end of his nose.

He attempted to pull himself to his knees—and felt the whole of his right boot, snowshoe and all, come off.

Fitz lay absolutely still for a moment. Then he sat up and tried to pry the boot free. To no avail.

"Bloody hell."

He frowned. To shout or not to shout?

Oh well, he wasn't that far from the cabin. It wouldn't be an easy go with only one snowshoe, but he'd make the best of it. And he could always raise the alarm when he got closer.

*　*　*

After they'd peeled off the three layers of heavy wool socks, caked with ice, Duncan had gently held Fitzcairn's right foot up so that Sam could see it.

The foot was black, from the toes to the ankle. It looked as if Fitzcairn had been walking in soot.

"Frostbite?" Duncan asked.

Sam nodded.

"It doesn't hurt, you know," Fitzcairn said. "It's—numb."

"It will," Sam said. "Bad."

Fitz made a face.

"I need to restore the circulation," Duncan said. He touched the foot. It was like marble.

"No rub," Sam said, sharply.

Duncan, who had been about to do just that, stopped.

"Toes break off," Sam explained.

"Oh, well—what's a toe here or there?" Fitz said, his voice high. "I can always grow new ones."

"I don't think so, Fitz," Duncan said.

"It's not possible then?" Danny handed Fitzcairn a cup of hot tea, laced with the very last of the brandy. "I'd thought maybe—"

"Danny," Duncan said sharply. Danny frowned, but he held his tongue.

"What does Siwash Sam say I should do?" Duncan asked the Indian.

"Best heat is heat of body. Skin to skin."

Duncan contemplated the foot. If Sam were not there, he would have been inclined to wait. Fitz was an Immortal. The frostbite would heal, eventually. He'd had no experience with the problem, so how long it would take was open to question. But like a wound or broken bone, it would heal and leave no trace.

However, Sam was awake. He had seen. So what had to be done had to be done.

"Fitzcairn, the next time you decide to take a barefoot stroll in the snow—don't."

"I wasn't barefoot," Fitzcairn replied, as Duncan loosened his shirt and drew the foot under his armpit. "Do you think me a complete fool?"

Duncan didn't reply. And in a short while, as the feeling came back to the frozen foot, anything he might have had to say could not have been heard over the sound of Fitzcairn's screams.

It was freezing in the room. That little minx Arianna had wrapped herself in the satin-and-goosedown coverlet, leaving him bare-naked. He rolled to his feet—

And Gina was there, running a warm hand over the cold flesh of his buttock.

"So lifelike," she murmured.

"So detailed," Arianna added.

A chorus of voices agreed. He looked down from his pedestal upon a garden of blooming beauties, bright faces turned up to him, eyes shining with appreciation.

Pedestal? How curious . . .

A hand—was it Gina's or Arianna's—brushed his manhood.

He didn't move. He couldn't move. He was a statue, lovingly rendered in the finest of marble.

The women continued to come and go in the room. They smiled at him. They spoke of Michelangelo and da Vinci. They caressed his perfect marble limbs.

Aisleen appeared. She smiled mischievously and began playing with his perfect marble toes, nibbling on them, tweaking them.

She gasped. Her eyes widened. She stepped back, his big toe held between her thumb and forefinger.

A cry of dismay rose. His right ear detached. His left hand cracked, dissolving into marble dust. One leg came off at the knee, shattering to bits as it struck the stone floor.

Then Arianna pointed to his groin and gave a strangled little cry. The crowd sobbed as one . . .

Fitz jerked awake in the chill darkness of the cabin.

It was only a nightmare, he thought. There was no need for him to worry. Of course he was still intact.

But . . .

Reassured, he rolled over, inching closer to the smoldering fire. He missed Vixen's furry warmth beside him. He missed the solid warmth of a good meal in his belly.

Most of all, he missed the sweet warmth of a woman beneath him.

Some nightmares, he reflected, seemed never to end.

Dearest Claire,

It pains me to write these words, but the truth of it is that all that keeps us now in this cabin is Sam. And he will not be leaving here alive. Sam knows this. He knew it before any of us, I think. Indeed, he told us. But I didn't want to believe him. We do what we can to make him comfortable, while we wait for the inevitable.

In the meantime, our days are taken up with our own efforts to survive . . .

Duncan flinched at the gunshot sound of a tree cracking in the cold.

He was some distance from the cabin, in a thickly wooded area, rifle in hand. The food stores, even with the addition of the salmon meant for the dogs, were running perilously low.

But so far, their hunting expeditions had yielded only a

couple of hares. And he was having no more luck this day. Of what use were tracking skills if there is nothing to track?

The forest was as silent as death, save for the occasional snap of a frozen tree limb, and the slight sounds he made moving carefully forward.

His stomach rumbled. Loudly. Well, if there were any game around, that would have flushed it out!

But—wait. Ahead and to the left. There was *something*. A sound, an animal sound of some sort.

He crept forward cautiously. A few hundred yards and through the winter-bare branches he could see what he had heard.

The dog Klute, feeding off the carcass of a dead moose. It hadn't been killed that long ago, he noted. The stains on the snow were still bright red.

Klute raised his head. He stared directly at Duncan. His lip curled back, baring his teeth in a guttural snarl. His muzzle was covered in blood.

Slowly, Duncan raised the rifle to his shoulder. The brute might know what that meant—he'd seen Pie shot—but he might not.

He did. He sprang back into the tree cover, fading into the general grayness.

No matter. If the kill didn't look diseased, Duncan would be quite happy to take Klute's leavings.

He pushed through the trees and knelt by the carcass. The moose had been old and scrawny, but there was no sign of sickness. It hadn't died from anything other than a torn throat.

The dog had gone for the entrails, ripping into the stomach. None of the meat had yet been touched.

Duncan set the rifle aside and unstrapped a large knife from his thigh. His stomach was rumbling again, and he could feel saliva starting in his mouth. Meat, even raw meat, had awakened every hunger pang in his body.

First, he had to finish up the bloody job of gutting. He reached into the torn stomach . . .

Ninety pounds of fury struck him in the back, sending him sprawling over the dead moose. He felt the dog's teeth ripping through the hood of his parka, lacerating the back of his head, seeking a death grip on his neck.

The brute's full weight was on him. Though he still had the knife in his hand, there was no way he could manage a clear thrust.

Oaths that he hadn't used in centuries, delivered in a burr that would have set Fitzcairn's teeth on edge, poured out of him. He got his hands underneath his chest, and pushed himself up, first to his knees, then upright. The dog still clung to him, teeth buried in the nape of his neck.

The brute let go, finally, dropping to the ground. Duncan fell on him before he could gather himself to renew the attack. The knife blade flashed, up and down, again and again. All of the frustration he'd felt the last few weeks exploded in a frenzy.

He could not save Sam. Despite his best efforts, the man was dying, in pain, by inches. It would have been far better for him if he had gone under the ice and drowned.

The dog was long dead when he stopped. He pushed back from the body, panting with exertion, covered with gore.

He knelt by the body, his hands resting on his knees. Finally, he dropped the knife by his side, and lowered his head.

He was Duncan MacLeod of the Clan MacLeod. He had just slaughtered a dumb animal as though it were a mortal enemy.

Because he could not kill the real enemy—this blasted land that could take a man's life in an instant—and his soul, too, if he were not ever-vigilant.

He raised his head and looked up at the sky. Today, it was

that damnable ghostly white that meant yet more snow was coming. He'd best get the meat back to the cabin quickly.

He was Duncan MacLeod of the Clan MacLeod. He would not give up.

Danny sat on the floor by the fire, his legs drawn up, his arms crossed on his knees. Hugh was out gathering firewood and MacLeod had taken the rifle in search of game.

The green-eyed angel was hovering over the heathen.

He could see them quite clearly now. Indeed, they were the figures from the great staircase window in his dream house, come to life for him.

Oh, Danny-boy, we love you so, the blue-eyed angel sang.

Before the angels had appeared, he'd been feeling a great loneliness here in this cabin. Hugh fretted on about the brown dog. MacLeod concerned himself only with the heathen.

Sure and it seemed that the two of them were forgetting the gold. The fortune they had with them, the fortune still to be dug out of the ground when spring came.

The green-eyed angel was sitting now on the dying man's chest.

Not a thought were they giving to the future. The fine things to be bought, the journeys to be taken, the houses to be . . .

But you must bide . . .

Waiting, waiting.

The man was not one of their kind. He was a mortal.

She leaned forward, brushing her wings against his mouth, back and forth, back and forth, in time to his labored breathing.

Danny rose slowly to his feet.

If the man did not die tomorrow, he would die the day after or the day after that or next week, or next year.

Or today, Danny-boy, the brown-eyed angel whispered. *He could die today.*

Danny crossed to the bed. He picked up a thick fur robe.

It's dead he well may be, the singer crooned.

The green-eyed angel rose to give him room.

He bent over the heathen.

"Danny! Fitzcairn!"

MacLeod's voice, calling from outside the cabin, shouting about fresh meat.

Danny clenched his jaw and tossed the fur robe back on the bed.

Around him, the angels sighed.

Siwash Sam knew that his time had come. It was, in fact, past due. If the Scotsman had not made him eat of the moose meat, he would have been gone days ago.

But now, no food or drink or medicine would matter. He could hear the call of the eagle, the grunt of the bear. He was ready.

He called the Scotsman to him.

"I will leave this place soon," he said.

"Sam—"

"Listen. Do not argue. I have no time for it."

The Scotsman knelt by the bed. He listened.

Sam spoke slowly. The pain robbed him of breath. But he made sure that the Scotsman could find the way to McPherson.

The Englishman stood now at the foot of the bed. Sam could see him dimly. His face was lined with worry.

"Fitz, I think—" the Scotsman said.

The Englishman nodded.

"I shook your hand. I made a promise," Sam said.

"Sam has kept that promise," the Scotsman replied in a low

voice. "He has guided us well. Because of him, these cheechakos have survived."

Sam smiled faintly. The Englishman had been shot and had drowned. The Irishman had taken a killing fall. They all had walked away from a bear fight.

He had heard them talking when they thought he was asleep.

He had seen the swords.

These three did not need the likes of Siwash Sam to survive.

He stared for a moment into the dark eyes of the man bent over him. If he were to ask him now, if he were to say *What manner of men are you?*, the Scotsman would answer.

It did not seem important.

But there was one last thing that was.

"Scotsman," he said weakly. "Come closer."

He took a deep breath as the man leaned over him.

"I am called Nia-sut-lin," he whispered. "Tell this to the fire."

Duncan melted snow and washed Sam's body as well as he could. He made a pyre of the last sled, and they put him on it, on a bed of the driest wood they could find.

There was no real sunset at this time of the year, but Duncan judged when it was evening by where the moon was in the sky.

Fitz had roasted meat, and brewed some of the last of their tea. They couldn't sit in the snow, so they stood by the sled, eating and sharing their memories of Sam.

Even Danny was there, though Duncan knew that he had been reluctant to take part in what he called "heathen rites." He assumed that Fitz had prevailed on him to join with them.

Fitz sang "Amazing Grace," all of the verses. Duncan marveled, as he always did, at how good his voice was.

He wasn't certain what Sam would have thought of the hymn singing. But Fitz had very much wanted to do it.

Then Duncan stepped forward. He lit a branch and walked around the pyre, setting the wood ablaze.

He didn't know the Siwash words, so he spoke Lakota, sending the spirit of Nia-sut-lin to join that of the bear. He prayed, as Sam had for his brother, that it would not be long before that spirit would be born again into this world.

The three Immortals stood together then watching as the all-too-mortal remains of the man they had known as Siwash Sam were consumed by fire.

Finally, Fitz turned away. "Look, MacLeod," he said softly, pointing toward the ridge behind the cabin.

Rip sat silhouetted against the snow. How long had he been there? Duncan wondered.

As the fire slowly died, the black-and-gray dog threw back his head and howled mournfully. The sound went on and on, an animal wail of grief more genuine than any human keening.

Then he rose to his feet and, without a backward glance, disappeared into the darkness.

Chapter 11

"No, Danny. We can't take the gold with us," Duncan said. "We have to travel with what we can carry on our backs. Three bags of gold are a weight that's not needed."

"After all these months, after all of the dying that's been done, you want to just walk away and leave it?" the young Immortal cried. "I'll not do it, MacLeod. I'll go without food, but I'll not go without what we've left of the gold."

"Danny, it's not as though anyone is going to stroll in here in the next few months. We'll take just a handful. That's more than enough to establish the claim. The rest will be here when winter breaks."

"No. I said it, and I mean it."

"Look, lad," Fitzcairn interrupted. "We can hide what we leave behind. Here in the cabin, or outside in a place that's well marked."

"Hugh, I won't see another summer as a poor man, I swear."

Fitzcairn paced between them, running his fingers through his shaggy curls.

"Fitz, sit down." Duncan spoke sharply. "You're giving me a headache."

"A minute, MacLeod," he responded. "We've come this far together. We'll get to that blasted fort together, too." He crossed to the corner where the three bags of gold were stored, all in a heap. One by one, he hefted them.

"Here, lad." He threw one bag across the room. The young Immortal caught it, nearly losing his balance.

"You've hardly any strength, Danny," Duncan said. "None of us do. We're not going to die from lack of food, but even our kind need proper nourishment. Gold," he added wryly, "is heavy."

"I can carry it," Danny said stubbornly.

"All right, all right," Fitz said. "You've spent time in diplomatic circles, MacLeod. Let's exercise the art of compromise here." He turned to Danny, who stood, still holding the gold.

"That bag there, you could carry that with some ease, could you not?" Fitz asked.

"And two more besides," Danny replied, his jaw set.

"That one bag?" Fitz repeated.

"Yes," Danny replied, reluctantly.

"All right, that's it then. MacLeod, there are three bags of gold left. There are three of us. You and I can choose to leave ours behind. If Danny chooses to burden himself with his, then we should let him be."

"Hugh—" Danny began.

Fitzcairn turned on him. "There are three bags and three of us. I would think that would be clear."

Danny's blue eyes darkened. But he said no more.

*   *   *

There was no dawn to speak of, but a man could tell the time by the wheeling of the stars. When the hour was right, they started out, headed still north and a bit west.

All three bore full packs—the remaining food, fur robes and blankets, a pot or two, some basic tools. And the one bag of gold. The other two had been buried under the back of the cabin, by the area where the wood had been piled.

It had taken some time to dig through the frozen soil. Duncan had fretted the whole while, but Fitz's appeal to diplomacy had struck a chord. So he lent his own diminishing strength to the effort, and finally the hole was deep enough to hold both bags.

As they walked away, Danny turned, as though he were bidding someone farewell. Then he shouldered his burden and followed the other two Immortals into the dark of the day.

Danny, sweet Danny, the brown-eyed angel crooned, her dark hair curling 'round her ears. *You needn't worry your handsome head. My sisters and I will guard your gold.*

"You'll not be coming with me then?" Danny asked, a tremor in his voice. The angels laughed, all of them, swooping around him. Their laughter sounded like fine crystal shattering on stone.

Oh, Danny. They spoke as one. *We'll not leave you. We're here for you. And there for the gold. You can trust us. We're all you can trust. Remember . . .*

They were gone, shimmering away. They left him with a sense of peace. He could trust his angels. He would remember.

Hours later, after they had camped for the night, Vixen appeared.

"Well, there you are, my fine beastie," Fitz said. He ignored MacLeod's frown and held out a bite of salted moose meat.

The dog sniffed it, took it daintily. Then she yawned and settled at his feet.

"Finicky?" MacLeod crouched down beside them.

"Fed, I would say," Fitz replied, patting her head. "Under the current circumstances, an educated nose is no doubt of more use in filling the belly then our opposable thumbs." He held up his mittened hand and waggled his right thumb. Vixen shifted and thumped her tail, expectantly. Smiling, he began to pet her again, running his hand through her thick winter fur.

"Nonetheless, she's lost some of her weight," MacLeod offered. "Now that we're on the move, do you think she'll stay with us?"

"Yes. Yes, I do think so," Fitz said slowly. "If she was going to answer—what was the term the Indian used?—the call of the wild? Well, if that were true, she wouldn't be here at all."

"It's your way with the ladies, Fitz. Two-legged, four-legged—"

Fitz laughed. "True words, laddie. Remember that sorrel filly I had when we were in Naples? Bonita, her name was."

"Oh, I remember," MacLeod replied. "She stepped on my foot running to you for a bit of apple. Broke it, as I recall."

Fitz shrugged. "When it comes to the fairer sex of any species, Highlander, if you can't lead, then you must follow. Or get out of the way. If you'd only realized that two hundred years ago, I'd be with Gina now, instead of—"

"Instead of here with me," MacLeod interrupted, "eager to go off into the forest and use your opposable thumbs to gather some wood."

"Exactly why would I be eager to leave the warmth of the fire, might I ask?"

"If the dog is here to stay," MacLeod answered, "we can build a rough sled and harness her. We'd make even better time without a load on our backs."

Fitz rose. "Lead on MacLeod," he said. Vixen opened one eye—the golden one—and looked up at him.

"Be at ease, beastie," he instructed, as he grabbed the lantern. MacLeod fetched the hand ax, stopping for a minute to tell Danny what they were about. The two went off then about their business.

The dog settled back to sleep with a sigh of contentment in a nest of blankets that smelled of Hugh Fitzcairn.

Don't even ask it, Danny-boy, the dark-eyed angel said.

"But with the brown dog here, all the gold can be carried," he protested. "We've gone but a day—"

They'll not go back, I'm telling you. They're rich already, the both of them.

"Hugh's not—"

The angel made an ugly sound.

So he told you. And you believed him, Danny-boy. You believed him.

The next day, just as Sam had said, they came to the Peel River. They need only follow it north and they would find the fort. Another two days, at most.

Another two days—unless . . . Duncan could not help it. His eyes sought the sky no matter how hard he tried to keep his attention focused on the way ahead.

He had seen that color before, he'd seen those clouds before, he'd felt the change in the wind.

A storm was coming.

Fitzcairn drew alongside of him, matching his pace.

"How long, MacLeod?"

Duncan tightened his lips. Once more, he thought of the man whose ashes darkened the snow by the cabin.

"I wish I was certain."

"Should we keep on? Whatever this wind is blowing in can't possibly be worse than that first blizzard."

"But we were stronger then, Fitz. I don't know about you, but I'm so hungry that I hurt."

Fitzcairn laughed sourly. "Last night, I woke up thinking Vixen was growling. And there she was, staring at me in the dark, her head cocked. It was my stomach doing the growling, so loud I'll wager I woke her."

"All things considered," Duncan said, "it would be best to take shelter, if there's any to be had. The far bank of this river is fairly rocky. There might be some break along the way. Keep your eyes open. And tell Danny to do the same."

"I'll tell him." Fitzcairn sighed. "But I make no guarantee he'll hear me. If there's such a thing as snow-deafness, then he's been suffering from it since we left the cabin."

MacLeod saw the cave first, an area of blackness that stood out in the snow-covered riverbank even in the general darkness of the day.

"A den?" Fitz wondered. "And how are we to know if someone's to home?"

"We'll know," MacLeod replied, "because I'll go and knock on the door."

Fitz held his breath—and the end of the rope coiled around MacLeod's waist—as the Highlander made his way across the frozen river. If the seemingly solid ice broke, they could pull him out quickly, at the least.

And then they could stand around and watch him freeze to death from the wet and the cold. Not an interruption to the journey that he cared to consider. So he raised a weak cheer when MacLeod made it to the other shore.

In the ever-present twilight, Fitz could see him cautiously approach the cave. The lantern he carried flickered and dimmed as it was blocked by his body. Then he turned and held it aloft, a signal that the cave was empty.

Splendid! Poppa, Momma and Baby Bear were occupied elsewhere. Was it too much to hope that they had left their porridge behind? He giggled, then sighed. *Get a grip, laddie. Only a bit of a way to go, and we'll reach what passes for civilization in this blasted land.*

He and Danny followed MacLeod to the opposite shore, one at a time. Fitz led Vixen, harnessed to the sled. At first, she whined and balked at the entrance to the cave. She stood, legs wide, nostrils flaring, checking the situation out thoroughly in her own way. Finally, she gave a short yip and was content to join the humans inside. As Fitz worked to loosen her traces, he saw a few flakes of white melting on her fur.

The threatening storm had begun.

Hear the wind blow, Danny, hear the wind blow, the blue-eyed angel sang. The quiet one hovered behind her, swaying in the mouth of the cave.

An animal had once lived in this shelter they had found. There was a hollow of earth dug out in the farthest corner. Clumps of fur covered the earthen floor. Bits of bones, gnawed at the ends, lay scattered about.

There were small skulls among the bones, rabbits most likely, and here and there some larger that Danny could not quite put a name to. They gleamed oh so white in the darkness, staring at him out of the empty hollows that had held their eyes.

Bone, they whispered in voices so tiny. *Beneath your flesh, you're just like us. When you die, you'll rot away to bone.*

He shook his head, but the words would not stop.

Bone, Danny. Naught but bone.

"Danny?" It was MacLeod's voice. "Danny, come on. You've got to eat."

"I can't die," he whispered. "I—can't—"

"No," MacLeod said, "but you have to keep your strength up. We all have to. We may be Immortal," he added, an edge in his voice, "but we're not invulnerable."

"If you prick us, do we not bleed?" Hugh murmured in a sleepy voice.

If you cut off our heads, do we not DIE? the brown-eyed angel fairly shouted in his ear.

AND ROT, ROT, ROT AWAY the mocking voices chanted.

Danny rose. "I'm going to live forever!" he shouted. He'd deal with them, he would. Small bones crunched beneath his feet, one larger skull he hurled into the swirling whiteness outside.

"Easy, lad." His teacher was there, pinning his arms to his side. Danny looked at the familiar face, pressed close to his. He blinked, and the skin, ruddy from the wind and cold, melted away, the bright blue eyes, sharp with worry, sank and vanished. A grinning skull it was that confronted him, mouthing words of concern.

He felt a great fear then, one he'd not known since Lucas Desirée had told him what he was.

It was a lie, what MacLeod said. They *could* die, their heads could fall on this frozen earth. And rot away, like discarded bits of meat.

There were swords here, there were knives here. And there was death, lurking in the shadows.

Over the shoulder of the thing that wore Hugh's bony face, he saw the green-eyed angel, beckoning him from just outside the cave. He shoved with all of his might, breaking free.

The wind outside was howling, fair like the banshees were said to do. It drowned out all other sounds. He stumbled through the darkness, snow cutting at his cheeks like a shattering of glass.

He was safe. He would not be a prize this day for what

waited in the cave. He need only keep on, and it could not touch him.

Haven't you forgotten something, Danny-boy? the brown-eyed angel murmured softly. *Something important?*

He stopped. The bag of gold—*his* bag of gold. His insides twisted at the thought of leaving it amid the bones.

And then from out of the blackness, two figures fell upon him, shouting his name, dragging him back into the danger-ous light.

The lantern, a pale illumination that barely penetrated the gloom, flickered and went out.

"MacLeod?"

"What, Fitz?"

"How long ago was it that I said we'd seen the worst of the weather in this land?"

A sigh in the darkness. "Two days?"

What firewood they'd had when they first took shelter was long gone. There had been no break in the still-raging storm, no chance to gather more.

"Ah, well. I never claimed to be one that could tell the fu-ture."

Fitz could feel MacLeod shifting. Without a fire, the cave was bitter cold. They all were wrapped in blankets, huddled together. Vixen lay on his left, MacLeod next to her.

"No one of us can. Immortal or not."

"When I was younger—before I died—the tinkers came through my village," Fitz said. "Had my fortune told by a dark-eyed beauty that I'd taken a fancy to." He laughed. "She said I had an amazingly long life line."

"I traveled a while with the gypsies," MacLeod said, re-flectively. "It's true that there were some among them who seemed to have—powers."

There was something in his tone that caught Fitz's attention. Under ordinary circumstances, he'd be inclined to ask a sharp question or two, to find out more about MacLeod's life among the tinkers. And the girl, for there must have been a girl.

But these were not ordinary circumstances. Asking questions took energy, and energy was a thing in short supply.

Firewood. Energy.

Food.

They'd left the cabin expecting to be at Fort McPherson in three days' time. The food they'd taken with them was enough to last them on the way.

If MacLeod's guess was right, they'd been two days already in this blasted den, which smelled more and more of dead animal the longer they stayed.

Two days here and two days before on the trail.

They were stretching what they had as much as was possible. But put plainly, if the storm did not soon abate, they would have to finish the journey on a diet of sugar water.

Danny, lying to his right, moaned in his sleep. Fitz pulled the fur robe farther over him.

"He's calmer today," MacLeod said. It was half a question.

"Aye. But he still won't say what it is he thought he saw that drove him out, though. The look on his face . . ."

"You said before that you had some notion of where his mind was when it wasn't with us?"

"So I did. But since that day he lost his sight—I'm not so sure."

"He's keen enough still when talk turns to the gold," MacLeod stated. "Other times, though, he seems to be some-how—*listening.*"

Fitz nodded, although he knew the Highlander couldn't see him in the darkness.

"It might just be the bloody wind. Or the silence, when it

isn't blowing." He sighed, and rested his head against the cave wall. "The silence is worse, I think."

MacLeod made a noise that he took as agreement.

Time passed. It was difficult to tell how long in the total darkness.

"MacLeod?"

"Yes, Fitz?"

"The rules we live by—do you think they cover the subject of a teacher who drags his student thousands of miles across a frozen wasteland, so that he can have the delightful experience of freezing to death while starving? Or is it starving to death while freezing?"

"I dinna notice ye having to do any dragging," MacLeod replied. "He'll survive."

"We'll all survive, MacLeod, none the worse for the wear," Fitz said. "But will Danny be thanking me for this adventure, I wonder? Even when his pockets are filled with gold?"

"Being a teacher—it's na about protecting him, is it?" MacLeod asked. "Or fighting his fights? When he felt confident that I would na lose my head the first time I was challenged, my cousin Connor never tried to keep me out of harm's way."

"A point well taken," Fitz said. "I do recall that Henry Fitz once volunteered us both to travel to England with messages for the young king from his mother. Isabella the Fair, they called her. And rightly so, I might add." He smiled at the memory.

"We'd joined her guard when she returned to France after old John finally died. She was not at all on good terms with the Council, so what we were about was risky business indeed. But when I complained of the danger, he assured me that we were safe, since only those born gentlemen need worry about the headsman's ax."

"Fitzcairn, I canna believe it—do ye realize that ye just agreed with me?"

"No doubt it's the severe cold, laddie. It's affected my reasoning—and your speech."

"And what might that mean?"

"If ye dinna know, I canna tell you," Fitz replied.

MacLeod fussed at that a bit, but soon fell silent. *What a fine state of affairs,* Fitz thought. *Here we are, lacking even strength enough for a good argument!*

He sighed and checked on Danny, who slept still. Vixen stirred, and he pulled her closer. Outside, the wind screamed on.

Oh, how he longed for a pipe!

My dearest Claire, Duncan thought, *at the moment we are still some forty miles from Fort McPherson. We are dying, but you needn't worry, since the condition will prove to be temporary.*

Not a letter that would ever be sent, of course. Still, it did describe the situation fairly.

The storm had finally stopped midafternoon on the third day. They pushed their way out through the foot of new snow that had filled the cave entrance. To find a fairy-tale landscape of crystalline purity, unsullied white extending as far as could be seen in any direction.

By then, their store of food, except for a few scant mouthfuls, was completely depleted. Fitz agreed that there was nothing to do but to let the dog go free to forage for herself. Duncan doubted they would see her again.

Once more they divided what gear they had and shouldered the packs. They left a few odds and ends behind to lighten the loads as much as possible, taking with them only the minimum of what they would need.

And they left the gold, except for a small pouch.

That had been an ugly scene.

Danny had shouted, then wept, then gone dead silent. But this time, even Fitzcairn could not deny the need to carry as little as possible. If they had any hope of reaching McPherson before their strength failed, they had to travel quickly.

It was not starvation that Duncan feared. Though they were weak from hunger, they were days away from being at the point where vital systems shut down for lack of sustenance.

Duncan had starved to death—he knew the signs.

No, what would more likely happen was that they would simply collapse in the snow, falling into the stupor that precedes death by freezing.

Sam had warned Duncan of those signs. In the spring, they would thaw and wake. And if they were found before then, there would be difficult questions to answer.

They were so close—he would not let them fail.

So, here they were, worn to exhaustion already, exhausting themselves still further breaking trail through the fresh snow. They were on the frozen river. It had been Duncan's decision to take the risk of the ice breaking as a trade-off for the clear path that the river provided.

Yes, it was easier, but there were still places where the drifts were waist-high. And the banks didn't break the wind—they seemed instead to channel it directly toward them.

The way was arduous and they were all tired beyond thought when Duncan called a halt.

So you see Claire, we won't actually die. But we may come to wish we had.

"Danny, we needn't even wait for spring to go back, you know?"

Come ye back when all the roses falling, the blue-eyed angel sang.

"We can rest a bit at the fort, then take a team of dogs back to the cave."

And you are dead, as dead you well may be.

"Danny." The man put his hand on Danny's shoulder. It was shaking, Danny noticed. "We're so close."

Danny pulled away. He lay on his back, feeling the life ebb out of him minute by minute. He closed his eyes and heard a voice with a soft Southern accent.

It's who we are, the voice said.

It's what you must do, the brown-eyed angel finished.

Fitz was mightily concerned. The morning after they left the cave, Vixen had re-appeared, sliding down the riverbank in a cloud of white. She leaped through the snow to join them, her tail held high. He was sure that Danny would want to go back now for the sled—and the gold.

But the lad seemed to take no notice of the dog nor of his surroundings, beyond what was needed to keep on the trail. He could not be engaged in conversation. His dark blue eyes were somehow vacant, his mouth slack.

Fitz had seen such reactions in the mortally wounded, just before they died. A shock set in, and their minds went somewhere else, somewhere safer.

Ah well. Fitz raised a cup of warm, sweet water to his lips and drank slowly. In truth they were all on that edge.

He had to believe that a full belly and a warm bed would bring Danny back. Then he could get the lad to talk, to speak about the fancies and fears that were plaguing him. Given time, he knew that he could set things right.

And unlike gold nuggets—Fitz thought as he drained the cup—time, for Immortals, was not a scarce commodity.

*　　*　　*

"You could leave me, MacLeod," Fitzcairn said. "Go on, the two of you. I'll wait here for your return. You have my word on it." He managed a weak smile.

"If you'd not shared your food with the dog all those days in the cabin, ye would be better off now," Duncan chided.

"And you weren't giving half of your ration to the Indian, I suppose?" Fitzcairn responded.

Duncan sighed. What Fitz proposed made sense. But he was loath to agree

"We'll na argue. I've got a plan."

"Ah, I see. You're Duncan MacLeod of the Clan MacLeod and you have a plan. Well, wake me when you're ready to tell me about it."

"Hugh Fitzcairn, of here and there, don't you fall asleep." Duncan slapped his face.

"Danny," he called. The young Immortal was standing a few feet away. His pack was at his feet, and he was staring off into the distance.

"Danny O'Donal," he repeated, to no effect. He rose from Fitz's side. Grabbing the young Immortal, he shook him fiercely. At last, his eyes focused.

"Help me move Fitzcairn to the riverbank," he ordered. "Then make a fire and brew some tea. There's a bit left in my pack. I'll get it for you."

By the time all that was done, Duncan did indeed have a plan.

The dog was back again. She was strong enough to pull a pallet. He could throw one together, use belts and pieces of rope—whatever was to hand to lash the wood in place—and harness her.

If they kept on through the hours of the night, by midmorning they could be at the fort. No matter if Fitz died on the way—he would be in a safe place when he revived.

Duncan left the two Immortals by the fire and scrambled

up the bank. There was a small stand of trees a bit farther back. The dog followed him as he headed off with the hand ax. She disappeared into the brush, hunting for her dinner, no doubt.

The tea was exceedingly welcome. The warmth of it coursed through him rapidly. He could feel it set his pulses pounding, making his heart beat faster.

Given enough tea, perhaps he might not need to be dragged along to McPherson like a sack of grain. He turned to tell Danny this.

The young Immortal stood on the other side of the fire. His sword was in his hand.

You take our opponent's head—and with it his strength. *Isn't that right, Danny-boy?*

He would live forever, he would take this one and the other.

He would live forever—and he would have all of the gold.

He stepped forward.

"Danny?" Fitz rose slowly. "I have no sword. Remember? If you are angry enough to challenge me—"

The lad did not seem to hear him, his eyes were empty, emotionless.

"Danny?" he repeated more loudly, an edge in his voice.

Danny paused, and frowned. "Hugh? I—"

NO, the angels shouted together. They flew all in his face, even the silent one.

LOOK!

It was not Hugh he saw. It was the bony thing from the cave, Hugh was gone, lost somewhere along the way.

There was no reason for this bony thing to live—and all the reason in the world for Danny to.

He would survive, as Hugh had taught him.

He raised his sword.

A scream, shattering the silence. Duncan ran clear of the trees and looked upriver.

By the light of the fire, he could see the young Immortal slashing at Fitzcairn who rolled away, narrowly avoiding the blade.

Duncan threw himself down the river bank, shouting first Fitzcairn's name, then Danny's. As he scrambled to his feet, one of his snowshoes, weakened by the fall, broke beneath him. He sprawled facedown in the snow.

As Fitz dodged the bright saber, he felt that surge of energy that a fight always brought forth. His hunger, his weakness, were forgotten as his body obeyed one single command—*live.*

But he had no sword, no weapon.

Wait—the katana! It was with MacLeod's pack. If he could reach it, and hold Danny off until Duncan got to them—

Edging around the fire, he kept repeating Danny's name. But the young Immortal's face remained closed and set.

The patch of light he stood in now was full of sound—the voice of the thing that wasn't Hugh calling his name, the shouts of the brown-eyed angel, urging him onward, the cry of the blue-eyed angel raised in battle song.

Of a sudden, everything went flat, like a scene done in bits of colored glass. He focused his attention on the two specks of bright blue that were the eyes of the thing he had to kill.

The sword sliced the air, cutting through his coat. If it had not been sewn of thick fur and hide the blow might well have taken his arm. As it was, he felt a sharp pain and a wetness that must be blood.

Blast! Danny was still between him and the Highlander's sword.

Where in bloody hell was MacLeod? He'd heard him call, he must be coming.

And if he got the *katana*? Could he stand against Danny? He did not want to hurt the lad.

But he didn't want to lose his head, either.

He risked a drop and roll, coming up with the battered pan of boiling water. He threw it full in Danny's face.

As the lad screamed in pain, Fitz rushed him, trying to throw him off-balance. They fell together to the frozen ground.

A scream rang in his ears. His scream. Pain and anger surged through him.

FIGHT, the angels chorused. *FOR YOUR LIFE.*

They rolled together through the fire. Sparks flew, bits of gold in the darkness.

The thing had him down, straddling him, shouting in his face. It claimed still to be Hugh.

But Hugh would not have hurt him so.

BEHIND YOU, DANNY BOY! The brown-eyed angel guided his hand along the rocky ground, to a large rough stone. With a wild thrust, he pulled his arm free and smashed the face above him directly between the two specks of blue.

The thing slumped silent. Danny pushed it off and retrieved his sword.

He stood over the crumpled form ready to deal the killing blow.

The angels swooped about, cheering him on.

*　*　*

Without snowshoes, the going was difficult and treacherous. Awkwardly, Duncan ran through the knee-deep snow, shouting all the while.

Ahead, he saw Danny poised over Fitz's prone body.

A cry of pain tore from his lips. Too far, he was still too far away!

From above the two figures, a streak of brown flew through the air, striking the young Immortal between the shoulder blades.

Vixen.

The fight between man and dog was brief and brutal. Duncan was witness to it all. Danny rolled to his knees. Vixen, with all of her instincts guiding her, went for his throat. He fended her off with one gloved hand, striking at her with the hilt of his sword.

But she was tenacious, holding on even as Danny got to his feet. He slashed at her viciously. She yelped in pain and dropped to the snow. With a roar that seemed to Duncan hardly human, Danny gripped the sword with both hands and plunged the blade into her body. She yelped again, and was still.

Brave dog, Duncan thought, a catch in his throat. *Fitz's sweet beastie.* Not only had she saved his head, she had also distracted Danny. The young Immortal had not even noticed Duncan until he stood, *katana* in hand, between him and Fitz's still-unconscious form.

"Daniel Patrick O'Donal," he said. "I'm Duncan MacLeod of the Clan MacLeod. And I challenge you here."

Danny faced him, blood dripping from his sword. Absently, Duncan noted that, like saliva, it crackled when it struck the icy ground.

The man before him was a stranger. His jaw was tensed, the plains of his cheeks stood out like carved marble. The sparse beard that had added some years to a face that would be forever youthful now seemed a mask, hiding the young man who was student—and friend—to Hugh Fitzcairn.

He gave no response to Duncan's Challenge save a sudden lunge forward. Steel struck steel. The battle was joined.

I am the angel with the sword. I will smite them all, all of
    my enemies.
Tom Kelly. John Kelly.
The list is an old one.
The Reb who killed me at Gettysburg. He is nameless, but
    he is on the list.
Michael Sheehan.
The list is a long one.
Jim Foster. Jeff Smith.
The list had grown with time.
Fergus Cooley.
I WILL SMITE THEM ALL!

Despite the wild emptiness in his eyes, the young Immortal was not fighting recklessly.

Duncan parried an overhead blow with the *katana*. Danny defended and fell back under a flurry of slashes.

The fight moved in and out of the flickering firelight. The play of shadow made it more difficult for Duncan to gauge Danny's movements.

The ground beneath could not be trusted. Twice Duncan slipped, the second time falling to one knee. Danny took advantage, dealing a blow so fierce that the *katana* rang with it, numbing Duncan's sword arm.

The horror he had felt when he saw Fitz close to a death he could not return from had energized Duncan. And the resources that he needed to fight this fight were always there, at the core of his being. They were a part of what made him Duncan MacLeod.

But he was tiring. The lack of food, the long deprivation of the trail had taken a toll on them all.

Yet Danny fought on, with an unnatural ferocity. As he had at the mock battle in the valley, he fought with a brutality that allowed no room for finesse.

There was no part of Duncan's mind that stood outside watching the struggle. All of his being was focused on the man he fought. If there were, he would have judged it not a pretty sight. The two went back and forth, slipping and sliding on the ice, foundering into drifted snow that held them like toy soldiers incapable of movement, forced to flail at each other in place.

Then Duncan recognized that Danny was setting up for the low thrust that he had learned from Fitz. He quickly moved backward as Danny lunged, then forward with his blade, aiming for the heart.

Danny dropped his sword by his side and fell to his knees. Blood seeped through his fingers as he clutched one hand to his chest. He looked up at Duncan, gasping for air, his breath frosting as it left his lips.

Duncan stood over him, the *katana* raised.

All of his warrior blood cried out to him to strike. But the heart of him said otherwise.

This man—this boy—on his knees before him was not an enemy. He was the student, the friend, of Duncan's oldest friend. What demons had possessed him Duncan could not say. But time could put them to rest.

His muscles slackened, his body began to relax. And Danny, moving more swiftly that Duncan would have thought possible considering his wound, snatched his fallen sword and stabbed upward with it.

Instinct took over. Duncan felt the blade pierce his side at the same moment as the *katana* bit into the young Immortal's neck.

Hugh Fitzcairn moaned. He raised himself on his arms. The snow where his head had lain was stained red.

He turned on his side. MacLeod stood just at the edge of the firelight. He held his side with one hand and in the other was his *katana*, a dark stain on the polished blade.

As Fitz watched, a swell of white light poured forth from the crumpled form at MacLeod's feet. It rose like a luminous mist in the darkness, enveloping the Highlander.

A wind rose, jagged lightning arched through the air.

He looked up at MacLeod, shaken in the middle of the vortex of wind and light.

And then he looked beyond. In the night sky, waves of colored light appeared. They covered the heavens, pulsating on and on, sweeping across the horizon.

The Quickening came to an end, all that had been Danny O'Donal was gone and done. MacLeod fell to his knees, still trembling with the aftereffects.

But the lights in the sky, huge and silent and splendid, continued to blaze. Rainbow bands, growing in intensity, until all of the sky seemed to be a riot of green and blue and gold.

Hugh Fitzcairn watched, weeping in sorrow. And in awe.

Chapter 12

"*Requiescat in pace,*" the grizzled old priest intoned.

"Amen," Fitz replied.

Duncan bowed his head as the two Indian boys they had hired slowly shoveled the still half-frozen earth over Danny's plain pine coffin.

"I wish I could have taken him to Darius," Fitzcairn said. "I'd promised him they'd meet someday."

Duncan put his hand on Fitz's shoulder.

A simple wooden cross, all that could be had, marked the grave. Fitz himself had carved the name on it. There were no dates.

Fitz sighed and turned to walk through the gathering twilight. Duncan followed him. Around them, Fort McPherson was waking from the long sleep of winter.

It was early May. The ice on the Peel was beginning to break, the hours of actual light grew longer as the sun climbed ever higher above the horizon.

They entered the small windowless room where they had sheltered for the past months. The dog Vixen, curled up in a heap of blankets by the potbellied stove, rose to greet them. She limped across the floor, wagging her tail so furiously that it nearly threw her off-balance. Fitz knelt to run his hands through her fur. It brought a smile to his face, Duncan was glad to see.

After Danny had—died, Fitz's grief had energized him to fight to save the mortally wounded dog. He had pressed Duncan to carry the beast the few remaining miles to McPherson. Somehow, he had found the strength himself to follow, though the way had been a nightmare of blood and tears that neither man would soon forget.

When they'd finally reached the Fort, both man and dog barely alive, Fitz had forced the doctor in residence to minister first to the stricken animal.

The Mountie captain had thought them mad then, and madder still when they had gone back into the wild some weeks later. They'd returned with Danny's body, carefully shrouded in fur robes, hidden away from mortal eyes.

But Vixen had lived, though she would never again be of use as a sled dog. And Danny O'Donal, whose frozen corpse had lain the winter through in the icehouse, had at last gotten a proper funeral, laid to rest in the corner of the fort given over to the dead.

They'd taken off their coats and were sitting at the small table in the center of the room.

"Fitz?" Duncan asked, filling a glass from the bottle in front of him.

Fitzcairn nodded. Duncan filled a second glass, sliding it across the table. He downed it in one swallow.

"Swill," he said, making a face. He slid the empty glass back. "More, if you please. If we're to have a proper Irish wake for Danny, we'll just have to ignore the quality of the whiskey."

They sat silently as the level in the bottle gradually lowered. The room had been filled with such silences for the whole of the winter, filled with the things that they were not talking about.

"I never told you about my first student," Duncan said, staring into his glass.

"The Frenchie with the fancy name? You most certainly did."

"No, not Jean-Phillipe," Duncan said. "My first student. His name was Devon Marek. When I found him, I was so pleased to have the chance to—well, to be Connor for another of our kind—" He paused.

"He was an evil man, Fitz. He took the best that I could give him and used it in the worst way possible." Duncan drained his drink. "It nearly came to a Challenge between us, but he ran."

"Danny O'Donal wasn't a bad man, MacLeod," Fitz said flatly. "It's not considered good form to speak ill of the dead at the wake, you know." His bright blue eyes were dangerous.

"No," Duncan said, hastily. "That's not what I meant." He spoke haltingly, choosing his words with care. "There were things driving Danny that you couldn't know, Fitz. Just as I couldn't know the terrible dark heart of Marek. Or," he added wryly "the thick head of Jean-Phillipe."

He faced Fitzcairn squarely. This man was his oldest friend. They had waged a war of words for centuries, but at the core of it, Duncan knew no one that he would want at his side more than Hugh Fitzcairn.

He had killed his friend's friend, his student. That would be forever between them. But it could be lived with, if they could get past the silences.

"If there had been any way, Fitz, any way at all. But—he'd gone mad at the end."

Fitzcairn looked up at Duncan, anguish on his face. "Is that the truth of it? It's surely what I want to believe . . ."

"Didn't you see it in his eyes when he was standing over you?" Duncan asked softly.

Fitzcairn slammed his empty glass down so fiercely that it broke, cutting his hand. "Yes, by God, I did. But why didn't I see it sooner? I kept making excuses, telling myself that he was sick from hunger and cold and exhaustion." He held up his hand, watching the blood run down from a deep cut in the palm.

"If I had only . . ." he whispered.

Duncan reached across the table to examine his friend's hand. The cut was already closing.

"We may be Immortal, but we're only human, Fitz. We have no special powers to see into another's soul. We take the measure of a man in the same way as any mortal would."

Fitz pulled his hand back. He ran his thumb over the thin line of blood that was all that remained of the cut.

"You saved my life, Duncan," he said. "Even if I'd had my blade, I don't know if I could have—" He paused. "This Marek you spoke of—would you have taken him?"

"I don't know, Fitz. I ask myself that still. To fight your own student . . ."

"I will say an Ave for you, Highlander, that you never need to answer that question." His eyes filled and he swallowed.

"Pass me the bottle, MacLeod," He said with a catch in his voice. "Let's drink together. To having all the time in the world. And to losing it."

They drank then, finishing one bottle and starting another. Fitz shared memories of Danny, and drew Duncan out further on the sore subject of Marek. Then the two talked of Connor and Henry Fitz, and of the stories Connor had told of his teacher Ramirez.

An hour had passed when Fitz rose abruptly. He took a few unsteady paces to the bunk beds on the back wall. Raising the thin mattress on the top bunk, he fetched out the small sack they had carried from the cave.

"Ah, well, MacLeod," he said. "It's past time to face up to it—we both know one thing that was driving Danny." He threw the sack on the table.

"It was driving us all, of course," he added as he sat down. "But you had the right of it from the beginning—the fever burned far too high in him."

"All that glitters . . ." Duncan murmured.

"Had we been as wise as bold," Fitz continued. "Or at least as wise as old . . ." He hiccoughed. "I should warn you, laddie. I may be a wee bit drunk."

Duncan smiled, and filled his glass again. "Had we but listened to Claire," he added.

"Yes. Indeed. The lovely Miz Benét. I've been thinking of her quite a bit, as a matter of fact." Fitz poked the sack with one finger. "Would my part of this be enough to enable her to be rid of her 'uncle,' I wonder?"

Duncan raised an eyebrow. One of the silences had been about the gold. They'd not talked of it at all. They'd not filed a claim nor made any attempt to return to the cave.

"I had a notion or two along those lines myself," he admitted. "I may well deliver the last of my dispatches to her personally."

"Well, I've no doubt that my consideration of her well-being greatly anticipated yours," Fitzcairn asserted.

Duncan smiled. "Indeed. I should know after so long a time that I canna possibly outdo Hugh Fitzcairn in gallantry."

"That's the bloody truth, all right," Fitz said. "And it's a further bloody truth that all Englishmen are gallant by nature.

For a Scot, such an attribute is mere artifice. Like—like a sheep wearing trousers."

"A sheep in men's clothing?" Duncan said. "I don't know if I should be offended or not." He felt absurdly happy. It was the first time in many weeks that Fitz had insulted him. It was a lame insult to be sure, but nonetheless welcome.

"Sheep—Scots—it makes sense to me." Fitz shrugged. "Perhaps you'd better understand silk purses and sows' ears, then?" he suggested, blue eyes wide.

Duncan sputtered, pretending great offense. Fitz laughed, and he joined in.

The sound of laughter had also been in short supply the last few months. It was also very welcome. Duncan was reluctant to break the mood, but he felt he had to ask.

"About the gold, Fitz." He gestured at the sack. "Are you saying that you want none of it?"

Fitz stared at it, sitting in the midst of the empty bottles and shards of broken glass. He seemed suddenly completely sober. He reached over and opened the sack, spilling out a fraction of the contents.

The gold gleamed in the light of the single lantern that hung on the wall in the windowless room.

One by one, he counted out five good-sized nuggets. Then he reached into the pocket on his shirt and took out a square of white linen, edged in lace.

He unfolded it and placed the five nuggets in the middle. Tying up the ends, he returned it to his pocket.

"Nothing gained," he said, quietly. "And a great deal lost."

The sack lay between them.

"The rest—the claim," Duncan said. "I should try to find Sam's people. And I did promise Amanda . . ."

"Do what you will, MacLeod." Fitzcairn shook his head. "I've seen enough of the Northern Lights. I'm set on seeing the lights on London Bridge. The sooner the better."

At his feet, Vixen thumped her tail. Fitz ruffled her ears.

"I know a buxom wench, a flower girl in Covent Garden." Turning toward Vixen, who sat up attentively, he cupped her face in his two hands. "She's always been dotty over dogs. This sweet beastie will make her eyes sparkle, I'll wager."

"If she's still there, Fitzcairn," Duncan said. "Even you can't expect every mortal woman you've ever known to wait forever."

Fitz chuckled. "Her grandmother was there, and her mother before her. So if she's not there, her daughter will be."

"But—" Duncan began a protest.

"They think I'm my own grandfather, you see. Or is it grandson? Oh, you know how it goes." He waved his hand vaguely in the air.

"Put the gold away for now, laddie." He got to his feet. "We'll talk more of this later. At the moment, we'd best hurry, or we'll miss what the cook so aptly calls 'evening mess.'"

"Go on, Fitz. I'll be along shortly." Duncan went to the door and watched as his friend disappeared in the darkness, the brown-and-white dog close by his side.

Then he donned his coat and walked some distance to the entrance of the fort. Slipping through the gates, he stood alone in the night.

The full moon was up, casting a midday luster on the landscape. The sky was pocked with stars, shining like gold dust thrown onto the cold ebony of the sky.

The still-white expanse of emptiness stretched away before him. He could hear, but not see, the cracking of the ice on the Peel as it flowed on northward, emptying finally into the frigid waters of the Arctic Ocean.

Three hundred. Seven hundred. Two thousand, like Darius and the others of the ancients.

Such were the spans of Immortal years, infinite compared

to ordinary men. Good men, like Sam and his brother. Bad men, like Smith and Foster.

And a brief candle compared to this ancient, untamed wild.

Mortal or Immortal, it mattered not. This was a land that tested men to destruction.

Mortal or Immortal, it mattered not, some failed that test. Duncan thought of ashes scattered on the snow, of a fresh-dug grave in the fort behind him.

Mortal or Immortal, some passed the test. The man who returned to Skagway for Minnie Dale was one.

Fitzcairn was another.

And he, Duncan MacLeod of the Clan MacLeod, had survived, his head and his wits intact. He felt no pride in this. Only a vast relief, and a wonder at it all.

On the horizon, the Northern Lights began their play. Like Fitz, Duncan had no more desire to see them. He turned and walked back into the fort.

As he did, it began to snow, a spring snow of large wet flakes.

By morning, five inches of white covered everything. In the corner of the fort that was holy ground, icicles hung from the rough-hewn cross above the newest grave. In the golden light of dawn, they sparkled like the finest, most delicate, most fragile crystal.

A cold wind gusted. The crystal broke, fell, and was lost in the whiteness.

AFTERWORD

All fiction is lies, they say. But historical fiction has some obligation to tell the truth, as much as possible . . .

On the evening of August 16, 1896, a man named George Washington Carmack, panning a small tributary of the Klondike River called Rabbit Creek, found a thumb-sized lump of gold. In short order, he found more—much, much more. Canadian law only allowed one claim per man, so after Carmack and his two Indian partners staked their claims, they spread the word.

Rabbit Creek was renamed Bonanza Creek, and men who had been prospecting the Klondike for years all rushed to the area.

But the Yukon winters are hard, and although fortunes were taken out of the ground in the next few months, it wasn't until the following spring, when the ice broke up on the rivers, that any news reached the outside world.

That news was reinforced in the most dramatic way possible. In mid-July 1897, the *Excelsior* docked in San Francisco and the *Portland* in Seattle, bearing men from the Northland. Men who were carrying with them literal tons of gold.

Within days, the Last Great Gold Rush was on.

Short, intense, and unprecedented in scope, the Klondike phase was essentially over by the summer of 1899, when it was discovered that the beaches of Nome, Alaska, were covered with gold dust. Those who still cherished the dream turned their attention west. (One hearty soul left Dawson City by bicycle. His departure—pedaling gamely across a snowfield—was captured on film.)

But before then, by some estimates as many as a million people from all over the globe, headed for the Klondike. (Although many, if not most, did not even know where it was.) Approximately a hundred thousand actually made it far enough to be "on the trail." Of those maybe forty thousand reached "the Eldorado city of Dawson."

Of those forty thousand a number did indeed make their fortunes—by opening stores and hotels, laundries and restaurants, sawmills and whorehouses.

Only a few thousand found gold, and of those, only a few hundred in any quantity.

For purposes of this book, Duncan and his friends are numbered among that few hundred, despite the enormous odds against them. The valley in the Mackenzies isn't on any map, though the theory of "looking where the rivers used to be" was a popular one among some of the prospectors.

Most of the rest of their journey, however, is as close-to-life as I could make it. In the Seattle/Skagway/Wilderness chapters, names of hotels, bars, ships, newspapers, restaurants, mountains, lakes, rivers, forts and some people are real. (Claire and her "Uncle," however, are not.)

The story of Jefferson Randolph "Soapy" Smith is all true.

Under the guise of an upright businessman, Smith ran a con on the honest citizens of Skagway and the thousands of argonauts who chose to travel the White Pass, for nearly a year. He had men—like Slim Jim Foster—steering hapless newcomers directly into the clutches of his thugs. He controlled the law, (what there was of it) at least one of the churches and a number of saloons and gambling houses, besides the Parlour. He amassed a fortune and on the Fourth of July in 1898, actually joined the governor of Alaska in leading the town's Independence Day Parade!

Four days later (as Duncan predicted) the good citizens of Skagway did come for him. A man named Frank Reid, head of a vigilante committee formed in March to stand against Smith and his gang, shot it out with Soapy on Juneau Wharf. Smith lost. His grave lies on a hill above Skagway. Frank Reid, who was mortally wounded in the fight, died a day later. He's buried nearby, under a monument praising him as the savior of Skagway.

I've taken two liberties in my story. The first is allowing Our Heroes to actually reach Dawson City before the winter. In reality, only a handful of the aforementioned forty thousand got through in 1897—many didn't because they were traveling without sufficient provisions. The vast majority of the gold seekers were stopped by the weather on the shores of Lake Bennett. They wintered there in an ever-growing tent city. The amazing flotilla—seven thousand boats of all descriptions—didn't take to the water until the end of the following May.

The second—and larger—liberty has to do with dates. Astute viewers of *Highlander* will know that the on-screen date for Double Eagle is 1888. I managed to not take note of that until I was some way into the book. The fact that Kit O'Brady left San Francisco for Alaska in a steamer that went down off

Portland, (an event that actually did happen in 1898) led me to mistake the late 1880s for the late 1890s.

But the story flows so well from Double Eagle that—inspired by Rebecca Neason, who moved the Chinese invasion of Tibet a decade in the interests of her story—I have concluded that in the world of Duncan MacLeod, the Last Great Gold Rush occurred some nine years earlier. (This is the same world where Lord Byron's friend the doctor is named Adams rather than Polidori.)

If you've read *White Silence* and would like to know more about the Gold Rush, go buy *Klondike* by Pierre Berton, Canada's premiere historian. His father crossed the Chilkoot in 1898 and hearing of that experience led to his lifelong fascination with the event. Some of the truths he recounts are as fantastical as—well, as the existence of Immortals.

I further recommend the novels and short stories of Jack London, from whom I borrowed my title. His fiction is as true as Berton's fact. London was there—as an adventurer and as a reporter.

The poetry of Robert Service, the other author usually associated with the time and place of *White Silence*, provided my epigraph (and Minnie Dale's name). Service wasn't there, until sometime afterward. Nonetheless, his verse—doggerel though it may be—is filled with a real sense of the land and the people.

In the rest of the book, all of the background information of Danny O'Donal's life is factual—details of place and events in New York City, both before and after the war; details of the aftermath of Cold Harbor and the siege of Petersburg; details of life in Temperanceville, which in 1872 became part of the city of Pittsburgh.

Other minor details—information about Native Canadian burial practices, the fact that Gounod's *Faust* was the most popular opera in America at the turn of the last century, the